SABATO
THE CROSS

TIES OF STEEL
BOOK FOUR

MJ FIELDS

Copyright © MJ Fields 2015

All rights reserved. No part of this publication may be reproduced, distributed, or transmitted in any form or by any means, or stored in a database or retrieval system, without the prior written permission of MJ Fields, except as permitted under the U.S. Copyright Act of 1976.

This is a work of fiction. All characters, organizations, and events portrayed in this novel are either products of the author's imagination or are used fictitiously. Any resemblance to actual events, locales, or persons, living or dead, is entirely coincidental.

1st Edition Published: March 2015
Published by MJ Fields
Cover Design by: K23 Designs
Cover Model: Bryant Wood
Photographer: Furious Fotog
Editor: Veronica Park
Editor: Kellie Montgomery
Formatting: IndieVention Designs

ISBN-13: 978-1511519618
ISBN-10: 1511519614

10 9 8 7 6 5 4 3 2 1

Disclaimer

This book contains mature content not suitable for those under the age of 18. Involves strong language and sexual situations. All parties portrayed in sexual situations are adults over the age of 18.

All characters are fictional. Any similarities are purely coincidental.

Each book in the Ties of Steel series can be read as a stand-alone.

TABLE OF CONTENTS

Chapter One 7
Chapter Two 24
Chapter Three 46
Chapter Four 60
Chapter Five 73
Chapter Six 83
Chapter Seven 92
Chapter Eight 102
Chapter Nine 110
Chapter Ten 119
Chapter Eleven 128
Chapter Twelve 140
Chapter Thirteen 150
Chapter Fourteen 159
Chapter Fifteen 165
Chapter Sixteen 175
Chapter Seventeen 184
Chapter Eighteen 192
Chapter Nineteen 201
Chapter Twenty 209
Chapter Twenty-One 216
Chapter Twenty-Two 226
Chapter Twenty-Three 234
Chapter Twenty-Four 240
Chapter Twenty-Five 246
Epilogue 255
How to tie the St. Andrews Knot 260
Playlist 261
About the Author 262
More from MJ Fields 263
Connect with MJ Fields 265
Memphis Black Excerpt 266
Sexual Awakenings: Vol 1- The Walz By Angelica 270
Merciless Ride by Chelsea Camaron Excerpt 284

SABATO
Nobody's Hero
May 27th

I prowl around the club in Florence. I need a release. Something warm to tease, taunt, titillate, tame, and tear up. It is not only the lifestyle I portray, it is truly who I am. It has never been my MO to waste time chatting up some romance novel junkie, saying all the things I know she wants to hear to get laid.

That is why I came here. It's not one of my places. I won't lose the respect of my girls, or my clients.

Tonight, I seek strange.

I've come to exactly the right kind of place. I know this because I planned it. I plan everything. I take in the leather clad wait staff with piercings and tattoos—some of whom are holding whips—this is a no-last-name kind of scene. All fetishes are welcome here. My eye catches on a tall redhead with a nose ring that's chained to her nipple ring—totally exposed, for all to see.

Make that welcome, wet, and waiting.

Nothing good happens on today's date. Hell, nothing good ever happens these days, aside from orgasms and creating desire. If not for causing the slow buildup to release, and the inevitable double-edged climax, I would feel nothing. But then, usually I like feeling nothing. For too many years,

I felt too much. Rage, sadness, jealousy, obsession, more rage...it was fucking exhausting, caring that much.

Nowadays, I am a shark, coldly calculating without allowing anything to touch me on a personal level. Ironically, this seems to make me irresistible to the opposite sex. It also makes me notice things that most people are too nervous, too excited, too full of desire, or scared to notice.

In one corner of the club, there's a man whose facial expression gives him away as a first-timer to the BDSM scene—eyebrows raised, wide shoulders cocked back defensively, and a scowl on his face that will likely keep any subs from approaching him. The way his eyes flit from side to side, it's as if he's trying to figure out how he got here, and what the hell is going on. I follow his gaze, more slowly and casually, expecting someone who works here to greet him, at least help the poor bastard feel welcome. But no one does.

As a businessman, it bothers me. But as an anonymous club patron—which I am tonight, I remind myself—I couldn't give less of a fuck.

I saunter over to the bar, sit down, and order a drink. Manhattan, with rye whiskey—the only kind of Manhattan that counts. When my drink is in my hand, I turn and continue scouting the crowd for talent.

The majority have not picked their poison yet, and the ones who have are clearly all about being dominated. It seems like the place is crawling with prey, but not so many hunters. Good, I like those odds.

The 'out of his scene' guy comes up to the bar and sits right next to me. He orders a glass of wine, cheap wine. I almost snort into my drink. Rookie move. Feeling generous, I turn to him and offer my hand. "I'm Sabato, how are you?"

Immediately, his shoulders go up. "Dude, I like pussy. Okay? I'm not sure what the fuck about me screams I'm willing to swing that way, but—"

"It's definitely the clothes."

"*Excuse* me?" His attitude is one I am not accustomed to. But then, after all, this is not one of my usual haunts.

I decide to cut the guy a break, since he's obviously clueless. "Look around the room." I gesture vaguely with my drink. "Tell me, what do you see?"

He shakes his head, looking confused. "Pussy." He snorts, shooting me a glare. "And a bunch of guys who want to tag my ass."

My patience is very quickly running out. "And, what else?"

He shakes his head again, more loosely this time. The wine must be getting to him already. What a light weight.

"Honestly, man, I feel like any second, half of these guys are gonna bust out doing the fucking YMCA. I mean...." He gestures agitatedly around the room. "You got the cowboys, the cops, the gay bikers—fuck, we're just missing the Indians in here."

I almost want to laugh, because he is right. "And if they see you checking them out, wearing...what you're wearing...how do you think they will approach you?"

He shrugs, looking offended again. I signal the bartender to bring him another wine, before he really gets his skirt in a twist.

"What the hell is wrong with my clothes?"

"Nothing," I tell him. "If you're going to a different kind of club." I gesture to his shiny, black silk shirt. "I mean, you have your *dancing shoes*," I can't hold back a mocking smirk, "that match your cute little *dancing shirt*."

"Fuck you, dude." His eyebrows push together, and he stares at me for a few seconds like he's seriously thinking about kicking my ass. Then, slowly, he smiles. Shakes his head. Holds his hand out for me to shake. "Zandor Steel."

I take his hand and shake it. I like a man who doesn't take himself too seriously.

"So, what brings you here tonight, Zandor?"

He shrugs. "Just thought I'd wander in. I'm not from around here, so...."

My eyes widen in mock surprise. "Really?"

"Fuck you twice," he laughs.

"Yeah, see," I make a tsk-ing noise. "You can't say that kind of thing in here, or one of these guys will take you up on it."

"Oh," he nods. "Good point. I meant 'Go fuck *yourself*, twice."

I find myself laughing, too, in spite of what day it is. It's been so long, I've forgotten how refreshing it is to have people tell you to fuck off to your face. Eyes narrowing thoughtfully, I take out my phone and send a quick, subtle text to have this Zandor Steel looked into.

When I look up, I see him staring at me, appraising me with a certain shark-like look to him. My shoulders straighten. I shouldn't have let my guard down so easily.

"I don't know if I should be taking your advice, bro," he says. "Doesn't look like you're any closer to slaying poon tonight than I am."

I like the ease of this conversation, but I don't like the innuendo. I nod to a petite platinum blonde woman who sits across the room, waiting for notice. In a blink, she is at my side. I nod toward the floor, and she drops to her knees in front of me, ready to service my every wish—in the middle of the club—if I ask.

"Well, fuck," Zandor says, eyes wide. "My bad. You want to be my Yoda man, I will be your Padawan. Gladly. Just show me how to use the Force like *that*."

I have no idea what he's talking about, but he looks like he expects me to. I shrug. Shake my head.

The look on his face is incredulous. "*Star Wars*?"

"Let me guess," I say, taking another sip of my drink. "It's an American thing."

"Actually, it's kind of the most epic movie series of all...you know what, never mind." He nods "Carry on, oh wise one."

I gesture down to the petite blonde. "What is your flavor?"

"My thing is pussy," he repeats, like that is helpful. "Warm, willing pussy, in all varieties."

I sigh with impatience. "No, Zandor. You're in a *bondage club*. I mean, what is your scene? What fetish are you into? Are you a top, a bottom, a group player? Dominance is not for everyone, no matter how...." I gesture vaguely at his physique. "Physically suited for it they may appear to be. Perhaps you yearn to submit. If that is the case, I can recommend some very talented dommes in the area."

Zandor Steel looks at me like I am deranged in some way—even though he is the one with the porn star name, who is wearing a 'fuck me, daddy' shirt.

"Bro, I just like to fuck and not have the bitch so enchanted or fucking needy that she pulls out the old sexual harassment card, trying to teach me some fucking lesson. I'm not into really fucked up. I'll spank an ass and play with some toys."

"So, no blood play? Animal transformation? Figging?"

"*Fuck* no." He looks vaguely nauseated at the thought—even though, I would bet good money he doesn't know what any of those things mean. "That's sick."

"It's not about mental health or sickness," I tell him, more patiently than I should. "It's about *control*. Losing it, and feeling free. Or maybe taking it, for the first time in your life. Every day, in all aspects of our lives, control is what we seek. Yet most people have no idea how to control themselves, and they don't try. They are slaves to their urges, instead of the other way around."

A feeling prods me then, something similar to guilt. What right do I have to be preaching to this stranger about self-control? After all, what am I doing here tonight?

But Zandor seems to consider—genuinely consider—what I've told him. "Not sure if you're being a dick, or sincere, but as I said before." He points to the blonde at my feet, who is still silently, patiently waiting. "I want something simple. Meat and potatoes. I want ass that goes away satisfied when I'm done and doesn't sit outside my door banging on it, begging for cock."

I can't help but laugh at the visual image he's created. "Begging is also a very big part of this scene, my friend. I wonder if you wouldn't be more comfortable at a nice trucker bar. I hear there is one down by the gas station, near the freeway."

"Don't tempt me," he says, rolling his eyes. "At least there, no one would have a chance at knowing who I was. Ever since my family came into some money, that shit has seriously fucked up my game. There's no such thing as 'anonymous' or 'no strings attached' anymore. Now, they're telling me I need to 'lay low?' That ain't gonna happen. So, like I said, teach away."

I'm intrigued by his story, and want to know more. New money is like blood in the water for a shark like me. But I'm also starting to like this guy, in spite of myself. So I indulge him, for the moment, and play mentor.

"You have to keep feelings out of it," I look down at the blonde, finally giving her the attention she craves. She is a textbook sub, willing to wait as long as it takes—because waiting for approval only makes her wetter. I point her to Zandor, and she crawls over, instantly transferring her attention—and adoration—on him. "The only thing you ask of her is obedience, until the game is done. Sexual obedience. Release must be earned, and given like a gift. It cannot be taken." Zandor slowly smiles, staring at the blonde's tits. "I *definitely* like control."

I nod to the redhead with the nose-to-nipple piercings, and she walks over to stand before me.

"Is Cindy to your liking, Sir?"

"She's hot," Zandor says. "So, yeah. I'd like to show her a good time."

"No," I correct him. "You want to take pleasure from her. In return, if she does exactly as you instruct, she will be rewarded."

I look down at the girl. "Present yourself."

She does as I say, without question. Whether they know my name or not at this place, it doesn't matter. They obviously know enough to tell a Dom when they see one.

Leaning back on her heels, Cindy widens her legs slightly, clasping her hands behind her back. The position causes her breasts to jut out, pressing her nipples out against the sheer fabric of her costume.

"You see how she is dressed?" I ask Zandor. "She is wearing lace, not leather. She will be a good partner for your first time. But make sure you agree to the rules, between the two of you, before anything happens. Her presentation shows her desires. She wants to be treated like a lady, but she needs for you to be in control. Like you, she is not so very experienced."

"What?" Zandor looks at me skeptically. "What do you mean? How can you possibly know that?"

I gesture for the blonde to leave us. "Go over there and wait for your master to claim you, Cindy."

Immediately, she goes back to where she was sitting before, across the room.

"Everything is in the rules," I tell him. "It's part of the world we live in, part of the scene. That is the kind of woman who wants a stranger to spank her and fuck her, but still wants the illusion of romance. She needs someone who wants to dominate her full time, and take care of her. If she asked for my opinion, I would have told her to go somewhere else. This is a place for temporary engagements. Whereas this one," I point to the redhead, who is smiling at me with open invitation. "Is a submissive of opportunity. She wants to lose control, for an hour...a weekend. But she is experienced enough to be comfortable in the scene, which tells me that she will be looking for something...special. A singular experience she can tuck away and revisit later, in her private moments."

My eyes burn into hers, and my explanation takes a turn into something else. Something meant only for her and I. "She is looking for an eye-opening, stinging slap that will drive her over the edge at exactly the right moment. She wants a man who will fuck her, mind and body, like pleasure is her only purpose in the world. And when she's screaming and begging for release, I will pull it out of her reach, at the last possible second. Because, more than anything, she wants the exhilarating feeling of being wildly...totally...helplessly...out of control."

By the time I am finished with my description, the redhead is almost panting with desire. I have no doubt that underneath her leather harness, she is dripping with need, ready and waiting for my cock to penetrate her. For my body to conquer hers, completely. I glance over my shoulder, toward the entrance to the private lounge area. I raise an eyebrow. She nods, eagerly.

I turn toward him with a start. I'd almost forgotten he was there.

"So...can I go fuck Cindy now?"

I nod, because I am done mentoring for the evening. I have my target now, and nothing else matters but the slow burn, the build, and the eventual quench.

"Of course. Just remember that control is a responsibility, not a right. It can be taken away, just as easily as it is given."

"Understood."

Satisfied that I have done my part for my fellow man, I turn my attention back to the redhead.

"Go to the cross and wait for me." I get up and slowly remove my jacket, folding it neatly over one arm. "It was nice meeting you, Zandor Steel."

With a nod, I leave him to his fun. I circle the bar and go into one of the side rooms, where a Saint Andrew's cross waits in the center of a dimly lit room. The redhead is there, on her knees, already assuming 'the Position.'

"Get undressed." I close the door behind me—but not all the way, in case there are any voyeurs who would like to peek in—and hang up my jacket. By the time I turn around, the redhead has taken off her scant leather thong, and is kneeling naked in front of the cross.

She is shaved bare, of course, and I can see for myself what my words have done to her. She is glistening already, and I have yet to touch her.

Behind me, I can hear whispers, and I don't have to turn to know a small crowd of watchers has gathered outside. It's not unusual for me, because they know who I am, I have a reputation, one I am proud of. Her chest is heaving, her nipples are hard and she waits in her pool of desire.

I unbutton the cuffs on my shirt as I look to my left and see Zandor, my new prodigy talking entirely too much to the girl wearing lace. I want to correct him but now is not the time. Now is show time, now is the time for me to release the anger of the date, to bring down sheets of glass and chaos on the lucky woman in front of me.

..*

Leaving the club, I see Zandor walking quickly up to me. I am physically exhausted but still wired.

"Wait up, Cross," he says and I stop.

"Sabato," I correct him.

"Fuck man, that was intense," he has obviously never witnessed sadism.

"Not your thing, I get it. But she is not bleeding and I can tell you she wouldn't have been upset if she were."

"Nah, not what I expected but if that's your thing, then ‒"

"It is not my thing," I stop and glare at him, "It is hers. Let me ask you, did you exchange numbers and set up a date with -"

"Nah, she had a list of shit she's not into."

"I knew she wasn't a true sub," I run my hands through my hair, "It was nice to meet you, Zandor."

"I'm gonna go grab something to eat, you wanna come? I'll buy."

"I'm not hungry-"

"After all that you're not hungry?"

"No." I answer and turn to walk away.

"Shit dude, just wanted to show some appreciation," he says with a bite.

I reach into my pocket and grab my phone. I read the message I get with the information.

Zandor Steel is associated with Benito DeLuca. I immediately get defensive and wonder if Father has planted yet another person to spy.

"Appreciation or are you being-"

"Hold up," he cuts me off and takes his phone from his pocket, reads something and laughs.

"What's so funny?"

"Your family ties man, seems they cross with mine in a fucked up way. But yeah, thanks for the advice earlier. I got it from here." He begins walking away and it irritates me.

"Explain," I demand.

He stops and looks at me, "Any friend of Benito DeLuca is no friend of mine. But again-"

"You're associated with the fucking idiot, I'm not. My father-"

"Is the fucking big Ragu, the Don, the fucking guys who run the underground-"

"My father is a self-serving asshole."

"He's the leader of the fucking Cosa Nostra. I'm all for head in bed, but I piss his boy off and I'll wake up with a fucking horse head in my bed and that shit ain't right. Plus, I have a knack for pissing people off," he chuckles.

"I'm hungry and-"

"See man, I fucking told you," he grins. "Look, you promise your old man isn't gonna come after me and I will still buy you dinner. I mean, after all we shared tonight I owe you that, hell little Miss Lacy could have gotten at least a meal outta me, but every time I was talking to her I felt your fucking eyes sculling me."

"I accept, but here's another thing, unless you want a committed sub, don't you offer any more dinners."

..*

Tonight I have invited Zandor to my club, *Privato DesIdErio'*, Florence. I like him. He seems relaxed and lost in an odd way. He doesn't need my money, he doesn't want a job, and he doesn't like Benito, therefore I am allowing myself to enjoy teaching him.

"Ciao," I answer my phone when I see Zandor Steel's number.

"Listen bro, you spoke English to me the other night, I now have expectations; don't fuck it up," he says in relaxed manner, one that I am comfortable with him speaking to me in.

"Fine, but don't show up here with expectations and for God's sake, leave those dancing shoes at home." I try to joke back. I think I pull it off.

"Listen. I'm not gonna make it tonight and I'm not gonna pull any punches and say some shit like, 'I have my period' or 'I need to wash my hair.' I like you man, you don't pussy foot around me like half this motherfucking country, so this isn't personal. I have a family who I need to protect. I'm not comfortable in a place that some Al Capone character is gonna get pissed 'cause I have a bigger dick and take it out on them. So how about you and I take off for a little trip? There's a shit load of kink clubs around and admittedly I need some guidance. I liked the way things went down the other night and I need a fucking break from my family ties, man. You think the Mafia is bad, you ought to take on Momma Joe."

..*

"What do you mean a vacation Sabato," my father barks. "You started seven clubs in seven years. I gave you the money to start them, now you wanna walk away?"

"No, I'm taking a vacation. The clubs have paid for themselves, they are owned by me. You gave me a loan, no different than you would anyone else. I paid it back along with the forty percent interest you charged me. They are legit and run smoothly."

"No, I need you around," he snaps.

"I wasn't asking permission. The only thing you need me for is a place to hide money—"

"You better watch yourself—"

"You better remember, threats mean shit to a man who doesn't value his next breath or fear losing it. You have the combinations to my safes, use them. I have people managing my clubs and surveillance cameras making sure they don't fuck up. You're the only one, other than me, who knows they're there and how to skirt around them. You'll be just fine."

I close my suitcase and stand toe to toe with him. It is not often I see defeat in his eyes, but over the past seven years I have given him very little to be disappointed in me about. I have even sensed from time to time that he is proud of me. I don't love the man but I know he works hard and that he is proud of that. For that reason, I have stayed connected with him.

'He is your father,' I remember Luciana saying to me.

I don't like to think of her, I don't like to think about my mama. I let them both down; I will never pretend to be anyone's *eroe* again. That way I can never be the cause of another's devastation.

* * *

After a few weeks, I am more relaxed than ever before. I return, having met a man who I can call my friend. He is different from me and I like that. There is no competition, no judgment, nothing but a good time. Zandor Steel is like a fucking party.

I have returned to an angry father and my help, my girls, are not the same as I left them. They are skittish and seem untrusting. They came to me this way and I fixed it. I have a responsibility to them; I will get to the bottom of the issue and make it right without causing them further stress. If he is connected, I will make him pay.

Two weeks pass and Zandor is going home to the United States; his family is apparently in crisis. "Fuckers are dropping like flies. One's married and the other is about to do the same damn thing. I gotta stop them."

* * *

Three months pass and Zandor comes back to visit. Apparently, he too got caught in that nasty little web. He is happy, truly happy and I am pleased for him. We still go out, except now he brings a girl with him. It is funny as hell to watch him 'control' her. She seems to like what control brings, but is resistant to it outside of the scene.

His family follows. I find them interesting. You can tell there is strength in their brotherhood but it is always foreshadowed by what the matriarch of the family says.

They respect her; she not only demands respect but she has earned it. I have heard stories now. It isn't often that I accept the invitation to dinner with all of them. Quite frankly, it's difficult and I find myself face to face with my past. However, the draw to them is undeniable and the bond they share seems extended. They are a good family. One I would never allow myself to believe I could have again, but being entertained by them is never dull. It douses a flame in me, but only for a moment.

When they return to the states, I don't feel like something was taken from me, even though I should miss them. I decide it is because I did not claim them. Doing that would result in devastation to them.

Within days, I am unaffected.

..*

It is a Monday night. *Privato DesIdErio' Laverno* is closed to the public. It's card night. I love to play poker and I love to take the money of men who bow to my father, yet feel they don't have to bow to me. I don't desire power in that sort of way but Monday nights give me a taste.

Dominic Segretti has been around lately. I don't trust him; he is Benito's relation and Benito is father's closest ally. I have allowed him to come because I want to figure out what it is he is up to. I also know he is considered a fierce competitor, practically un-beatable and when I take his money, he'll know I am not to be toyed with.

He is a formidable opponent, very hard to read, unlike the other clowns were tonight. He is hanging around the club, yet seems unaffected by the women and I know he's up to something. I watch him. He's had three drinks in the past two hours; he hasn't touched the women, he is watching me and I want to know why.

When he walks up to me in the corner table, I dismiss the girls and he sits down.

"You took all my money," he half jokes.

"You seem to be playing a different kind of game." I expect him to deny it but he doesn't.

"I need your help."

"Why would I give you my help?"

He looks around, "Is it safe to talk here?"

I don't answer. I stand up and walk to the back; he is following, I know it without looking. I walk out the back door, "Is this your car?"

"Yes," he answers.

"Have you had it swept?"

"I have, but it's been here for a few hours, can we walk?" He starts walking without waiting for an answer.

My curiosity is peaked and I follow.

When he stops and turns, he runs his hands over his head. "My cousin Zandor seems to like you, trusts you, says you're a good person."

"Keep going."

"I need your help."

"In?"

"I'm going to bring down Benito DeLuca. In doing that, I am going to more than likely bring down your father and in doing that, you may be in danger too. The clubs you run—"

"Own, they are not his, they are mine."

"Fine, which makes it worse. Benito is laundering money and millions of dollars are being shifted from DeLuca—"

"I am going to tell you this once. I don't give a shit what you do. Don't come back here and because you are Zandor's friend—"

"Cousin. He doesn't even know what is going on here."

"Walk away and I will act like this conversation never happened. You keep me out of this—"

"They're stealing from your friend's family's company. Is that okay with you?!"

"It has nothing to do with me!"

"Your businesses are a fucking cover for it."

"That's where you are wrong, my businesses are legit and legal."

"I hope so, for your sake," he starts walking away and stops. "I am taking them down. My family started this company and it will once again be called Segretti. I will do this with or without you. Do not stand in my way. Do not tell Zandor, by doing so you'll put him and his family at risk."

"Then why the hell are you doing it?" I am angry.

"Something was taken from me a long time ago and I want it back."

"Opening doors to the past is never a good idea."

"That my friend, is a personal preference." I turned to leave and stopped. "You have a couple weeks. Make sure you have everything in order."

"Don't threaten me," I caution him.

"It's not a threat, it's a kindness."

I am not panicked I know I will be fine. I have taken precautions. I am, however, wondering what I will do with myself and some of my girls if I end up shut down.

I will think of something, I always do. I never get too comfortable. That is a luxury. I just have to figure it out.

..*

"Hey bro, long time no hear from," Zandor answers the phone.

"I am considering a visit."

"Well fuck yes, come on over!" He laughs.

"And I am considering expanding."

"Nice, what do you have in mind?"

"Do you know of any fool that bought a club thinking he wanted to be just like me and then dropped like a fly?"

"Fuck you. You saw my Kitten."

"Oh yes, the one with the sharp tongue to match her claws?"

"She's learning, so am I. Fuck man, I want it all. Best of both worlds," he's spewing off like a teenage girl with all the happy ever after shit.

"Great, sell me the club." I interrupt.

"You really want Steelettos?"

"I want the club; the fucking name, not so much." I can't help but laugh, "That's why you like those dancing shoes, huh? Let me guess, it's all lights and bling."

"Screw you man, it's actually fucking perfect."

"Then sell it to me."

"I get to come play in one of the private rooms, a VIP and you have yourself a deal."

"Perfect.

* * *

I stand outside father's office, my blood is boiling, and I am going to kill him. I am going to kill him with my bare hands. I am going to do it slowly and in the most painful way I can devise.

My phone vibrates in my pocket and I see a message.

This is Dominic. *Are you in or out?*

It doesn't take me long to respond, *I'm in.*

I thought so, heard you bought a place in Jersey. How did your old man take it, will it make him suspicious?

No. It will be fine. He will never know what hit him.

New City,
New Beginning,
New York

Growing up, I was the voice of reason in my close-knit group of friends.

I was always the girl who told my girlfriends that second chances were granted only in certain situations—but not something that a guy you date should ever feel entitled to. I was the girl who set a three-drink limit on herself at a party that lasted four hours, because I had to make sure that everyone got home safe at the end of the night. But I've also always been the girl who will cut those ties, no matter how long I've been friends with someone, if I feel like they're starting to drag me down.

Because, unlike most of my friends, I know that people can't truly change, unless they *choose* to. I'm never rude or disrespectful about it, and I never push my personal beliefs off on anyone else. But if they can't accept that I'm not going to waver, no matter how long or hard they push, I have no problem walking away.

My first boyfriend, Ryan, was someone I grew up with. I dated Ryan from my freshman year until my senior year. I loved him—or thought I did, at the time—but I knew I wasn't ready to have sex with him. He pushed, I pulled, and finally the tie that bound us together, broke.

Honestly, I think in retrospect I always knew he wasn't *the one*. Not the one I wanted to go 'all the way' with, at least. If he was, I feel like there would have been a fierce attraction, an undeniable, unbreakable need to be with him. To want to kiss him, and be touched by him, all the time—but there just...wasn't. My attraction to Ryan was more like the way you would feel about orphans in Africa. You hope they're doing okay, and you don't want to see them get hurt, but...you're probably not going to give up your entire life to go live in a hut, just to be with them.

In all honesty, being with someone felt more like an obligation, or a line on my resume. In a relationship: three years. *See? Not crazy, or defective. I've got skills. I can hold down a boyfriend for three whole years. Hire me.* Or something.

That was all it ever was, with anyone.

One would think, that after attending four years of college and majoring in a field that makes you feel like you have a purpose, you'd be content. I was never a rule breaker, but I had my fair share of fun. Always while staying true to my own moral compass.

Then, a month ago, everything I thought I knew about myself changed.

I no longer wanted to be *just* a social worker. Suddenly, making a difference in people's lives, one person at a time—everything I used to think I wanted to do—wasn't enough. I no longer wanted to be 'just' a social worker. I wanted to change the world, change laws, and make life better for generations of people for years and years to come. Before anyone really knew what was happening, I'd already been accepted into the summer pre-law program at Cornell University, in New York City.

It came as a shock to everyone around me. Though, had anyone really been paying attention, it would not have come as such a surprise. If there's one thing I've learned, it's that people don't take notice of much—not when they're too busy living their own lives. I don't mean to pass judgment; it's just how the world works. People will act in their own self-interest, even if you give them an option to do something more, because people are self-centered creatures.

So here I am, on my own, naturally—as nature intended. Moving to New York City, while getting ready for an interview with the admissions department and looking for apartments.

I say it aloud to myself often: I'm going to be living in New York, the greatest city on Earth. NYC. *New York City!*

Well, I guess if I'm being honest, I'm not actually alone. I mean, I do have friends in the area. Sort of. My best friends, my high school best buds and college roomies. We were inseparable, until now. Nikki lives in New Jersey, just a short ride from me and Laney has just landed a job in the City too. I am hopeful Paige will find a reason to stay while here and we will all be close, again.

Laney doesn't know I'm in town yet, so tonight, Paige, Nikki, and I are going to surprise her at dinner.

Nikki's man, Abe, planned it while she and Laney went apartment hunting.

As I'm getting ready, there's a knock on the door of my hotel room. I glance at my watch, but I'm pretty sure it's Paige. I jump up off the bed and run to the door, flinging it open.

"You're here!" I screech, wrapping my arms around her.

"Sure am," she returns the hug and laughs. "Holy shit though, did you see Laney's IG?"

"No, why?"

"Hubba-hubba hotness, she's definitely over that redneck." Paige holds up her phone so I can see the guy.

I can't help but laugh. "She's got a new ride, now. Giddy up, motherfucker."

We both giggle as we search through his Instagram feed. There is a picture of Laney's guy standing with another man.

And while Dominic is no slouch in the hubba-hubba department, the other guy is *stunning*.

Even in his photos, his heavy-lidded, dark-eyed stare leaves me feeling pinned, like there is no way I could possibly hide from him. But then, why would anyone ever want to? It's like he is studying me through the screen, like he can see what is inside of me, my darkest secrets, my deepest desires. Just looking at him makes me feel...*naked*. No clothes, no skin, my very soul is exposed.

A chill runs up my spine and goose-bumps cover my arms. I want to look away, but I can't. His jaw is strong, his jaw muscles tensed in a slight frown. Whoever took the picture must have caught him off guard. Those muscles lead down to a thick, strong neck. My mouth waters, and I swallow hard as my eyes start to burn, unwilling to blink for fear I won't ever see him again. His cheek bones are high and sharp, his nose perfection. His lips are almost pornographically full, top and bottom in perfect proportion. His shirt hangs open, just a few buttons loose, the muscles in his shoulders and upper pectorals defined and so strong....

"Did you just *come*, Melyssa?" Paige laughs.

I feel my face burn for a different reason: embarrassment.

"No...." My voice cracks and she laughs again.

"He's hot," Paige agrees. "But...from what I'm seeing here, he may already be taken by one of our girls. So...let's just put this away, shall we?"

When she tosses her phone back into her handbag, I feel like I've experienced a deep, personal loss. Not because I fell in love with this guy at first sight, or anything lame like that. It's more like...finding out a priceless painting has been stolen. Like, I feel pain for all those people who won't get to experience the beauty of it.

I for one, am pretty sure I'm never going to see a man that perfect, ever again.

"We need to get going," Paige says, snapping me out of my moment of funk. "The restaurant is only ten miles away, but traffic around here is a bitch, and I wanna get there before Laney and Nikki."

..*

When Laney and Nikki walk into NY Steakhouse, Nikki shrieks, startling several unsuspecting diners as they make a beeline towards us. Paige and I meet them half way, just as excited as they are. We hug and laugh, annoying more uptight New Yorkers in the process.

After the big greetings are over, I hone in on Laney.

"Okay spill it," I grab her hand and pull her to the table, to sit next to me.

"When did y'all get in? This is crazy, no one told me."

"Yeah, yeah, yeah," Paige says, as she sits on the other side of Laney. "Who cares? The *man*, the one with the abs, like...."

I notice Laney scowl and kick Paige under the table, "Ouch, Mel."

"Will you introduce me to your friends, Laney?" We look up to see the man from Laney's Instagram, the one who has allegedly shared her bed, standing there, staring intensely at her.

She doesn't even look at him. *Uh oh. Trouble in sex paradise?*

"I'm Dominic Segretti, a friend of Abe's." He introduces himself to us and shakes our hands.

"I'm Paige."

"I'm Mel."

"Pleasure to meet you." He speaks in a thick Italian accent—*delicious!*—and I can't help imagining that's what the dark-eyed guy from the picture must sound like.

"I think we've already seen you," Paige says. I kick her again, harder this time. "Ouch!"

Dominic smiles. "You're referring to the photo I posted last night. I should have told Laney, I am a jealous man."

"Well, Giddy up mother—ouch," Paige snaps and looks at me, shooting daggers with her eyes.

The waitress brings wine to the table. Dominic only has eyes for Laney. "This is a much better brand than the one from the hotel bar. I think you'll enjoy it." He pours a glass for her first and then fills ours as well. "Is she always this quiet?"

"Only when she's pissed," I answer.

"I'm going to see where Nikki is." Laney stands and walks toward the ladies' room.

"Please excuse me for a moment," Dominic follows her.

Paige and I look at one another, both of us clearly confused.

"I'll drink to that," she lifts her glass of wine.

"To what?" I ask.

"I have no clue, but whatever the hell is going on around here isn't going to ruin this wine for me," she says. "It's delicious, so let's drink to the wine."

I raise my glass to Paige's awkward toast and then take a drink. That's when I finally get it, the meaning of Page's toast. I almost choke on the next sip.

If only I had someone to follow me into a bathroom stall. Sigh....

"Hello," I look up at the voice, and am immediately speechless. My mouth dries up like the Sahara, and my stomach does the Macarena. I feel butterflies, tingles, the swell of a thousand-voice choir of angels, you name it.

It's *him*.

The effect he has on me is out of this world. I am suddenly anxious that he'll know how I feel, yet...at the same time, I want him to look at me, to see me, to see what he does to me—because I couldn't hide it if I wanted to, and as much as I have kept those inner desires secret for most of my life, somehow I know...he knows *exactly* what I secretly want.

My eyes are trained on him, and nothing else. Also, I'm pretty sure my mouth is hanging open.

"Mel," Paige whispers.

"Yes?" I whisper back, still looking at him.

"You okay?" There is a playful note in her voice. I regretfully tear my eyes away from him, to look at her.

I scowl, I know I do, because I want to see him the moment he looks at me, I want to see that I hold the same kind of interest to him. I nod and grab for my glass, watching him bend over to talk to Abe. They fall easily into conversation, ignoring us ladies completely. I've never really considered myself an attention whore, but at the moment...I really want to make a scene. Something. Anything, to get him to look at me.

Finally, he sits down at the table. I wait for his eyes to meet mine. When they do, he sizes me up for only a moment, and then looks at Paige. He nods to her, even though he didn't nod to me. He isn't interested. My stomach drops to the floor. Yet, somehow, even knowing that doesn't quiet my desperation. The desire I feel for him might be one sided, but damn if it isn't strong.

Abe introduces him to the rest of us as Sabato Efisto. Even his name is sensual, and I want to whisper it to myself to see how it feels on my tongue. No one hears me, and I feel a little thrill at the thought of getting away with it. I half listen to his and Abe's conversation and pick up on a passing mention of a dinner at his club in New Jersey.

My heartbeat quickens, knowing he will be so close to me. I allow myself to imagine studying until the wee hours. Sabato coming to me after, when he closes his club. I imagine he is interested in what I have to say. That he brings me coffee and quizzes me on torts and case study before kissing me, touching me, wanting me.

I imagine Sabato naked, filling me with his...oh, God, am I drooling?

"You ladies are more than welcome to join us tomorrow night," Sabato says, deep eyes looking only at Paige. The club will officially open in a week. Tomorrow will be more of an...intimate evening. Drinks, dinner, and entertainment."

His last word—entertainment—is the only word directed at me. Sabato's dark eyes seem to slice through me when he says it. My mouth opens slightly as I try to stifle a gasp of surprise—and excitement.

Laney and Dominic return to the table then, but she doesn't look happy. Maybe Paige's suspicions about what was going down in the restroom—or, who was going down—were wrong. They had to be, right? Otherwise, there's no way Laney would not be looking happy.

Dominic looks at Sabato. "What brings you by?"

Sabato doesn't reply. For a long moment, he just stares at Dominic.

Finally, I blurt out, "He invited us to a dinner at his new club, before he officially opens."

I look out of the corner of my eye to see how he reacts to my voice, hoping he finally feels the connection I do. I mean, how could he not? I'm such a stunningly gifted conversationalist. Right?

But...no. Nothing.

"Opening sooner than expected?" Dominic asks.

"Things are moving faster, yes." He looks uncomfortable with the conversation—almost annoyed. "Father and his associates are coming in two days."

"Here?" Dominic's voice is concerned.

"I think it will actually work out better than planned." Abe winks.

"So, will you ladies be joining us?" This time, when Sabato asks, he is looking at me—*only* at me.

"Probably not a good idea," Dominic says. I am immediately deflated.

"Why is that?" Sabato asks, as his eyes slowly continue skimming up and down my body.

"We can discuss it later," Dominic is annoyed now, too.

"Did you find a place today?" Paige asks Laney, changing the subject.

I know I should be interested in the conversation, but I am still watching Sabato look at me like I'm suddenly the most fascinating thing in the world.

His eyes practically molest me as his fingers strum on the table. He turns his body towards his friends, but keeps glancing at me every so often. I make sure he knows I haven't forgotten about him, either. My pulse quickens as I watch his hands move. They are beautiful, just like the rest of him. I wonder desperately what they'd feel like on my....

"Mel has news." Paige says.

What? I do? Oh, yes. Right.

Again, I am forced to rejoin reality, stepping outside the fantasy I have going on in my mind.

I clear my throat. "Yeah, I was accepted into Cornell's accelerated pre-law program, starting this summer."

"So, you're really going to do it?" Laney looks genuinely happy for me, in spite of whatever's going on with her and Dominic.

"I think so. I have a meeting with admissions on Monday. My focus won't be that much different. I see it as social work, but on a larger scale. I will still focus on women and children's advocacy though, you know, fighting for the greater good."

"Your parents must be so proud."

"They are." I look up at Sabato, whose eyes are fixed on me. I can't tell what he's thinking. He looks away and I think I see his eyes roll.

I am crushed.

*   *   *

Paige has been asleep for hours, but I am still wide-awake.

I've fallen into an Instagram rabbit hole, cyber-stalking Sabato. God, I love his name. In Italian, it means someone was born on a Saturday, considered the Sabbath. Apparently, it's a good omen.

And, I think it's safe to say that I am fixating.

I am a good person, most of the time. I want to be a good person. I try to be a good person, but lately...I have changed. No one has noticed the change, because I've hidden it well.

In college, I dated… a lot. I wanted to feel that earthquake-inducing attraction everyone always talks about. I wanted that 'once in a lifetime' chemistry to happen to me, so badly. So I forced it. First I would fixate on a guy, flirting with him until he asked me out on a date, and another, and another. Finally, when that build up of physical temptation was nearly too much to handle, when I was sure that all of this desire for me was real, I'd let him kiss me. And kiss me. And kiss me.

When the kissing stopped getting me hot and bothered, I would let him touch me. Always breasts first, nothing below the waist. If that felt good, I would let him lay on me and rub against me, Levi-loving style. Some call it 'dry humping.' Doesn't really matter what you call it, though, the aim is the same:

Friction.

Friction, I discovered, felt good.

I would lay there, eyes closed tight, getting dry humped into oblivion and thinking of Zac Efron, or Theo James or either of the Hemsworth brothers. And yes, sometimes I felt a slight fizzle of heat between my legs, but that was always contained by the fabric between us.

There were only twenty, real-life men who I allowed myself to get close to, in a sexual way.

Twenty men who I dated, kissed, allowed to touch me, and rub on me.

Twenty men who pretended to fuck me, while I pictured someone else.

Twenty men tried to get in my pants, and I denied them access.

Twenty men all eventually grew tired of trying to fuck me.

And twenty men who had told me to my face, in one way of another, that I wasn't worth the effort.

I, Melyssa Chance, am a tease.

In my defense, though, if the build-up to a kiss, that sweet burning anticipation, is inevitably *snuffed* by said kiss? Then why on Earth would I have sex with a guy, just to find out that experience is also much worse than I imagined? Not to mention, after the disappointment, comes the disappearing act. Once they got what they wanted from me, poof! On to the next challenge, the next 'unattainable' girl.

I don't care if a girl has fifty partners. I'm not here to judge that. Let me remind you I have been ready to give it up twenty times in four years. But if you don't *feel* it, then why *do* it? It's not like you have some kind of written obligation to see it through, and finish what you start. Though, God knows some guys will make you feel that way. Expectations are made to be let down. Feelings, emotions, attachments, and broken promises lead to hurt. I have spent years avoiding hurt, and yet, I still managed to pick up some scars along the way.

For the longest time, I was afraid I was cursed to live without lust. Then I realized, I had the drive, but my vagina was a tricky vehicle to operate. No one bothered to give me a user manual, so I just spent years feeling like I was broken.

I am sure I have been cursed with the Elsa of vaginas. I may thaw out a bit, get worked up, but when it came right down to it. I was—frozen.

But I gave it the 'old college try,' as they say. Now I'm left facing the fact that my dirty desires will probably always be much better off, just living in my head.

I did it again tonight, with Sabato, whose name still makes my long-dormant nether regions purr with excitement.

I lay back and try to erase him from my mind, but no matter how many Hollywood hunks I try to replace him with, nothing works.

* * *

We pull into an empty parking lot, stopping in front of a sign that reads: Steelettos.

Paige bounds out of the car like an excited puppy—or a dog in heat, take your pick—while Laney just seems annoyed. I know she likes this Dominic guy, but typical of Laney, she acts like she's more pissed off than she really is. My kind of girl, she likes to make them suffer and beg, so she knows it's real. Apparently, Nikki is already here with Abe. He didn't want her to go with him, but she insisted.

Laney warns us that this club is different.

"Okay, so some of the things we see in there tonight might seem kind of...hard core. But don't worry, nothing is going to happen to you. At least, not without your permission."

She looks at me—the virgin of the crew—like I should be upset, but I'm not. Actually, I am very intrigued. According to Laney, Steelettos's staff is made up of scantily clad Amazon women who don't speak English. Very exotic! And...well. There is always Sabato.

Sabato.... I tease his name with my tongue, and it teases back.

I adjust my boobs as we walk in. My intention was for them to play a bit of peek-a-boo, but now they're kind of spilling out of this balconette bra. I chose to wear a shorter and slightly more revealing than normal black dress, too, hoping maybe it would call attention to the assets Sabato was checking out before.

Inside, the lighting is soft, there is artwork on the walls and a large, dark, wooden table set up in the middle of the room. I find that odd, for a club. Shouldn't there be a bar in the middle, or a dance floor, instead? I assume, because it's set, that dinner will be held here.

Across the room I spot Nikki, Abe, and another man I don't recognize. Nikki waves us over and we join them. When I am introduced to Benito, he shakes my hand and kisses it. It makes my skin crawl. His eyes are black with no life in them.

Sabato and a man walk out into the club next, from a room just beyond the one we're in. From what Dominic said before, I assume it's Sabato's father, but the resemblance pretty much stops at...tall. Sabato introduces him to everyone, and when he introduces me, I nearly shudder at the way his tongue caresses my name. After the introductions, the older Efisto kisses my cheeks—the foreign way, and then walks over to Benito and nods towards me. They make no attempt to hide the fact that they're talking about me.

"Voglio mangiargli la fica." Mr. Efisto says, and they both look me up and down. I catch a glimpse of Sabato from the corner of my eye. His lips curl in distain and he looks away from me. What they said upset him, and I want to know why. I also want to know what 'Voglio mangiargli la fica,' means.

But I don't get a chance to ask Laney to ask Dominic; because we never get a moment alone and also...they're apparently still fighting. We all sit to eat. Sabato ends up across from me. I look up at him and he leans back in his chair and stares at me.

Stares. At. Me.

Three women come in through a side door, carrying trays of food. After what Laney kind of explained to us before, I thought I would be prepared. I wasn't. Amazon had not been a joking term. We might as well be getting invaded by an army of Victoria's Secret models. They are dressed in leather, strappy one-piece thingies, with matching thigh high boots.

I glance back at Sabato to gauge his reaction, but miraculously he is still staring at me. I swallow hard, but refuse to look away.

"Is that them?" Paige whispers into my other ear, and I nod, once. "Wow, this place is *that* kind of club huh?"

When I don't answer, she nudges me, forcing me to look at her.

"How do you think they pee in those things?" Her eyes look like they're going to pop out of her head. I can't help but stifle a giggle.

When I turn back, one of the women is bending to whisper in Sabato's ear. *Christ! No way can those be real!* Oblivious to the boob explosion, he nods and waves her off. Then he looks back at me. My jealousy dies out in a fizzle, when compared to the heat in his eyes.

Burn, baby, burn!

"The tour of the club seems to be taking a little longer than it should, wouldn't you say, Sabato?" Benito chuckles. "My wife must be entertaining. It's a good thing I'm not a jealous man."

Laney turns slightly green as Dominic and a black haired woman appear from the back. She excuses herself and gets up. I start to go after her, but Paige holds my hand, stopping me.

"She's upset," I whisper.

"The new ride is going in after her. Come on it's Laney, let her deal with this her own way."

It's not easy for me to sit on the sidelines, not when I can see my friend is hurting. I scowl. "He has two minutes to fix it, then I'm going in."

While I wait, I sit back and take a drink. There's a part of me, a small part, that is starting to wonder what the hell

I'm doing here. This place, these people, none of this is who I am. Or, who I was. Hell, I'm not sure if I even know which is which, anymore.

Abe and Nikki come back and conversations start flowing around the table. Some are speaking Italian, others English. I am not speaking, but drinking wine.

Wine: the universal social translator, since ancient Rome.

Three glasses have gone down already, when one of the Amazons brings over bread and drops it on my plate.

"*Mangia.*"

"*Excuse me?*" I don't speak Italian, and with wine comes the inability to use a quiet voice, so everyone is looking at me.

"Eat," Sabato says. His voice is silk, strong and smooth.

"I'm really not hungry," I say. "But thank you."

His eyes squint, like he's judging me, and quite frankly it makes me irritated.

I roll my eyes. Sabato raises his eyebrows, as if I am challenging him. Or at least, that's how I take it.

"She gets no more wine, unless she eats," he says, in plain English, to the leather clad Amazon chick.

"Let the girl drink, son," Efisto's voice booms. "She'll enjoy the night much more if she loosens up."

"Salute," I throw out the word like I know what the heck it means, then take the glass, lift it in mock cheer and drink it up. All of it. I may want this man's attention, and maybe there is a part of me—the darkest part—that wants all sorts of his other parts in my...but, I *do not* want to be told what to do. I set the glass down, a little too hard. "Ah, excellent."

Sabato stands slowly, his beautiful face turning to stone. He looks just like something Michelangelo would have sculpted. Or maybe it was Leonardo. One of those Ninja Turtle guys, I'm pretty sure. Shaking his head in disgust, he follows Abe and Giddy up away from the table. Nikki goes, too.

When they are all far enough away, Efisto and Benito stand. Efisto makes his way towards me, grabs the bottle and refills my glass, "How about you ladies join us in the other room? The entertainment is about to start."

Before I can say anything, Paige is getting up and following behind Benito and his wife. Not wanting to be alone with Efisto, I stand, wobble a little, and then quickly catch up.

Looking around this new room, I feel like a deer in headlights. There are small platforms around the perimeter, and if there was any more doubt that this was a sex club, it's gone. Several of the platforms have these x-shaped crosses, made of worn, wooden beams. There are rings attached to the walls and ceilings, and some of the stages have what I'm pretty sure are sex swings.

Okay, well I'm more than pretty sure. I know they are sex swings. How do I know this? Let's just say I have watched a few 'adult clips' on the Internet. Okay, maybe more than a few.

The room is practically dark, lit only with sinful red lighting. It screams sin, sex, and Sabato. The wood grain is so dark, it must be expensive. It matches his eyes. There is no doubt in my mind who chose the furnishings. One thing I wasn't sure about, but now I know.

Sabato is a wicked, wicked man.

In the center of the room, there is a form of seating. Large, round leather pieces of furniture, all positioned so you only have to turn your head, and everything is visible.

Paige sits on one such leather couch-thing, pulling me down next to her.

"Holy hell," she whispers. "Kinky."

Nikki comes in and sits on my other side. "Mel, Abe wants us to leave. Do you want to come with us?"

"I'm fine, Nikki." I laugh her off, but as soon as Sabato comes out with the smallest of the three Amazons, I start to feel sick.

Sick, not because I drank too much, but because I can't look away from him. He is shirtless now, and I swear if he was on the ground, I would pour wine on his eight-pack stomach and drink from it like the dirty little dog I am—I mean, like I try really hard not to be.

His dark green cargo pants hang dangerously from his hips. The top button is open and I see dark hair following the curve of his muscles down to...*gulp*. His 'V' is as deep as the Congo River, and I know from the outline that it isn't a little water snake hiding beneath the surface of those pants—it's an anaconda. I ache everywhere, from my breasts to my vagina. I cross my legs, seeking pressure, knowing it will at least take the edge off.

I am sick, too, because there is a blank look in his eyes. There is no depth, nothing but focus in those dark pools between his lashes. He is completely focused, almost to a surgical degree—and by the way he is wrapping her wrists in rope, securing them to the rings suspended from the ceiling, it's obvious he has done this a time or two...or twenty.

Biting my lip until it hurts, I have to look away when he shortens the ropes, causing her to stand on the tips of her toes. She winces in pain and pleasure, and so do I.

When another woman—Benito's wife, I recall— joins the show, I sneak a glance at Laney. What's her name...Mrs. Benito...she wears a tiny red robe, and is leading another disgustingly beautiful girl. The girl wears a collar—and not much else— which is attached to a leash. Laney is starting to look a little ill now, too. Nikki has her by the hand, and they are standing, getting ready to leave. Paige grabs mine, and we follow them out the door. I look over my shoulder, just as Sabato's eyes lift from the suspended woman, and zero in on me. Not breaking eye contact, he runs the whip in his hand along her thigh, up between her legs, and slowly back down again.

He watches my eyes follow his movements, watches me react, and doesn't look away.

When we leave the room—or, when my friends drag me out—Benito's wife follows us. Her laugh is evil, taunting. "What? You are leaving, before the show even begins?"

"The ladies are ready to retire," Abe says, turning his back to her.

I watch the way she looks at Laney and I know I will be forcing this conversation soon. Laney will be pissed, but I don't care. I won't lose her, too.

I hear Dominic whisper to her, "You look beautiful tonight."

"Do you think that makes this easier?" She waves her hand through the air, refusing to look at him. "Goodbye, Dominic."

..*

I lie in bed at the hotel, for what seems like the entire night.

Paige is sleeping in the bed next to me, and I know I should be sleeping too. But I can't stop thinking about him. *Him*. The way he looked at me—hell, the way he *looked*, period. Over and over, I replay the looks on his face, and the little things he did or said when he was irritated, or amused, or interested. Any time he let his guard down and showed some little hint of emotion. All of those little moments seem important to me, telling, even though he seems to be an expert at hiding how he feels, who he really is.

I know I am obsessing. No...I am officially obsessed. But I can't help it. I need to know more. I need to know everything. I need to solve the mystery that is this man.

When I finally bother to look at the clock, it's well after midnight. But I am still dressed, I am still awake. I no longer feel drunk, at least not on alcohol. I cannot stop thinking about the desire I have, for him. I want to go back. I want to see if he is finally alone. I want to be that woman he has suspended, I want to feel the caress of his whip and the slap of his hand on my...and I really, really want these thoughts to go away.

Since we got back to the hotel, around nine, I have tried to talk myself out of making this mistake. For another twenty minutes or so, I wrestle with myself, trying to push the thoughts away. Finally, I fail. I embrace the darkness.

It takes me less than twenty minutes to sneak out of my room, go down the elevator, walk out to my car, get in, and drive back to the place that made me feel so sick before. Back to the one place I know I should not go, back to see the one person I know I should not see.

Sabato.

I pulled in the driveway and go around back. There are only two cars left in the lot: a black Land Rover and a black sports car I don't know the name of—but it's a very *expensive looking* sports car. The other three vehicles that were there when we left earlier are gone now.

Yes, I noticed. Why? I don't want to admit that to myself. Maybe...because deep down, I knew I would be coming back. This draw, this pull, it's strong—and like nothing I've ever felt before.

I've always been able to tell when a man wants me, and I've always loved it. But I've been focusing on that feeling for years, instead of the actual person who inspired it, because otherwise I know I would feel nothing.

Sabato, though. He pulls at me, he tugs at places in me I never knew existed. I don't want to ignore that. I can't. I want to explore it. As I walk toward the club I feel sexual, hungry, needy.

I did not come here for *that* tonight. At least, that's what I tell myself. I came here to face these feelings, to let them wither away in the harsh light of reality. Like they always do, when I eventually realize that the person I'm fixating on couldn't possibly live up to my fantasies.

Tiptoeing to the side window, I peek inside. Sabato is sitting in a chair, alone, at the big dinner table.

For the first time, he doesn't look relaxed or in control. In fact, it's kind of the opposite. His eyes are darting around the room, and he keeps running his hands through his hair. From where I am I can hear nothing, but I see his jaw twitch and he leans back, seemingly trying to calm himself. His hand runs through his thick, dark hair again, and he sits up agitatedly. The powerful, controlled man I've seen before, he's not here now. Instead, I see a reflection of myself. I see myself, or what I must look like, when I struggle with my innermost, darkest secrets.

I see his mouth move then, he speaks to someone angrily, and two of the women—those damn, sexy club employees—are suddenly at his side. One hands him a glass, as the other kneels at his side. He stands and says something, a directive, and the girl on her knees starts to pull down his pants. The other girl pulls a chair to sit opposite his, letting her robe fall off. Sabato sits and spreads his legs apart. I see his erection, jutting proudly, impressively away from his perfect body. My body hums, vibrates, and tingles all over.

The second girl sits across from him, and spreads her legs to him. Sabato takes the whip from beside him, the same leather-ended stick from earlier, and rubs it against her until her head falls back. He doesn't react, though, he just watches her. He says something to the woman on her knees, and she moves between his legs. In a flash, her mouth is on him, wrapping around his manhood. She moves slowly up and down, and he leans back, moving the whip up and down against her bare skin in perfect time. I feel it too, in that moment, I feel it. And I want it.

At another command, the kneeling girl straightens, turning her body toward the other woman. Sabato smacks her ass with his whip, until she is on all fours. He smacks it again, and she begins licking the woman's vagina.

Sabato reaches beside him, allowing the whip to drop, and bends over. He picks up his pants and pulls something out of his pocket. I know it's a condom. He is now positioned, facing in my direction. I watch him rub himself up and down the woman on all fours, and then without word or warning, he pushes into her and stills. His body stiffens, and his jaw clenches. He grabs her hips and lifts, positioning her exactly how he wants as he pushes in and out of her. When her head raises and her mouth forms an 'O,' he swats her ass, then moves quicker. Back and forth, back and forth harder, he rocks into her.

As I watch it happen, I am wet, soaked, filled with desire. But strangely, not jealousy. Not in the way I thought I would feel it. I want that to be me. I want him, in me. So I pretend it *is* me he's fucking, as I rub myself, over my clothes. Friction.

I watch him for what seems like an eternity, until my hand becomes tired. The woman is now on her elbows, no longer between the other one's legs. The other woman is on the floor next to her, caressing her breasts. Still thrusting, Sabato's body trembles and his eyes finally open wide.

He is looking in my direction. I know he doesn't see me, but I pretend he does. It makes me feel dirty. It makes me feel free. It makes me feel everything I don't want to admit that I want to feel.

His teeth clench together as he rams into her, looking at me—well, in my general direction.

One, thrust, two, three, four—I feel every one. When Sabato comes, I pretend I can feel that, too. He doesn't stay inside her, when it's over. He stands and pats both of their heads, before kissing the tops of them. He picks up their robes, helps each woman up, and puts the robes over their shoulders. He pushes them towards each other. They embrace, and kiss. Sabato looks pleased as he watches them. Then he dismisses them. Each girl gives him a soft kiss on his cheek before they leave the room.

After they leave, he looks towards the window again, toward me. When he starts moving toward me, I run around the building and get into my car. I start it up quickly, but leave the lights off as I pull out of the driveway. Once I am out of the lot, I turn the lights on. He saw me. He was coming toward me. Wasn't he?...Was he?

No, I shake my head, trying to control my breathing. I try to convince myself that it's all in my head as I drive back to the hotel. I hope that Paige doesn't wake up when I sneak back into the room.

A part of me is angry at myself, but another part is glad I did what I did. Now, when I lay down, I can concentrate on the ugliness of what I just witnessed, and how it made me react.

Tomorrow, maybe this curiosity will completely fade away, into the blackness, and I will no longer want to follow it.

At least, that's what I hope, and wish will happen.

SABATO
New Jersey

It's three in the morning, and I am driving back to Steelettos, finally allowing myself to think about the night I've just had.

My father was far too close for me to be comfortable.

In Italy, I kept my distance from him. He did the same. I ran the clubs. I saw him only when he traveled to one of them, and normally I was aware of his schedule and would make sure not to be there when he came in.

I've always despised the man, my whole life, but now things are different.

Before, I was just biding my time until the bastard finally died, of natural causes.

Now, I am waiting for the day that I, the sinister son, will personally bring the most feared man in Sicily to his knees. I plan to destroy him, just like he once did to the young boy I was. While I am at it, I will make sure that he feels each shard of pain ripping through his skin, while he looks into the eyes of the once innocent victim of his mayhem.

Watching him laugh and joke tonight, while trying to keep the inferno of hatred hidden inside, was close to impossible. But I made it possible, barely, by fixating on a young blonde haired woman with green eyes who clearly wants to get my attention. She wants it, bad.

Every time I caught her staring at me tonight, she would hold eye contact and try to appear calm. She was not. She fidgeted with her hands, bounced her knee and tapped her wine glass. The longer I allowed her eyes to connect with mine, the more her signs of arousal became evident. Her pupils visibly dilated with anticipation. Her lips parted slightly, and her breasts would heave, just enough for me to notice. Her back would arch slightly—pushing her body toward me, proving she was subconsciously craving my touch—and then, I would look away.

Pleasure for me is found in a woman's desire—in prolonging, heightening and amplifying it. Giving pleasure is one of the few luxuries I allow myself to revel in. I give everything, and nothing, keeping my own pleasure at bay.

When I heard my father speak of her the way he did, I detested him even more. Unlike me, my father cares only for himself, his own needs. His own emotions, his own drives, his own pleasures. It's a short-sighted, stupid, and dangerous way to live—and an even worse way to rule. His inability to acknowledge anything beyond his self-serving nature incurs the secret wrath of his henchmen, weak men who only do what is asked of them, because they fear repercussions.

One day though, one day soon, that fear will dissipate. And my father's power will dissolve, right along with it. I will use my father's greatest weapon against him.

Most men fear death. I have been flirting with it for as long as I can remember. Over the years, I have come to relish the thought of finally giving in, of succumbing to that final and eternal release.

Other than death, there is nothing to fear, and so I fear nothing.

Tonight, I watched my father watch me, as I watched her. More than I knew her want for me, I knew that he would want to take her away. That's what he does. So when he requested entertainment, I knew it was his way of keeping me busy, to clear the way for him to pursue the girl who wanted me. The girl he thought I wanted back. Melyssa.

Sweet, innocent Melyssa, so clearly unaccustomed to dealing with men motivated by...darker desires. I was pleased that Dominic and Abe seemed to be taking care of her, to find that they aren't that kind of man. I was the one who had invited the women, but that was before I had gotten a true read on them. It was careless of me.

It will not happen again.

I pull into the darkened lot and make one pass around the property, to ensure that my father has not yet returned.

Once inside, I sit and pour myself a drink.

I can't help remembering the look on her face, at the beginning of the suspension, before she left the room. She wasn't horrified or shocked, but intrigued. That's why I left, shortly after, to follow her back to her hotel. I had to ensure she made it home without running into my father. Without being followed by someone whose intentions were...less honorable...than mine. If that was possible.

My carelessness in choosing the bait seems to have caused another problem. Melyssa's interest in me is stronger than I realized. I saw her watching me from the window. I knew she wanted me, to the point of desperation.

Strangely, I did not feel concerned by this.

I enjoyed knowing that she watched as I pleasured the staff. I looked into her eyes as I came. I don't know how it's possible that she did not know I was watching her, too. After my problem has been dealt with, maybe I will allow her another indulgence in her fantasy—or even a taste of the real thing—before I go home.

But first, I need to untangle this web of complication that surrounds my central goal. All the pieces are there, but not all are in place. Zandor Steel, my friend. Dominic Segretti, his cousin. Jules DeLuca, Benito's wife, who very conveniently has a thing for Dominic. All of them secretly—

or not so secretly—loathe my father, each in their own way. Most of them also loathe Benito, his right hand and most trusted friend.

Benito, who has been laundering money through the company he controls, which rightfully belongs to Dominic's family.

Benito, whose wife is a manipulative and power-hungry woman, who yearns to fuck someone else.

Benito, who is the weak link in my father's chain of control—a link I plan to help Dominic and the Steel family exploit, to the fullest degree.

I lean back and close my eyes, basking in the knowledge that all will begin to crumble, very soon. A few minutes later, I hear a sound at the door. I stand and walk to the entry, where just a while ago Melyssa stood, watching me through the window. This time, it is my father and Benito. I look at my watch, annoyed. It's nearly four in the morning.

My father looks angry. They both do. It gives me a sick satisfaction. I open the door and stand in their way, facing my father with cold determination.

"We have new girls coming in," my father says, "in two days."

He tries to push past me, but I don't move, and they are forced to go around me.

"We aren't ready for more girls yet," I say, shutting the door and turning around.

"They're already on the—"

"I said no." I look at him with a blank face. "This place will be run my way. The women will be hand-picked by me, and me alone."

"They are coming in from Eastern Europe." He stands taller, puffing out his chest.

"This is not Italy," I tell him, shaking my head. "Here, there are laws."

"Fuck the law!" He and Benito laugh, congratulating themselves. "Now, get me a damn drink, son, and thank me for helping fund this little American dream of yours."

"Get your own drink," I tell him, gesturing behind me. "The bar is right over there. I am going to bed."

I feel my hands begin to tremble, and I know I need to walk away soon, or I will kill him with my bare hands. I turn away, disrespecting him with my body language.

"You!" I hear the click of a gun hammer being choked back. "Turn around, and tell me again, you little—"

I turn slowly, and laugh. "You don't get to tell me what to do. And one last time, I am not afraid of you. Your threats are bullshit."

My father's eyes narrow, and Benito smiles, like he knows a secret.

"Well, maybe you do and maybe you don't. But that girl, Melyssa?"

"Is nothing," I finish his sentence for him. But even as I bluff the words, my heart rate increases. I feel hatred creep up like bile in my stomach.

"You know," I say. "I'm beginning to think you're the one who is afraid."

"You." The gun in his hand is shaking with his rage. His face is almost purple. Benito takes a step back. "You bite your tongue, boy."

I lunge for him then, knocking the gun from his hand. I hear it clatter on the wood floor as we exchanged blows, rolling around in a murderous heap on the ground.

Benito moves toward us, reaching into his jacket. I reach out, allowing Salvatore to continue beating on me, as I grab for the gun. Once I feel it secure in my hand, I reach up and shove it into my father's mouth.

A reckless darkness overtakes me, then. Things may not have gone according to my plan, but I am ready to die. Provided I take him down with me.

"Now you're done fighting, you pussy?" I taunt him, watching gleefully as blood trickles out of his mouth.

"Sabato, son, don't!" Benito yells.

"I'm not your son!" I push the gun in further.

I love the surprise that blossoms in his eyes as I look into them. He tries to fight me, but I only thrust the cool steel deeper in.

"All these fucking years," I whisper. "You sick, son of a bitch. I blamed myself for her death, for wanting to go to the museum that day, and you let me. You encouraged me. But it was you, wasn't it? You're the one who killed her?"

A sharp blow to the back of my head, and I am stunned. Benito pulls me off of him, but even at death's door, I will not let him win. I roll to my side. Benito is aiming a gun at me, but I don't care. The man I always wanted to believe was grieving in his own way, slowly pulls himself up, and carefully wipes the blood from his mouth with a silk handkerchief.

"Shoot him." He turns his back on me.

I pull the trigger.

Salvatore falls to the floor on his knees, as blood begins to spill out of the hole in his shoulder. The hole I blew in him, with his own gun.

Another shot rings out, but it's not mine. A hole appears in the floor, right next to my head. Benito is slower than I am, and apparently not a very good shot, but that doesn't mean I'll survive. I keep aiming, determined to put as many bullets into my father as I can, before his henchman drops me for the last time.

"Freeze!" I look up, just as the place fills with police officers. All with guns aimed on all three of us. Benito drops his gun. I immediately drop mine, raising my hands. Salvatore Efisto falls forward, in a pile on the ground.

A faceless police officer pulls me to my feet and jacks my arms behind my back. I can feel myself smiling, viciously. It's over. Just like that, it's finally over.

But my satisfaction dies when I hear the words, "He has a pulse. The bullet went through his shoulder. Let's get him to a hospital, now."

A man walks up to me then, and I hate him, for stealing my revenge.

"Are you Sabato Efisto?"

I shake my head, no. I am no one's son.

Not anymore.

* * *

I refuse to speak to anyone as they search my club.

The policeman in charge, whose questions I refuse to answer, makes phone calls and orders a bunch of uniformed men around. I sit silently, watching my father as he is cared for by the paramedics.

It's not until they start to wheel him out on a stretcher, that I finally find my voice.

"Marcisci all'inferno, bastardo!"

Across the room, I watch his lips turn up and even though he seems unconscious, I know the fucker hears me. And once again, as always, he is taunting me.

"Sabato!" Zandor comes toward me through the crowd of officers. One of them grabs his arm, stopping him.

"Nick D'Angelo called me."

The man who appears to be in charge—Nick D'Angelo, I assume—comes towards him, nodding to the uniforms to let him pass.

"Is this Sabato Efisto?" he asks Zandor.

"Yeah." He puts a hand on my shoulder, like a concerned brother might, if I had one. "You okay?"

"He's alive," I tell him, through gritted teeth. "So, no."

Zandor's face fills with concern—but also warning. "Bro, you need to keep that kind of thing—"

"I should have shot him twice, three times, as many as I could."

"Okay," D'Angelo seems to have heard enough. He nods at one of the officers. "Get him out of here."

"Nick, man, come on," Zandor says. "He's—"

"Refusing to answer questions."

Amelia, Rosalie, and Cassandra come in from the back, looking terrified. I feel my blood boil, as I realize they were there the whole time. In danger. Not to mention what would have happened to them after, if Benito had shot me. If my father had been left alone with them.

"Zandor." I nod in their direction.

"I got it," he says, looking over. "Don't worry, they'll be fine. Though, I may be on the shit list later." He grumbles the last part under his breath.

"They need to come in too, and answer some questions."

I start to object, but Zandor makes a face at the detective. "Look, Nick. They were clearly sleeping when all this went down. This is his place, and those two fucks were clearly not welcome—trespassing, even. Do you really need to treat them like a bunch of suspects?"

"*Fine, I'll question them here.*"

"*Le ragazze non parlano inglese,*" I say then, glaring at the cop.

"*E 'una buona cosa che parlo italiano,*" the detective responds with a growl.

"If you dare try to trap them, or manipulate their words, you will pay."

"Jesus! Shut the hell up, Sabato!" Zandor is pissed, but it still sounds like a plea. "I'll check back in with you when this is taken care of."

"*Spero che muore,*" I tell him, as they cuff me and push me out the door.

..*.*

Two days later, Zandor picks me up from the police station and brings me back to the club.

"*Sei a casa!*" All three of the girls greet me enthusiastically.

"*Sono a casa.*" I nod. "*Ho bisogno di un bagno. Unitevi a me.*"

After our shared bath, and much needed releases by all, I send them off to rest. They haven't slept since I left, I can tell. They no longer feel safe here. Soon, I know I will have to send them back. The sooner the better.

They aren't happy when I tell them they are going back, but I make it clear that the subject isn't up for discussion. I book them on a flight, to leave for Italy in the morning.

They will be safer there, if not completely safe.

I decide I will send them to a man who is better than me.

Amelia, Rosalie, and Cassandra had already been employees of my father's, at the very first club I took over. I did my best to change their lives, for the better. They were still so young, and so damn afraid of everything. And as long as they are in a position where my father can reach them, I realize now they will never stop being afraid.

The next day, I say goodbye to them for the last time, and return to an empty club.

Finally alone, as I should be, I stand in the middle of the floor and look around. His blood is still on the floor, even splattered across some of the chairs. I decide I will spend today fixing that, since I could not fix his fate.

First I fill the hole that I assume held the bullet that failed to kill him. The police took it away, as part of their investigation. I would have loved to keep it as a souvenir. Zandor seemed close to the detective; maybe he could pull some strings. In the meantime, I need to busy my mind. I can relax for a bit, but only for a moment. Even though I know he can't come after me this second, I know damn well it isn't over.

I decide to try and drown my anger with music—loud, harsh music. I go behind the bar and slide through my playlist. Lacuna Coil fits the bill. With the music pounding in my ears, I grab a bottle. I will drink, work myself into exhaustion, and then sleep.

There is nothing else I can do, not now anyway.

I grab the putty, tools and paint I need to fix the floor. Then I decide, fuck it, I'm just going to paint the entire room.

Red.

Blood red.

Lacuna is on repeat as I work through the rage. When the music stops suddenly, I turn around, welcoming the threat of an intruder.

"Lacuna Coil?" The girl smiles and walks up to me with her hand extended. I look at Dominic, and then back to her.

"Valentina Segretti."

"Sabato Efisto." I hold up my hands. "Paint."

"I'm not afraid." She smiles and pushes her hand closer.

"Good to know." There is something about her, something familiar.

"Valentina?" Dominic comes up quickly behind her.

"Lacuna Coil," she continues. "I love that song, 'I'm Not Afraid.' I saw them live three times. They're amazing." She wraps her arm around Dominic's waist, which immediately seems to put him at ease.

"I remember the pictures on Instagram. I also remember being relieved that Franco was there." Dominic laughs.

Ah. That's where I knew her from.

"Sabato, this is my sister, Valentina."

She smirks, and I know she remembers me too. I wonder if Dominic knows his sister has a taste for the dark side.

"What brings you here?" I pull a handkerchief out of my back pocket, wipe my face off, and then tie it around my head.

"Just came in last night, and wanted to see how you're doing."

"Fine." I walk past them to the bar. "Drink?"

"It's nine thirty in the morning," Dominic laughs. "We're all set. Where is your staff?"

"I sent them back to Italy. Didn't want them to get caught up in the storm."

"The storm?"

"Father is being released from the hospital tomorrow."

"And going to jail," Dominic adds.

"Yes, of course."

"You don't seem too sure of that."

"My father has ways around everything."

"Benito does, as well, but he's in jail." Dominic folds his arms. "And he's staying there."

"That's wonderful." I fill my glass with whisky and drink it down.

"You're painting? So, you plan on staying?"

"The wall had a hole in it, and blood stains. I thought I'd fix it. Not much else to do today." I pour another drink. "You sure you don't want one?"

··*

I am glad Dominic got what he wanted. But I am still angry at myself for not killing the man whose sole purpose on this Earth is to make my life hell.

After I finish painting, I decide to install a security system. Next time, when my father appears, I will kill him in self-defense. I will not go to jail again.

When I am done, there are cameras in every room. Very few areas cannot be seen by those cameras, but if there is a God, the areas with blind spots will serve my purpose well.

Now I sit at the bar, as I have since I finished, and I look around at the results of my work. Looking at it now, you would never know that this was where I drew first blood against my enemy.

I glance up at the window and I meet her eyes again. I have had a lot to drink and now I consider that I may have drank too much. This may be an illusion, and when they disappear, I assume I'm right. I hit 'random' on my iPhone, and Arctic Monkeys begin to play. The song makes me think of fucking and I want to fuck.

I look back to the window and there are eyes again. I decide to go find out if my eyes are deceiving me, or if it is really Melyssa staring at me with those curious eyes.

I am quiet in my movements, cat-like, and drunk.

I stop dead in my tracks when I see her outside, squatting down with her hands fisted in her hair. She is frustrated, and so am I. I assume for the same reasons.

I open the door quietly; slip out until I am standing above her. She is unsuspecting, and I like that. When she looks up, she jumps and screams. I grab her, and she tries to pull free.

"I am not in the mood for games."

"I'm not playing one," she hisses.

I lift her and stumble back through the door.

"What are you doing?"

"I don't feel like doing this outside," I tell her. "There are people."

"Your father!" She sputters. I immediately set her on her feet and step back. I say nothing. I am angry now.

"It's on the news." She looks around, confused. "You painted."

"Good observation," I say, icily. "Is that the reason you were looking at me through the window?"

She doesn't say anything, but her face burns brightly. This amuses me.

"Yes." Melyssa looks down and straightens her blouse. "You were gracious enough to invite us for dinner, so, I thought I would, um...." She stops and looks up, squares her shoulders and clears her throat. "I wanted to repay the kindness. I'm new here, too. I just thought maybe." She stops and her shoulders begin to turn in again. She tugs once again on her blouse.

"How about we cut the shit, Melyssa," I say. "You want me to fuck you."

Her mouth drops open. I reach up and close it for her.

"You Americans." I shake my head. She looks confused. "I need to fuck as well. So let's just get to it, shall we?"

I take her hand and lead her to the 'playroom.' Then I turn to her.

"Where shall we start?"

She appears stunned, too stunned to respond.

"Melyssa, I am exhausted and have had too much to drink. I do not wish to play games. Remove your clothes."

She doesn't move though, so I give her what she needs: instruction. "Now."

She stands straighter, and I step to her, my body an inch from hers. I watch her eyes, and they tell me what I need to know. She's nervous, excited, titillated, yet unmoving. I watch her eyes, waiting, waiting, waiting until her pupils react.

She finally lets a bit of tension release in a slow exhale of sweet mint.

"You want me?" She attempts to open her mouth to speak, and I hold my finger just in front of her lips. Not touching, not yet.

"Your breasts are tender, there is a knot in your lower abdominal area, here," I let my hand slowly fall away from her mouth. Her lips move towards me, as if magnified.

Tremante.

I put my hand on the material of her blouse, but not touching her body.

"There is a deep pull between your thighs, and you want to squeeze your legs together to ease the pressure that is mounting. But you know that if you do, it won't be enough. Your pussy is wet and getting wetter by the minute."

Her eyes grow heavier, lids fluttering.

Bisogno.

"You want my touch as badly as I want to give it to you, yet you resist. You want to touch my cock, but are afraid to touch me because you know what I can do to you. You've seen it with your own two eyes, and you are afraid that after you've had me, you will crave more. I promise, you will. I will touch parts of you that no one ever has. I will show you places on your body that will drive you almost insane. I will turn your sweet, wet pussy into a raging inferno. Every dirty fantasy you've ever had about me while you finger fuck yourself, at night, lying in bed, dreaming of my touch, will become a reality."

She is panting for it, now. Her back is arching and her nipples are pushing against her shirt. I hear a slow deep intake of breath, and I know she is ready.

Suscitato.

"Tell me why your clothes are still on." I push her with my words. "No, better yet, take them off now, Melyssa. Before I grow too tired of this game. Before I decide I would prefer to tie you up and pump my cock in my hand, while you're on your knees denying yourself. Until I come all over your face."

Esposta.

She whimpers, and her eyes roll slightly.

Orgasmica.

"I am going to make you come, Melyssa. Present to me."

She reaches down and begins to unbutton her blouse. I take a step back and sit down, watching her prepare.

Ho bisogno di questo.

She presents herself to me.

To
The
Cross

He could have told me to leave, when he caught me outside. He could have made me feel ashamed. He could have, but he didn't.

Instead, he told me, in the crudest possible way, that he wanted to fuck me.

No man had said those words to me before—not in the heat of the moment, or otherwise.

Sabato looks expectant, and his eyes are less masked now that he is in control.

I close my eyes as I fumble with my buttons. I allow his sexually arousing words to continue to replay in my head. They don't just make me hot. They make me feel sexy. They make me hungrier, needier, than I ever have been.

I am quivering.

He sits and watches me, and slowly unbuttons his pants. I remember the light sprinkling of hair beneath his zipper. He pushes his hand inside his pants and squeezes himself. I don't hold eye contact, because I can't. He feels this too. I know he does.

I am in need.

I reach up and tug at my sleeves. My shirt falls to the wooden floor. I hope my movements are sexy, teasing, and not just rushed and desperate. I want to be sexy. My hardened nipples push against the fabric of my bra. I ache. I want him to touch them.

I am aroused.

I pull my white, lacy bra straps off my shoulders. I don't look at him. I can't. I have never been totally naked in front of a man. To calm my nerves, I think of what he said. I focus on the sensual sounds of his words and how they felt even more arousing, because of his accent. I kick off my flats, then I unbutton my pants and shove them down.

Sabato stands. I finally look up. He pushes his pants down. His cock is hard, and big, and beautiful. He nods, and I know he is waiting for the last piece of fabric to be removed. I push my panties down and step out of them.

I am exposed.

He reaches out and the feather light touch of his finger circles my left nipple.

I cry out his name. "Sabato!"

I am orgasmic.

He runs one finger up my chest, to my collarbone, across my neck and finally allows it to rest against my lips.

"Shhh." He steps into my space. I feel the crown of his thick, warm cock as it nudges my belly, in exactly the place the knot rests. I bite my lip, trying to remain quiet.

"Bella," he whispers. His lips hang centimeters from mine. They are not touching mine but I feel their weight.

I need this.

Finally, I gain the courage to lean up into his lips. But he pulls back and shakes his head, no. He steps back, holding his hand out to me. I take it. The electricity of our touch is jarring and his steps falter momentarily.

He needs this.

He leads me to the cross. I know what it is. I've seen it before, and not only here in this room.

I am not afraid.

Sabato stops and turns around, reaching for me again. His fingertips move from my hipbone up my side slowly. I watch his eyes appreciatively take in my naked form as he lightly rubs up my rib. I giggle, and he gives me a stern look.

His head bends forward and without warning he clamps his mouth down on my nipple. I cry out and reach for him to brace myself. He grabs both wrists and pulls them above my head. He turns my body in one swift move, until my back is against the cross and his body is pressing firmly against me. He sucks hard on my nipple. I thrust my pelvis against him, seeking pressure against my throbbing, sensitive spots. When it's not enough, I pull on my hands to get free. But he holds firm, pushing my wrists against the hard, cold wood as he continues sucking and biting on my nipple.

When it's too much, I test his strength by allowing my body to go limp. He catches me with his weight against the cross. Then I surprise him by wrapping my legs around him. He releases my hands and takes my waist. I wrap my arms around him, as my now passion-possessed hips grind on him. I cry out and my head falls back.

I'm going to come, Oh God, I think I'm going to—"

"Stop," he growls, and pushes me back.

"No," I challenge, holding tightly to him.

I have no idea where this voice is coming from, this need is coming from. But stop now? No way. Hell hath no fury like a twenty-four-year-old woman seeking her first real orgasm.

He grips my hips tightly and forces me back. I look at him angrily. He drops me. I scramble to keep from falling to the floor, grabbing the cross for support. He steps away, folding his arms.

Humiliated and naked, I pull myself to my feet.

"Well, I guess I'll just be going." Blushing, I try to walk past him.

His hand catches my elbow. "Did I dismiss you?"

I feel a chill run up my spine, but I don't answer. He grabs my hips from behind and once more I am slammed against the wood. He is like a jungle cat, fast, sexy and efficient. He has my arms spread against the wood and his lips are touching me, ever so softly, behind my ear.

He growls dangerously, "Did. I. Dismiss. You?"

I don't answer, but I look up as I feel leather cuffs wrap around my wrists. Before I can say a word, his head is between my legs. But not the way I want. One ankle is shackled in leather, then the other.

"There is no other way with you," he grumbles. I watch him walk away, circling off behind me.

I hear drawers open and shut, and anticipation mingles with desire and adrenaline. I try to look back behind me, but I don't see anything.

"Sabato?"

"Not another word."

He is behind me. I feel a sharp, stinging spank to my ass. Then his hand is kneading the spot he just hit. "You need to learn control. This is not what I need tonight, but it seems to be what you need." I feel him against me, and I feel material on his body. His lower half is no longer exposed.

His hand reaches around and cups me, and I jump in surprise.

"Sabato."

He nips my ear. It stings and he sucks on it.

"*Bagnata.*"

I don't know what it means, but his finger is now between my folds. Oh god, yes. My knees shake with desire, and I'm so close. But then he moves his hand away and steps back.

"*Pazienza.*"

I can't see him, but I can hear and feel his hot, heavy breath on my neck. I arch back, hoping to get closer. He sighs heavily, and I strain to look back at him, out the corner of my eye. He looks angry.

"Eyes forward."

"Why?"

"Focus," he growls.

"Focus on wh—Oh, god!" I look down to see the flogger in his hand.

He rubs it up and down my side and I am overwhelmed by the sensation. His hand comes up to cover my mouth as he shoves his finger inside.

"Show me what you will do to my cock."

I suck greedily on his fingertip. His lips are on my neck, his tongue caressing my ear. He moans.

My legs spread apart and I rub myself against the flogger's tail. He flips it and pushes the handle against me. My body tenses up. He pulls his fingers from my mouth and moves them between my legs. He is rubbing my clit now and I am on fire. He pushes the leather handle further inside me.

I try to close my legs. No, this isn't right. I want him, not this.

"Stop!"

And he does. Suddenly, he isn't touching me at all.

Before I know it, my ankles are removed from their restraints and then my wrists.

I turn to see him shirtless, glowering, pants undone. The tip of his cock peeking out, laying against his belly button. His arms are crossed, and in his hand is the black leather flogger.

I take in a deep breath, digging deep to grasp the courage I need—but then I realize, I don't need it. Desire trumps all feelings, all thoughts and all insecurity.

I take two steps to close the distance between us and reach out, running my hand lightly over his bulge, letting my thumb stroke over the head of his beautiful cock.

Sabato doesn't change his expression, but I hear a deep rumble in his chest. I look up at him, leaning in until I am centimeters from his lips. His expression is still unchanging. I wet my lips and push up on my toes. We are nose to nose, eyes looking into each other's eyes. His chests rumble intensifies and I know he is going to kiss me.

I want his kiss, more than I've ever wanted to kiss anyone. Knowing somehow that his kiss won't disappoint. I take his arms, and with a little effort, I move them so they are at his sides.

I am in control now. I am filled with desire. I am ready to give it up. I press my lips to his and feel them tighten underneath mine. My tongue is denied access to his mouth.

I won't allow this to stop me.

I lick his lips, then down to his strong, square jaw. I open my mouth and slowly move my lips down his neck. My tongue traces his Adam's apple, down to his chest. I nip at his skin, licking his hard, muscular abs.

Then I am on my knees and I look up at him. I yank at his army green cargo pants and his cock springs free, to hit me in the lips. Without thinking, I sweep my tongue across it.

His jungle cat-like reflexes kick in then. He crouches down, roughly grabbing my tits, squeezing my nipples, pushing them together. He rams his cock between them. I gasp. He doesn't stop. He rolls, pinches, and tweaks my nipples as he fucks my tits. His eyes are half-closed and I see fire in them.

He is relentless.

His hand grips my hair. "Open."

Fear rages through me and his eyes widen as his cum hits my chin. I am shocked and enthralled. He immediately releases my hair, then takes a step back, looking stunned. After a moment, he regains his composure. He reaches to the floor and grabs the flogger.

"Present," he snaps.

I am unsure what this means. I try to think as I wipe his cum from my chin.

"Lay back Melyssa and spread your legs. I will make you come now."

Desire's embers are still burning through my self-consciousness, so I do. I don't care about holding back, not anymore. I want to give this away.

Sabato drops to his knees at my side and spreads me by pulling my knee onto his leg. He leans over and holds the flogger so that the beaded tassels dance against my sensitive skin.

His wrist flicks. Gently, he swats my pussy with the flogger. It doesn't sting, but it burns. Not where he strikes, but deep inside. The embers of arousal erupt into flames when he does it again.

My hips gyrate and he flips the flogger in his hand. The handle is at my opening. I try to close my legs, and he holds my knee and he rubs the flogger up and down my slit, applying pressure against my throbbing clit. Over and over, he taunts and teases me until I am delirious with desire. He is watching me squirm, quiver and practically convulse under his sex-pert moves.

He has brought me to a place no one ever has before. I'm trembling inside, knowing I am going to come—finally—I am going to come. I arch my back and his mouth surrounds my nipple. He tugs, sending me spiraling over the edge.

"Yes, Oh god! Oh god, yes!" I cry out.

Pain shoots between my legs.

"NO!" I cry out and pull away from him.

"No?"

"No." I sit up and look at him.

The look on his face is stunned, confused, almost...hurt? *Oh god*, I think as I collect myself. *What did I do?* I stand up off the cold wooden floor and dart to my pile of clothing.

"What the hell just happened, Melyssa?" He follows me as I pull up my pants, pocketing my panties.

"Answer me, damn it!"

I can't look at him. I grab my shirt and throw it on as I shove my feet into my flats and walk quickly to the door.

As I reach for the doorknob he blocks me, while buttoning his pants.

"I asked you a fucking question."

"I wanted you," I try to explain, through my hysteria. "Not, not...." I feel tears threatening and I clear my throat. "You can keep your silicone and strap-ons, Sabato. That's not...I'm not into that. Now, please excuse me."

"It was *Italian leather*," he says, sounding offended, "not silicone, Melyssa. My equipment is of the finest, all-natural materials."

Obviously, he doesn't get it. "I want to leave."

My head is held high, eyes blank. I know he'll let me.

"I would like to understand," he snaps.

"You didn't kiss me, you made no attempt to."

Sabato looks incredulous for a few seconds, then he closes his eyes. With his thumb and forefinger, he massages his eyelids. When he finally opens them again, he is angry.

"I never asked you to come here."

I nodded. "Okay, well, I am asking to leave."

"Fine," he hisses. "Don't come back."

I'm not prepared for that kind of response. It hits me like a kick to the gut. My eyes sting, but I don't let him see.

"I won't."

Once I'm alone in my car, I let the tears flow freely. I start the car, back up and drive to the lot opening, waiting for a break in the passing cars.

I wipe the tears away and look to my left, toward the club. Sabato fills the doorway. His shoulders are slumped, hands buried deep in his pockets. He no longer reminds me of a jungle cat. Now, he's definitely human.

As I drive home, I decide he is even less than that. He's just a number. Number 21 on my list.

Once back at the hotel, I run a bath for myself. It's late and Paige is asleep. I am nervous the sound of running water will wake her, but I feel dirty and I don't want to wait. I step in to the hot, steaming water and sink down until everything but my nose is covered. Floating, I try to clear my head.

But I can't. I think of all the feelings I experienced tonight. Everything was in vivid detail, etched in my mind. All the smells—fresh paint, wood, leather, musk and mint—all the sensations, all the need. Everything I have fantasized about for years. But nothing like my fantasies, at the same time. At the time, it wasn't 'dirty,' it was erotic. Not for one second did I feel like it was wrong.

What's wrong with me? Maybe it's me. Maybe I'm what's wrong with me.

I am dirty.

I scrub my body, too hard, until the buildup of emotions finally explodes. Hot tears trickle down my face for the second time within an hour. I sob silently into my hands, until all those emotions dry up.

When I step out of the bath, I notice the mark on my neck. It's not a hickey, per se. But it's definitely a mark. I try to be angry. I even scowl at myself in the mirror, but it's my first mark from a man. I look down and my left breast is marked as well.

I am a dirty, dirty girl.

So why do I feel better, on some level, than I ever have before?

* * *

I tell Paige I am sick and stay in bed all the next day.

We watch television and she dotes on me. I reschedule my interview with Cornell and am once again warned it's not a guaranteed spot. I can't tell them what I've come down with, because this illness is more a deep-seated, mental kind of sickness. They allow me to reschedule for the next day.

I have taken enough classes on human behaviors to know that this is pure, indulgent, narcissistic self-loathing, at its finest. I am allowing feelings and reactions to my experiences run me, and they are running me into the ground. I just need to find a new focal point—something other than feeling bad about my body, my sexuality, my newly-acquired and less than stellar personality traits that have made me start to question who I am. Before this, I was never indecisive. But now, even just looking into the hotel closet and trying to figure out what to wear to the interview, I realize that I am bordering on true depression, not just sadness.

Somehow, I get it together enough to attend the interview. I even manage to convince them that I am sane, that I am normal. That I am not fundamentally broken.

A few days later, I find out I've been accepted into the program, which should put me on a high.

But it doesn't. Instead, I find myself looking over my shoulder, wanting him to be there. A few times, I want it so much I even delude myself into thinking I feel him, watching me.

But then I am reminded by the more sensible side of my brain, the one attached to Elsa's darkest urges, that he has banished me. Dismissed, with no more sexy Italian requests to 'present myself,' or promises to do things that make my head spin, and all because I preferred to have him inside me, instead of that sinful—yet sensual—tool.

I keep catching myself, just standing frozen, eyes closed in an attempt to drive away the sexual demons that haunt my every waking thought. Though I might seem frigid on the outside, inwardly I am a hot mess. Silently, I beg for it to go away. But I keep fixating on the way his lips never touched mine. I brush my finger across my lower lip, feeling the weight of Sabato's deep, shadowed brown eyes. I wonder how long it will take for me to forget what color they are.

I manage to get through the next few days without being lured by my vagina to his club. Paige has asked me several times if everything is all right. Of course, nothing is. But I can't tell her that.

To placate my conscience, I focus on one thing that is right, and answer with at least a halfway-truthful response, like, "Yes, new city, new life, new beginning. What could possibly be wrong?" Then I smile a big smile, the one my friends are used to seeing. *I am Pollyanna, Polly positive, Polly.... Well, I guess that's it.*

"Don't look at me that way, Paige," I say, smiling like an idiot. "We have a busy day. It's time to go check out some of these shoebox-sized apartments."

"It'll be fun," she laughs, grabbing her purse to follow me. "Just pretend they're like the dorms."

..*

We walk back to the hotel carrying a huge stack of folded boxes.

Paige huffs behind me. "Are you sure?"

"Of course I am," I tell her. "I'm so sure, that I am moving in later today. It's a great little place. Off-street parking, second floor—"

"With a scary-ass fire escape."

"And a bad-ass security system."

"It's a forty minute commute to your school," she points out. "Why couldn't you stay in one of the places in Manhattan?"

"Because...reasons. Five times the cost, one third the size, for a few." I roll my eyes. "Paige, it's a done deal. Let's grab our stuff and go shopping."

Later that night, we sit together in my new place, looking around warily. The furniture store just outside of my little community was going out of business, so I went a little crazy. Thankfully, they were able to deliver my new bed, chaise, desk, side tables and television.

It's official. 7 Deep Place, Staten Island, New York will be my home for the summer. If all goes as planned, I might even be staying longer. Laney is moving in across town tomorrow, and we'll both be living about the same distance from where Nikki and her fiancé live, near the Jersey Shore.

"This bed is so big!" Paige flops back, bounces on it and laughs. "I can't believe you bought it. It just screams 'seduce me.'"

I laugh and flop down next to her. "*Seduce me?* How so?"

"Four poster bed....just add some handcuffs and...."

"Half-price," I remind her. "And only fifty dollars more than the one *you* liked. Plus, I like the canopy. I can hang curtains around it and pretend it's a bedroom."

"I think the sleeper sofa would have been more sensible."

"Sensible can suck it. I slept on a crappy twin bed for four years. This is a queen," I roll to my stomach. "And look at that! I rolled over and didn't fall on the floor."

Paige reaches over and smacks my ass. "Don't get too comfortable, we have walls to erect."

She grabs the basket with the bedding and material we bought, then washed and dried while waiting for the delivery truck.

"Slut red," she says, holding up one of the sheets. "I like it."

The color perfectly matches the room Sabato painted at the club. I haven't really thought of that, until now. Even my subconscious is on dirty Elsa's side's... side.

I shrug. "It'll do."

After dressing the bed and moving furniture around, Paige and I order Chinese and have it delivered. We sit and talk about what the summer might bring for both of us. Paige is planning to go home, take the summer off, chill with her family and look for a job. She majored in marketing and wants to be part of the entertainment industry—badly. She doesn't think her odds are good, but I know she can achieve anything she sets her mind to.

We zone out on TV for a few hours, then fall asleep together in my queen sized bed/bedroom.

..*

It has been a few weeks now, and I am sick. I walk out of the clinic with a prescription. They think I have bronchitis. My chest is sore; the pain is not intolerable.

What is intolerable is the fact that I swear, I still feel the weight of his stare, all the time. Like he is around every corner. But I know he's not.

I still fight to keep myself from going to him and I am sinking even deeper into a self-loathing state. My only reprieve comes when I distract myself with my classes, or my chats with Laney, Nikki, and Paige.

Laney knows something is going on. She asks me often and I tell her I am just overwhelmed with school—which I am. Earlier this week, she set up a time for me to meet Dominic's sister Valentina. I'm guessing it's her way of drawing me out, by double-teaming me with another strong-willed girl.

SABATO

No Sleep
No Life
No Fear

I don't like her new home.

It isn't safe.

I don't like that I know she is in danger.

I hate that it is my fault.

It's strictly physical, I keep telling myself. Guilt, at the very most.

I don't like how my dick jerks whenever I think of her.

I hate the fact that I have been watching her for two weeks now and I haven't touched her, not once.

I want her to come to me. I need her to come to me. I need her to come on me. I hate that I need it, almost as much as I need to know where she is at all times.

No woman has ever denied me, or made me want her, this much. Not for a long time. Even then...it was different and that was long ago.

Salvatore is going to court tomorrow. He is behind bars and I should get some sort of satisfaction out of it. But like coming, true satisfaction is found at the end, the very last thrust, the very last release. Until that point, you cannot be truly satisfied. When that motherfucker is dead, when he'd finally been fucked right out of this world, then and only then I would truly be satisfied.

Zandor keeps offering money, but I continue to decline. There is no income to be made here. Not now, possibly not ever. He pushes and argues and looks at me like I am insane. He has even offered me a job, which I declined.

What none of them know, is that I have a trust fund of my own making. I have money, I have property, and I have more than I need. No one can touch it. No one knows about it. Soon it won't be connected to me.

Also, I have a secret: I am about to become a married man. My wife will become a millionaire and hold more power than she could ever imagine. But first, she will have to submit.

I sit at the bar, staring at the window, which is still uncovered. As if somehow, she will come and peer through it at any moment.

I fantasize about binding her to the cross, so she can't squirm beneath my touch. Blindfolding her so she doesn't see me, stinging her ass with my flogger, then a whip, then fucking her with every tool in my cabinet. I want the words 'no' and 'stop' to be cut from her vocabulary. I want to force my cock down her throat and hear her choke on it. I want to come on her face, in her mouth. I want to bury my dick in her ass, then leave her alone and wanting for hours, to contemplate what she can do to earn more of my torture.

I want her so sated, exhausted and submissive that the word 'no' never again falls from her lips.

She lied to me. That night at dinner, her eyes lied to me. She will pay for that lie, I've decided. Then, I will be able to move forward as planned.

My birthday was a few months ago, but this will be a belated present, one I give to myself.

Before I realize it, I am drunk. I decide to lay my head down and think about those sweet lips, that skin, those thighs....

I hear footsteps and pull my head off the bar. I look at my watch, eyes bleary. It is seven in the morning. I hear it again, the sound of footsteps and I recognize them immediately.

The hair on the back of my neck stands up and every cell in my body vibrates. I look next to me, where my gun rests, ready. I look up at the newly-added skylight. It took two weeks and several thousand dollars to complete. Etched across its surface is a perfect replica of Peter Paul Rubens' 'Adonis.'

I shift my eyes to look in the mirror behind the bar. He is in perfect position. I reach for my gun.

"I wouldn't do that if I were you," Salvatore hisses.

I don't care what will happen. I shouldn't care. I'm not afraid. I shouldn't be afraid. I fire into the skylight, over my head. Then I dive out of the way as bullets fly from Salvatore's gun. There is a loud shattering sound and then Salvatore screams out in pain.

I roll, dodging the bullets from his men as I dive behind the bar. Most of them are smart enough to stop shooting and get out of the way. Salvatore, though, he's always let his anger get the best of him. I watch his reflection in the mirror as he keeps shooting, as the glass rains down on him, thick shards impaling his shoulders and arms.

I smile as I run, dodging bullets as I make for the back door.

"Forget him," I hear Efisto gurgle. "Get me out of here!"

Something in my leg burns, stings, but I continue making my way through the back parking lot and into the trees. I can't stop, even though it fucking hurts.

I have gone over this scenario at least once an hour, every waking hour. I've dreamt of it often. It went exactly as planned. I push on and make it through the woods, across the street, to the copper-colored Mercedes Benz GLA that was purchased with cash, weeks ago. I reach for the hidden key under the bumper, unlock the door, jump in and take off down the road.

Once I pull onto the main road, I turn at the light and see a large piece of glass buried in my leg. I pull over on the side of the road and yank at it. Pain rips through me and the bleeding increases. I push against the wound, gritting my teeth against the pain it causes, but knowing I need to apply pressure to slow the bleed.

I can't go to the hospital. I only know one person who may be able to help, but she is an hour away. I press harder and hit the accelerator. I try to breathe slowly, aware that my heart beating so quickly can't be helping at all. I want to focus on something that calms me, but nothing does. I turn on the radio, finding no comfort in music. I think back to a time when I believed I could be happy. Luciana's face pops into my head. Aside from my mother, she was the only one who ever loved me.

My heart races and the pain intensifies.

The picture of the last time I saw her, kissed her, held her, is far from calming. It was the day my last bit of hope in humanity died.

I look ahead, ignoring my pain, focusing instead on the pain I caused her. Luciana, the first girl who told me she loved me. I told her once that I would make her my queen. I would protect her from the war that raged in my family. She took comfort in me. I took comfort in her. Eventually, I found the longer I gave her pleasure the longer the look of awe remained in her eyes as she looked at me.

Luciana made me believe what my mother had said to me the day of her death. One woman may have been enough, after all. But I couldn't protect her, be her Adonis, her eroe any more than I could save my Mama from my father's evil schemes.

I fight to keep my eyes on the road, as the oncoming headlights begin to blur together. My phone. Where is my...?

"Fuck." I slam my hand against the steering wheel, smearing it with blood.

I pull into a parking garage in the city and pay the attendant for an all-day pass. I park between two vans, behind a cement pillar. I know the dark tinted windows will keep me invisible to anyone walking by. I kill the engine and recline the seat. I am thankful it is cold and that the bleeding seems to have slowed. If I die today, I will die knowing I have made him bleed twice.

The same amount of times he has made me bleed inside.

..*

I wake shivering, in a pool of sweat. It is night and I know there isn't any reasonable explanation as to why I am still alive, but I am. I get out of the car in the darkness and hobble across the road. As I stand looking up, I think I see her standing on the balcony above, staring at the sky.

Miraculously, she senses me. She looks down and calls out my name. I hop into the alley. What the fuck was I thinking, coming here? She will call the police. She yelled my name, for anyone to hear. *Stupido, stupido*. I slide down the brick wall, ready to succumb to the darkness, when I hear footsteps and look up.

"Oh my God, you're hurt!"

"Please don't call for help," I plead, weakly. "Don't call the police. No one, Valentina. Not even your brother."

Yet another fucking secret to keep.

"Good timing, then. Franco is out. Let's go hide you in my place."

I groan as I push myself up. Valentina slides under my arm and helps me inside.

When we are in her apartment—though I can't remember getting there—I feel the need to tell her something. I look at her, blinking against the darkness.

"When I pass out...."

"No, don't you dare."

"It won't hurt so fucking bad when you pull out this glass," I move my hand away from the wound and she cringes.

"Do your animal doctor shit, or look it up on YouTube. No hospital, no help. No one knows but you understand? Promise...I need you to promise."

Valentina rolls her eyes. "Sure thing lover. But you are gonna owe me. Big."

"For God's sake, not now."

I groan as I hop beside her into the bathroom. She makes me a pillow out of towels and helps me lower myself into the bathtub.

"You know," she says, looking down at me. "This actually isn't all that...."

Everything goes black.

* * *

I wake in her bed. It smells like Italy. I look over to find her beside me, asleep. I look to the other side, and the clock blinks 3:00 AM. I vaguely remember waking up, and her insisting I do so, throughout the night. But I don't remember how I got into the bed. "Are you all right?"

I groan, shaking my head. "Hurts like hell."

"Here." She sits up and grabs a bottle of water and two pills. "This will knock you out."

"How was it?" I ask, nodding to my leg before swigging down the pills and water she offers.

"Disgusting." She shudders. "It's a good thing I look forward to my payment, because I can't stand blood."

"You went to veterinary school."

"You remember?" She looks shocked.

I roll my eyes. "I've looked into you since the other night. All the players in this game have become persons of interest. Do you know how many of you there have been?"

"One."

"Valentina Segretti, you and I are the same. We know that fucking is just fucking. I've been with you once—"

"Twice," she corrects me.

Really? Shit. "Okay, twice. I'm sorry, I didn't remember."

"Well, I do," she says. "You don't just fuck. You perform. Regardless, it's memorable. Plus, I've been going through a dry spell lately. I expect two encores."

I feel dizzy. "Demands will get you nowhere."

"I'm going back to sleep, then." She shakes her head at me and lies back down. "By the way, they're looking for you."

"Is he dead?"

"They haven't found a body." She pauses. "Did you kill him this time?"

I close my eyes. "I hope so. Thank you Valentina. I am going to…"

"Lie down and get some more sleep. I have to score some antibiotics tomorrow, or you'll get an infection and lose your leg."

* * *

The next time I wake, I have a fever.

Valentina is frantic, talking to someone on the phone.

"How the hell is it possible to score painkillers in two minutes, and then when you try to get your hands on legitimate, non-recreational medication, it's like you're trying to buy national security secrets?"

"I'm fine." I try to sit up and she puts her hand on my chest.

"You're on fire."

"The fever will break." There is a knock on the door and we look at one another, with the same fearful expression.

"Whoever it is, get rid of them."

She doesn't answer, but I hear the beep of her phone receiving a text.

"Praise Jesus, Sabato! Apparently, Laney's friend, who was here a couple days ago, lost her prescription when her purse dumped on the couch!"

With that, Valentina gets up and runs out of the room. I don't understand what the hell is going on, but maybe that's the fever. Maybe I'm sicker than I realized.

I blink, or maybe pass out and wake to the sound of a man's voice. It's a voice I feel like I should recognize, but I can't place it. I want to get up and make sure everything is all right, but I feel so weak.

Valentina's voice drifts in from the hallway.

"Sorry, Franco. Just tell her...tell her that she must have dropped it somewhere else. ...I don't care, just tell her not to come over. I'll look between the couch cushions later."

A few moments later, Valentina comes into the room, wearing a self-congratulatory smile. She's shaking something in her hand—a bottle of prescription pills, one of those orange ones.

"Look! Free antibiotics," she says.

In the depths of my fever, I try to reason through what is happening. "...What friend?"

"Just some girl." She shrugs. "More like, friend of a friend. She came to have drinks. Nice enough, but kind of boring. Blonde. It doesn't matter, just take some of these and get some rest."

I take the pills she's holding in her hand and for the first time in as long as I can remember, I follow a woman's orders.

..*

I don't know how long I am out this time, but when I wake it is dark.

The pain is still there, but the fever has broken.

I sit up and look around. I get out of bed and pain shoots up my leg. I push through it. I have felt pain before, true pain. Compared to that, this is nothing.

I make my way to the bathroom and open the door. Valentina is naked, pinning her hair up.

"Wow, you're awake." She smiles, not shy about her nakedness. She shouldn't be. "How do you feel?"

"Better," I say as I push my boxers down.

"Wow, so it'll be just like that, huh?"

"I'm hard, you're wet, and the shower is running. Let's take care of this need."

"We need to wrap your leg," she says as I walk up to her.

"I need to come. You need to come. Do you have condoms?" I reach to fondle her breasts.

She arches against me, then reaches down and opens a drawer. "Plenty."

She hands one over her shoulder to me and I quickly put it on.

"No games this time, I need to feel." I push her forward and she moans. "Pleasure, to take my mind off the pain."

"Of course," she purrs, and I ram into her. She cries out. I reach around and pinch her clit, fucking her hard.

"Fuck, you are hot," I groan, and smack her ass. I need more, harder. This is not the usual for me.

"Again," she cries, and I smack her ass again.

I grab her hair and pull it toward me so I can see her face as I make her come.

"More," she growls. I strike her ass again, and again, and she cries out over and over.

Within seconds, she comes. But I continue holding back. The agreement was two orgasms and I am built to please. I fuck her, tweak her nipples and pinch her nub between my fingers. She whimpers. I refuse to deny my release any longer, she screams and I come hard.

The door flies open then, and I am snatched back by Franco, her bodyguard.

"Leave us!" Valentina screams as she grabs a towel.

"He is wanted!"

"He is hurt," she says. I jab out and my fist connects with his face.

He stumbles back and I make my way past him, fleeing naked to the door. I look up and into the eyes of Melyssa.

"What the fuck are you doing here?"

Emotions flood her face and behind us I hear Valentina screaming in Italian to the man, Franco, to leave.

"My medicine," she says. "I came back for...." Then she turns and runs to the door.

I grab my clothes and throw them on, adrenaline numbing my pain as I make my way out the window and down the fire escape. My wound throbs, but I don't care as I jump to the ground. She is at the corner stoplight now and I push myself hard to get there. I needed a place to hide, to lay low and I will make sure she pays for fucking up my plans.

I open the door of her car and slide in, just as the light turns green.

"Get out!" She is crying.

"Drive," I tell her, pointing my gun at her. "Don't do anything stupid, Melyssa. Just do as I say."

DRIVEN MAD

I am shaking, almost too much to drive straight.

Sabato rests a gun on his leg, pointing it toward me and fear races through me. I look out of the corner of my eye when I hear him hiss. He is holding his leg with his other hand and there is blood everywhere.

"You need to go to the hospital," I try to sound strong, but my voice betrays me.

"No. Take me to your home."

I put on the turn signal, immediately heading in the wrong direction. I will not let him know where I live. I will drive in circles until I run out of gas. I've read and seen it on TV, what happens when a crazed man with a gun gets into a woman's car. It always ends badly and I do not want it to end badly.

Especially not with him.

"This isn't the way, don't toy with me, Melyssa," he leans toward me, but my vision is only trained on his gun. He grabs the steering wheel, "Watch the fucking road. Better yet, pull over. I'm driving."

When I don't do as he says, Sabato raises his voice. "Pull over."

I try to come up with something, anything, to avoid going to my place. "They'll look for me there. They'll look for you. It's not a good idea."

"Bullshit."

I start to shake and choke back a sob.

"Go back. Turn around. There is a parking lot a block—"

"I can't!" Tears start to fall and he moves the gun. "Don't!"

"Christ, Melyssa!" He waves the gun around and there is no control left in his eyes. I barely even recognize him.

"Please, just don't hurt me!"

"Pull the fuck over and get out."

I do as he says. I pull over and jump out. I'm ready to run, but with his jungle cat-like speed, he is in front of me immediately.

"There's a cop car coming this way," I threaten. "He'll see you. Please, just take my car and go. I swear, I'll scream. I will scream and you will go to j—"

His mouth crashes against mine, hands riding up the back of my shirt. I feel the barrel of the gun against my skin. When I try to pull away, his free hand captures the back of my head and his tongue enters my mouth. I cannot move away. I don't want to move away—but I have to. With a feeling like a cold bucket of water hitting me in the face, I remember why I ran. Sabato was inside another woman, just a few minutes ago.

I pull my lips from his and he doesn't fight it. His hand leaves my face. Suddenly exhausted, I go to rest my head against his forehead. He steps back. When I look up, he looks away.

"Now get in the damn car." His voice is sharp, hard, like a slap.

"No," I say, trying to be strong.

"You seem to forget I have a gun," he reminds me.

He does. I can still feel its pressure against my back.

"Now climb in, across the seat."

"No." I repeat, hands shaking.

"I promise you," he says quietly, dangerously. "That word will get you nowhere with me, but bent over my fucking knee."

I decide then to do as I am told.

He slides in behind me and winces as he pushes on his wound, "When we get to the car, you'll get out of this one, without a fuss and into the vehicle I tell you to. Then you and I are going to spend some time together."

"They'll look for me."

"Not where we're going, they won't."

He pulls out onto the street and drives. He drives perfectly, just below the speed limit, using his traffic signals and never looking at me once. I know he's in pain, but he doesn't seem to let himself feel it, or even acknowledge it.

"You can't force me to stay with you?" I don't mean it to, but it comes out as a question.

"I can," he laughs. The sound is conceited and cold and I hate it.

"Where are you taking me?"

"Somewhere nicer than your place."

A chill goes down my back. "How do you know where I live?"

"I make it my business to know the business of the people who peek in my windows. Now enough questions. Or so help me God, I will gag you."

"If you gag me, how will you shove that...that, big, intrusive tongue in my mouth?"

My boldness surprises me. I hold my breath as I wait for his response.

He looks at me briefly, out of the corner of his eye.

"I don't intend on doing that again."

I know I shouldn't want it, but it doesn't take the sting out of the fact that he seems unaffected by a kiss. Our first kiss. And our last, I'm now sure.

"Good, that wasn't a ten for me either, you know," I say, just above a whisper.

He shakes his head. "It served its purpose. The cop who drove by saw *amanti,* and not a wanted man and a sassy little girl, who seems to be hiding around every fucking corner."

"You kissed me because...." Oh.

"Of course I did. What, did you think...." He laughs. "Incredible."

My head is flooded with emotions. I'm scared, turned on and embarrassed at the same time. Sabato Efisto is a wanted man. And I am a stupid, naive, dirty girl.

He is a suspect in killing his father. I just returned from being sent back to my hometown in Georgia, to be 'kept safe' by Nikki's fiancé, Abe and his cousins. Apparently, Sabato's father was not just a random crime boss, but *the* head of the Sicilian mafia. Like 'The Godfather.' But in real life.

When I was tricked into having drinks, then whisked away from Valentina's place and put on a plane three days ago, it was scary. I questioned myself and swore I would never put myself in the position I had been in that night at Sabato's club.

I told myself I fell into wanting that experience by pure accident—or *impure* accident. I tried to feel shame and regret and all the things people tell you to feel. I wanted to feel like the woman in those videos felt. Yes, I Melyssa Chance, was once addicted to online porn. I suppose I will always be drawn to the darkness.

I had never seen a man in real life—meaning outside the computer—who made me feel that way, until I saw Sabato Efisto in person. He is dark, clearly dangerous, and I am a strong, educated young woman who carries the moral ideals of a nun—aside from the closet porn fetish, that is. Then again, who knows what those nuns do in their spare time? Yet, I am so enchanted by the darkness that I find myself wanting to embrace it, ready to be taken in the way I know only he can take me.

Every way, any way, body and soul, corrupted. Claimed.

While I was home, I dug down deep into the bottom of my heart, my soul. I cried, sometimes for hours at a time, I even knelt and prayed at one point. That was when I realized what a hypocrite I was being. I wanted him to claim me, but only on my terms. I wanted to be pure, but only in the way I thought I was supposed to be, because of the way I was raised. I half-assed sex, wanting it to be clean and controlled, like a fantasy—or a video. I didn't want it to be messy, or scary, or God forbid, kinky.

Even if that was how, deep down, I know I would secretly like it.

So, I sat in front of my father's old home computer and I obsessed. I searched 'Salvatore Efisto,' and not just pictures this time. What I found shocked me, more than I'd thought was possible. There was never an arrest made against the man, but he certainly was a suspect in a lot of truly horrible crimes.

Then I saw him. I saw him at seven years old. I read his story and I cried again. Not because I was forcing myself to, or because I thought I should feel guilty, but because my heart was breaking. My heart broke for seven-year-old Sabato. Then it broke again for eighteen-year-old Sabato and the girl he'd loved and lost, Luciana.

Now, knowing what I know, even though I want to, I can't hate him. I try, but I can't. Even if he is a monster now. Because it's true, that saying: sometimes monsters aren't born, but made.

So I keep my mouth shut and I let the monster drive.

..*

The next day, Salvatore Efisto's body is found in the woods behind Sabato's club.

We've been driving for almost an entire day, stopping only long enough to eat and pee and buy bandages and pills for Sabato's leg. I've kept my mouth shut, meekly going along with his unspoken plan, the entire time. But when the news comes on the radio, I can't keep silent any longer.

"Did you kill him?" I burst out. "Your father, did you kill him?"

The tires squeal loudly, as Sabato jerks the wheel. We go off the road, dust kicking up and wheels spinning as we almost go into a ditch at the edge of a dirt-filled parking lot. I scream, terrified, and then immediately start to cry. It's true. He killed his father and now he's going to kill me.

I had this coming, I realize. The minute I let him near me, let him into my head. He's a monster and I knew it and I fell for him anyway. I brought this on myself.

"No, no, no, no. You are not to cry." Sabato's voice is softer now, gentler, but still firm.

For some reason, that makes me cry harder.

"Melyssa, we don't have time for this."

Sabato's eyes dart around the parking lot, nervously taking in our surroundings.

"You and I are going to get in this car over here," he says, more calmly now. He points to a new BMW in the next spot over. "Then we are going to go have a chat about what our expectations are of each other. Come now."

"I just want to go home."

"That's just not in the cards today, but maybe tomorrow."

The word tomorrow brings hope.

"You aren't going to hurt me." I don't ask him, I tell him.

"No," he says as if he's annoyed by my question. "Let's go."

"Do I get a say in—"

"No."

I get out of the car and for some reason, I believe he won't kill me, even though the gun is still shoved in his waistband.

He grabs a key fob out of his pocket and hits the unlock button, his limp intensifying as he makes his way to the passenger door.

His hand has not left his waistband and I am aware that it's meant as a threat.

"Let me drive." He starts to speak, but I bravely cut him off. "Your leg, Sabato."

He tries to read my face, my intentions, looking for any sign of rebellion. "If you don't do as instructed, I promise you—"

"I understand."

Once in the driver's seat, I adjust it to my height. It is a beautiful vehicle, brand new and luxurious. I adjust the mirror and fasten my seat belt. I look over at him, waiting.

"Is there a problem?"

"Your seat belt."

"I don't need it," he says with displeasure.

"I'm sorry, but it's the law." He starts to interrupt and I raise my voice. "If I am going to be subjected to your demands, could you at least give me the kindness of bending, on just a few little things?"

"I have a gun and yet you think that you have any—"

"Please."

He looks a bit stunned, but then quickly shakes it off and buckles his safety belt.

He bends over and plugs some directions into the car's GPS.

"You're to drive straight there. If you waver off course, I will know. If I fall asleep, do not think that gives you an excuse to pull a stunt. I am a very light sleeper. Can I trust that you can follow instruction and do the right thing?"

"The right thing?" I can't help making a face.

"Just do as I say," he snaps. "You'll be rewarded. This will all be well worth your time. Just a few more days, and this will all be over."

"But, I have class!"

"Desperate times calls for," he cringes as he adjusts his leg and continues, "Desperate measures."

"That's unfair," I whisper.

"Life isn't fair, Melyssa," Sabato says, as he leans his seat back.

"Can I at least know where we are going?" Following the GPS's annoyingly calm voice, I pull out and turn left.

"All in due time," he says. "Just get us the hell out of this city."

* * *

It has been totally silent for two hours.

Sabato is asleep and I am driving down US highway 1. I look over frequently, almost staring at him. He is even more beautiful when he sleeps, I've decided. He looks younger, more innocent, and sweeter. But no less mind-blowingly alluring.

His eyelashes are thick, long and dark. All those words can be used to describe every part of his body. His skin is tanned, he is tall and his body has more ripples and waves than the Atlantic Ocean on a stormy night. A stormy night.... I find myself thinking about that night, long ago.

"Watch the road," he says, not even opening his eyes.

"I am," I use a defensive tone, one I probably used a time or twenty with my parents when they asked if I was doing homework while I was messing around with my smart phone. Not the tone one should take to a man with a loaded weapon.

Then out of—hell, I don't know where—I reach over and touch his forehead. He flinches and tenses up. Stone cold.

I quickly take my hand away. "No fever."

"That broke yesterday." He groans as he sits up.

"Will you tell me where we are going?"

"Are you tired?"

"I couldn't sleep if I wanted. I feel restless, like a little kid on Christmas Eve. Except, you aren't Santa Claus and I'm pretty sure this doesn't end in hot chocolate and presents."

"We'll pull over around four in the morning, when no one is around."

"I have to use the bathroom."

"Pull over now, then."

"And do what? Pee in a ditch?" I half laugh.

"Right." Sabato runs his hand through his hair, looking irritated. "All right then, find a rest stop. Actually no, I like the ditch idea better."

I huff angrily. "I'll just wait."

"You're going to hold it for five hours?"

I shrug. "I'm also thirsty."

"What plans have you conjured up?"

"I have been driving. I haven't had time to devise an evil plan, Sabato."

His eyes meet mine in challenge, but I hold.

"I'm not afraid of you."

He lets out a malicious laugh, one I suppose is to intimidate me. So I laugh, too. Then we both fall silent.

After another twenty minutes, he points to a sign.

"Two miles. Little café with bathroom facilities. Melyssa, I am telling you. Do not fuck this up. This is not a game, this is my life."

"So, did you kill him?"

There is no break or regret in his voice when he answers. "Yes."

I'm not sure what to say to that. About two miles later, I spot the diner—or café as he called it—and my skin immediately crawls as I pull in. I hate public restrooms.

"If I get an STD, it's your fault." I quickly unbuckle my seat belt, jump out and run towards the restaurant.

I reach into the back seat and grab my gym bag. Inside is a pair of drawstring pants. I kick off my boots, preparing to change.

My fucking leg is throbbing and I am stuck inside this little vehicle trying to change my clothes because I honestly don't know if she is in there calling the police. I need to hurry and be ready for anything.

I grab the t-shirt and throw it on, then quickly shove my feet back in my boots and get out. I look back to grab the keys and she has taken them. It rubs me the wrong way for two reasons; the first is that she took them. I mean, how the hell did I let that happen? How would I get away if she did call the police? Second, because it's a sign of ownership and I have worked hard to become who I am and earn what I have. The only reason losing it all will not be hard is because there is no greater satisfaction in the fact that he is fucking dead.

Part of me is terrified that she will betray me. But then, the rest of me is just exhausted and numb at the thought that I might finally be free. Except for being wanted by the police, possibly for murder, now.

Honestly, I don't even really care about that.

At this moment, I really only care about one thing: Salvatore Efisto is dead.

He is lifeless, powerless, gone. His reign of terror and corruption is at an end. And, most important of all, I have finally avenged my Mama's death. I can finally go to sleep knowing that I did one thing to earn her pride in heaven. I may not have been able to save her, but I at least could avenge her.

Feeling light-headed with hunger and hope, I stretch my arms and survey the little roadside 'cafe.'

I picked this place because I knew that there was no way in fuck that they would have cameras. It was a dump. I would never have thought, in a million years, that I would pick a place like this to celebrate the news that Salvatore was dead. But now, it doesn't matter where I am. All that matters is where I am not—under his sway.

And, I suppose, it does not hurt that Melyssa is with me.

When I walk in, Melyssa is squatting down, helping an old woman pick up at least a hundred straws that are scattered across the chipped tiles on the floor.

"There," she smiles, handing over the last handful and patting the old woman's back. Although I hadn't made a sound when I came in, she immediately looks up at me.

"Hi."

"You were gone for a while."

"Oh yeah, well...Nadia here was trying to convince me she served the best chicken and dumplings in the world." She looks back at the woman with great fondness, even though they were strangers moments before. "She thinks I look hungry."

"Looks?" The gray haired round woman shakes with laughter. "No, sounds. Stomach like monster, rumble, rumble, rumble. You both sit, eat."

"I think we should probably—"

"No," she interrupts me, and I give her a look. "No stink eye, either."

I am at a loss. The old Czech woman—if I'm not mistaking her origin—laughs and walks away, towards the back of the shack.

"Let's go," I say quietly.

"She wants us to eat." Melyssa sounds like a pendulant child. "Besides, I'm hungry."

"Then we go somewhere that doesn't smell like—"

She walks to a booth and sits. I follow her.

"Are you disobeying me?"

She nods and raises her eyebrows. "What will you do, kidnap me? Threaten me with a gun? Oh, wait."

"I will punish you. Just as soon as we get out—"

"Sit, boy. Is ready!" The old woman walks out of the kitchen carrying two heaping plates of food. "He hard to hear?"

Melyssa laughs and shakes her head. "He's just in a rush."

"Well, he need nourishment before." She stops, cackles, and flashes a toothless grin. "Make baby."

"Oh no, that's not—"

"Thank you, Nadia." I sit and look down at the plate, and then up at Melyssa, who is unwrapping her silverware.

"He grumpy all the time? Life's too short. Beautiful man, beautiful, sweet young woman, embrace it!" She waves her chubby little nubs in the air. "It is not much, but it is ours. All we have is *Nadeje*, and we praise Lord for this."

I give her a polite smile, the best I can muster. Finally, she wobbles away and I look at Melyssa. "You're truly not going to eat that, are you?"

She sticks her fork into the mountain of food, shovels it up, smiles at me and pushes the whole glob into her mouth. Her eyes light up, her lips curl slightly and she sighs as she chews. She sets the fork down and grabs her glass of water, bringing it to her lips.

"If you get sick...."

"It's delicious," she mumbles. "Seriously, you should eat."

"This place is not clean."

"On the contrary." She waves her fork. "Smell the air, you'll smell Clorox. That bathroom is the cleanest public restroom I have ever been in. I almost didn't even bother lining the toilet with paper. Heck, I even thought about sitting down instead of straddling the thing."

She takes another bite.

"So, if you get an STD, it is no longer my fault?" I smile slightly, but my amusement dies as I stare down at the plate, pushing the food around with my fork.

I look up when she coughs. She grabs her glass and takes another drink. Then she gasps.

"Are you all right?"

"Fine, I'm—" She coughs again.

She is clearly not fine. "Your face is bright red. Melyssa. Are you sure you can—"

"I'm fine." She scowls down at her plate. "Actually, I'm not fine."

I start to stand.

"What are you doing?" she whispers.

"Do you need something, Melyssa?" I try to remain calm. If she causes a scene, the old woman may get suspicious.

"No," she whispers. "I have no idea what you want from me. I can't even fathom what's go—"

"Okay." I sit back to appear calm, because I don't want her to get worked up. "I will tell you. I need something from you. You will be well compensated."

"I'm not a hooker," she tells me, eyes wide.

"I never said you were," I lean forward again, putting less space between us. I've learned that when Melyssa is nervous, she tries very hard to give off the impression that she is in control. But inside, she is exactly the opposite, a complicated bomb of emotions. I should run for the hills.

This never happened to me before. I was always a very good judge of a person's desires. But with her...she is what Americans call a 'hot mess.' She doesn't seem to know what she wants, from one moment, to the next.

"Will you let me ask you a few questions?"

"Will you let me?" She leans in, furrowing her brows, like she is trying to intimidate me. I am growing tired of the game she plays with me. If she were one of my girls, I would tie her up and flog her ass. Possibly even fig her.

"Why don't you just tell me what it is you're waiting for," I say.

This seems to catch her off guard. "I'm waiting to be let go," she says. But she doesn't sound sure. "Maybe you're right. Maybe I should stop waiting. Heck, I could scream, cause a scene, call the cops—"

I am getting angrier by the moment. More at myself than at her, though. It seems I was very wrong about her before; she isn't as intelligent as I believed her to be.

"I could pull the gun out and blow Nadia away." I say, calmly. That shuts her up immediately. "No one would know for days. I mean, look at this place. Then, Melyssa, I could do whatever the hell I wanted to do to you, and no one would know."

She looks off-balance and afraid once more.

I smile. "Eat."

"No."

I don't say another word. If she wants a fight, childish behavior is not how she will get me to rise to the challenge. I look away, down at the food again and finally decide to take a bite.

"Are you in love with Valentina?"

I nearly choke at her words. "That's insane."

"Not really." She picks up her fork and pushes her food around. "She's beautiful."

"Attraction is physical, Melyssa," I say and take a drink. "Love is an illusion."

"She likes you. She brought you up a few nights ago, when I was over there. She said you were a 'stallion.'"

"Is that so?" I dispassionately take another bite.

"She said you two have been together before, in Italy, at a concert."

"Why is this important?"

She shrugs and forks more food into her mouth.

"Valentina is a pleasure seeker," I tell her. "She likes anything, as long as it gets her off."

"So...she's a submissive?"

I hesitate, because I do not feel like going down this path. Not now. Not with her.

"No. She's no more a submissive than you are. Let's eat and get out of here."

She glares at me accusingly. "You like it."

I raise my eyebrows.

"The food, I mean."

"It's fine." I shrug.

"Right." She rolls her eyes.

* * *

I decide it is best for me to drive from that point on. We strike out again, in search of a seedy little dive where truckers and married lower class people go to hide an affair.

I spot the place an hour from the time my decision is made, but then I drive past it and find one of those discount stores. Because if Melyssa is afraid of contracting a disease from a public toilet, I know she isn't going to be at all pleased with where we will be staying.

I park in the lot, keeping a sharp eye out for security cameras.

"What are we doing?"

"Picking up some supplies."

As we walk toward the super store, it is more than clear that we are not a couple. With my limp and her scowl, I worry that people will start to notice us. Standing out at this point would be a very bad thing.

"Melyssa, take my hand," I hold out my hand for her.

"No thanks, I'm fine."

"It wasn't a request." I take her hand and tug her toward me. "This way, we won't look so suspicious."

"And when you get arrested, I will look like an accomplice," she hisses into my ear. "This isn't fair, Sabato. I didn't ask for this."

She was right, she didn't.

"That's neither here nor there. Do as you are told."

"Say please."

I am amused when it hits me, she always whispers when she is feeling brazen. This gives me hope that her behavior can be worked with, with proper training of course.

"Please," I say and keep walking.

"That's better," she whispers again.

Once inside the store, she points to a cart. "We'll need one of those."

I admittedly have never in my life seen a shopping cart that was not a picture in the upper corner of a web page. I have never done my own grocery shopping. And I never will again, if I have any control over it.

"You have to let go of me, so I can push this thing." Melyssa pulls her hand away and starts pushing the basket on wheels. It squeaks and one wheel keeps trying to go in a different direction than the others.

"If you're going to blend in, you should probably try to look a little less disgusted."

I nod, slowly.

"So," she huffs. "What are you after, sir? Bullets, duct tape, rope?"

"Sheets, bedcovering and disinfectant." I lean in and whisper seductively, "also, clothing."

"Clothing?" she sputters. "How long do you plan on...keeping me?"

"As long as it takes," I answer as we push the cart forward. "Let's get going."

She walks through the store as if she already knows where she is going. I am alarmed by the amount of people she is weaving in and out of. No one is paying attention to us. I am disturbed by the fact that so many parents would bring their children to a place like this. Although, when those parents are wearing pajamas and socks with sandals, I should just be impressed that they know how to procreate.

"Everything okay?" Melyssa asks. We stop in an aisle, waiting for a little fat kid to stop rolling around screaming, throwing a tantrum because apparently he wants birthday cake flavored Oreos. I watch as his mother drags him by his chubby little wrist across the filthy floor. Disgusted does not begin to explain how I feel. Though...I suppose she did better by him than my father would have by me, if he'd ever taken me shopping.

I shake my head.

"Yes, let's continue."

A few moments later, I am standing in front of a wall of bedding, feeling lost. None of the brands I am used to are here. I look at Melyssa for help and she looks somewhat entertained.

"Is there something you prefer?" I ask, shifting my weight off of my injured leg.

She looks down at my leg. "Does it hurt?"

"It doesn't feel good."

She looks away again, to the wall. "We'll get skin adhesive for your leg. And I don't care about sheets, you choose."

"I would prefer if you do it."

"What size?"

I have no idea, so I just tell her to get the biggest size, and a mattress pad.

We walk away with dark blue sheets with a thread count of 200, a comforter and pillowcases, all sold together in a bag. A fucking bag! I am already well aware that sleep is going to be nearly impossible.

"Toiletries." I say when she looks at me again, questioning.

"And pharmacy," she adds. "You need to get something for pain. Also, bandages. The wound needs to be cleaned and dressed and—"

I shake my head. "Valentina took care of it."

Her lips formed a straight line and she looks like she wants to hit something. I try not to smile. It is amusing that she seems jealous of Valentina. I know I can use that to my benefit in the future.

"I'm sure she did," she whispers, in that brazen way that makes me want to spank her.

We are in the pharmacy aisle next, when she starts throwing things angrily into the cart: alcohol, hydrogen peroxide, antibiotic ointment, pain relievers, skin glue and bandages.

I looked down the aisle, and go to the condoms, grab two boxes, bring them back to the cart and set them in.

She looks at them, for a long moment, then up at me.

I meet her gaze with a challenge. "Is there a problem?"

She looks around and then leans in. "Why?"

"You're the one who is worried about STDs," I say. "I don't want you to worry."

"Hold up," her face is slowly turning red, as she whispers. "You...you think after all this, I am going to sleep with you?"

I throw another box in the cart just to fuck with her.

"Don't play games, Melyssa. You and I both know we have unfinished business. I promised you I'd punish you, remember? So you'll be getting what you asked for. Unless...you've decided on the flogger? Where do you suppose they keep them in this store?"

She gasps in horror, then turns and pushes the cart down the aisle, leaving me standing there to feel impressed with myself. She didn't even whisper a snide remark. Adding to that the way her nipples pushed against her shirt and my dick stirred, I think the next few days may turn out to be bearable, after all.

I hurry to catch up to her and she is still red faced when I do.

"I need to know how long." She bites her lip, staring only at the toothpaste.

"As long as it takes," I answer.

"How will I know what to get?"

"Get a week's worth of supplies. If it takes longer, I will make another trip."

"A week!" This time she is loud enough to cause an Asian couple to stop and stare.

I try to grab her hand, but she pulls away. "Why me?"

"Why not you?"

I am now annoyed and in too much pain to indulge her pretense.

"Let's go."

We walk by the same woman with the chubby kid who was rolling on the floor fusing over cookies. I grab a box of condoms out of the cart and throw it in hers.

"Oh my God," Melyssa gulps.

Cabin in The Woods

After we leave the store, Sabato seems to decide on the spur of the moment, where we will be staying.

About five miles down the road, there's a turn off leading to a very isolated camp ground, with a few tiny cottages. According to the peeling wooden sign out front, all of the cabins have a small kitchenette and a separate bedroom. I suppose it's better than a seedy motel would have been, but it isn't very homey, either. Homely, maybe, but not homey.

After we check in to our very own shitty cabin, I open the curtains and sit down on the bed, hugging my knees. I look out the window at the forest and finally decide to try and process the events of the day. More importantly I was trying to process my feelings about the day—or, days, actually—since all this happened. Mostly, I thought about the fact that I was being forced to be involved in…whatever the hell was going on here.

When Sabato walks into the room behind me, I refuse to look at him. I can't face his careless disdain, not when I feel like I'm about to start crying and never stop.

"We need to talk." He crosses the room and closes the curtains. "We need to keep these shut."

I don't reply. I'm too afraid that if I do I'll explode.

He pulls the chair from the corner to the foot of the bed and sits down.

Now that he's taken my view of the trees, I keep my eyes glued to the floor.

"Did you hear me?"

I nod once. My face gets hot. I can feel his eyes penetrating me.

"I have a business proposition for you, Melyssa. It is one that is mutually beneficial." He sets a gym bag on the foot of the bed and opens it, pulling out a large file. "I know that you are carrying a lot of student loan debt from your time in college."

I am completely taken aback, so surprised that I forget I'm supposed to be ignoring him. But the shift in tone is so abrupt, I can only stare. And frown. And stare. "You have nothing to say?" He sighs. "You're not curious as to why I looked into you?"

"Oh, so now you give a shit about my education?" I snap. "I am enrolled in an intense summer program, which costs more than I can even wrap my head around and you are literally screwing me out of that education right now."

"You don't even *want* to be a lawyer, Melyssa," he snaps back.

I am incredulous. I let go of my knees, dropping my feet to the floor.

"Yes I do," I sputter. "Otherwise, I wouldn't be working my ass—"

He holds up his hand. "Let me make one thing clear: lying to me is a waste of time."

"Go to hell," I tell him.

"It would be a nice vacation at this point, but unfortunately, I'm here now. So are you. Even though my plan was based on some assumptions I made of you the very first day I met you. Assumptions which, I'm not so sure about now."

"What? What do you...you mean, at the steak house?"

"Yes, at the steak house. I met a young, intelligent woman who seemed focused, driven and very much trying to gain my attention."

I feel my face get redder than ever, and I want to tell him he was wrong, but...he wasn't.

"Then at the club, you watched me." His eyes burn into me, lighting me up inside. "I saw you, and you weren't repelled. You saw me for what I am and you still came back, revealing your voyeuristic tendencies by watching me fuck. I knew then that you were perfect, that this arrangement would be perfect."

"I'm *not* a voyeur."

He laughs. "And I'm not a Dom."

"I'm not!" I arch my back, meeting his eyes defiantly.

"We'll have that discussion at a later time," he says, not rising to my challenge. "But for right now, I need you to understand that there are seven properties in Italy, which are currently being sold. All of my clubs. I can't go back there now. So I am stuck here, in the U.S., where I am now hiding from the police. The money from my clubs will soon be deposited in an account; those funds would clear your debts, times a thousand. Our agreement will take care of your college debt and pay for law school. If all goes well and you are careful with your spending, you could even open your own practice. But, like I said, I know that's not really what you want to do with your life."

Doubt niggles at the back of my brain, but it only makes me more set on arguing.

"Don't pretend to know me, Sabato. If you did, you would know that I haven't received as much as a parking ticket in my entire life. So whatever shady, tax-evasion, mafia thing you're trying to involve me in—"

"And this is where the screaming is going to come in," he continues, as he opens the file. "My wife—"

He's not wrong. "You're WHAT? You're married?! Well, screw that!" I stand up. "Just so you know, you don't have attorney-client privilege here, buddy. I'm not a lawyer yet, and even if I was...well, I sure as hell wouldn't work for you! So I don't want to hear another word. I want *nothing* to do with this. No involvement, no way, no thank you."

"Melyssa, you're already involved. Now, sit down, or so help me I will make sure you can't sit for a week."

At that moment, I pause. Not for long, but it's enough to make me truly hate myself. God, even his empty threats to spank me somehow manage to make me stroke out with desire.

"Screw you," I say under my breath, already heading toward the door.

He springs up like the jungle cat he is, filling the doorway before I can reach it.

"There is no escaping this. What's done is done, you just need to accept it." He looks me up and down and stalls at my boobs. I hold my breath, hoping he won't see that yes, my nipples are hard. Because yes, oh yes, I am still turned on by this rotten, evil man. He rolls his eyes and shakes his head.

His hands go to his belt, and he starts unbuckling. I am shamefully turned on, but also scared. It's a heady and confusing mix.

"Let's get something out of the way," he says. "Maybe then, you'll be able to focus and we can move forward."

I try to step around him, but he is quicker. His hands capture my hips and he lifts me. I grab his biceps, afraid I may fall. He takes three steps and deposits me on the bed. He kicks his pants off and my eyes widen. Apparently, he doesn't ever wear underwear. He pulls his shirt over his head next, then grabs my wrists and pulls me up, into a seated position. He pulls my shirt up, but I fight him by holding my hands over my chest, thinking that he won't be able to remove it that way. He seems annoyed, but then he reaches down behind me and in one swift move, the shirt is over my head.

My mouth opens in protest, but nothing comes out. I want to say no, but I also want to see what he'll do next. Also, I'm a liar. I don't really want to say no.

Head spinning, desire pooling, I have to admit to myself that Sabato is still so, so beautiful and I am still so, so, stupid. Nothing has changed between us, except the scenery. Circumstances don't seem to matter, not to the Elsa. So I decide to... *let it go.*

Sabato takes my pants next, pulling them off in one swift move.

He isn't gentle when he grabs my hands and pushes me down on the bed. He pins my wrists in one hand as he grabs a condom out of his pocket, then rips it open with his teeth and rolls it onto his massive, fully-erect cock with one hand. He grabs my leg behind the knee and pulls it up, pinning it against his hip. As he lines himself up, I try to close my legs.

"No more games, Melyssa." Sabato's thick, gruff voice fucks all my senses at once. "You said you wanted my cock, not some tool. Now, I'm giving it to you. Yes or no?"

I am floating in a cloud of desire. My whole body is telling me no, except for the parts that want him, so bad...okay, every part of me... I nod once and he shoves himself roughly inside me.

I feel a sob creeping out and stifle it as the tearing pain sears through my body, feeling like I imagine a dull knife would. A knife I begged for, but still.

"Fuck Melyssa, when is the last," he pulls out and then rams into me again, "when was the last time someone fucked your tight little twat?"

I close my eyes, turning my head away. I can't look at him. I can't face him. Tears start pooling and I try to bury my face in the pillow that my head is no longer on, as he continues driving in so deep that it takes my breath away.

This isn't the man who took me to the cross. This is not what I expected. But it is what I asked for.

When a sob finally escapes my throat, I hear a quick intake of breath and he pulls out immediately.

"*Cosa ho fatto*, Melyssa?"

He pulls his weight from me and says it again, "*Cosa ho fatto*? Answer me, damn it!"

I roll to my side, pulling my knees up to my chest. I grab the blanket from behind me and bring it around myself to cover my naked body.

The bed sinks beside me under his weight.

"Tell me what made you cry. Tell me now!"

I shake my head, no. He rolls me onto my back, cups my head in his hands and stares into my eyes. I can't take it, so I close mine.

"Now, it is you who is not being fair, Melyssa. Answer my question. Or is this another thing that I have misread about you?"

I swallow down my tears, feeling suddenly angry. "Leave me alone."

"No. That's not how this works. This is not part of the plan. This—"

"Leave. Me. Alone."

I feel his hands begin to shake against my face and for the first time, I am truly afraid of him. Then I feel his breath against my face.

"You said you wanted me. You said...." He stops. "At my club, you were angry. You were angry, because I didn't fuck you with my cock." He is trying to let himself off the hook, even though he has no reason to be on the damn thing. This was on me, all me. Me and my stupid, foolish inability to control my desires.

I lose my train of thought when he whispers, as if to himself, "Kissing, that's the other."

I feel his lips gently caress my face and I choke back another sob. Now they are against my lips. His breaths are short and jagged.

Pain.

I feel his pain.

"Melyssa, *lascia che ti bacio*," his tongue teases my lips, but I turn my head away.

"Let. Me. Kiss. You."

"No." I open my eyes and look into his, which are still confused. "I'm not feeling well. I need to be alone."

"That's not what you need," he says, as his hand wraps around my waist.

"Don't pretend to know me." I snap.

His face darkens. "Fine. I will give you a few moments, but then you and I will be discussing this, this, charade you've been putting on."

He gets up and walks into the bathroom. I use the opportunity to turn and cry softly into my pillow.

* * *

When I open my eyes again, it's dark. It's dark and I feel cold. It's dark and cold, and my chest feels tight.

I push myself up off the bed and I see a pile of clothes folded neatly on the chair next to the bed. I look down to the end of the bed and see Sabato, sitting in the chair. His eyes are closed and his head is bobbing. I wonder how long he's been sleeping like that. I quietly reach across the bed, trying not to wake him and pluck the first t-shirt I see off the top of the pile. I scoot to the side of the bed, searching for my panties and pants, the ones he took off of me only a few hours ago. At least, I think it was a few hours ago. I don't have a watch, or a phone, or—

"Melyssa."

I jump when I hear his voice and the blanket falls away. He looks me up and down, until I grab the t-shirt and pull it over my head. I blink back at him nervously, but he is emotionless as he stares at me.

"Did you sleep well?"

"Yeah, sure. Where are my pants?" I say in a rush, looking around.

"In a bag out there," he points his finger towards the doorway. "But you need to have a seat. This discussion needs to happen."

"I would like my clothes first."

"And I would like a fucking do over. I don't like to leave a woman, or myself, unsatisfied."

I quickly cover my mouth, to stop myself from gasping—or starting to cry again.

"Not acceptable. Do you understand?"

I am beyond angry that this little blonde thing has played me.

The intelligent, educated, sensual being I met at dinner has tricked me. The voyeuristic sexual deviant who gleefully watched me fuck, then came back for some hands-on experience has fucked me, mentally and physically—but not in the way I like. My head did not need to be any more fucked up than it was before.

If she doesn't accept my terms, I swear to God, I will...I don't even know. That's how upset she makes me. I have run out of ideas.

I stand up and drop the folder on the bed in front of her.

"The first time I met you, I decided you were the perfect candidate for this. It would have been mutually beneficial I thought. I was sure of it. But now, you have forced me to rethink everything."

I open the file and push it toward her. There are photographs, dozens of photographs, depicting the two of us in a relationship.

She looks down at them, clearly confused, but then shakes her head and looks away.

"After that, what just happened—I don't want to see your wife, Sabato. I don't want to see that. I feel trashy enough right now, that I allowed it to happen."

"Could you explain to me what coming to my fucking club was to you?"

I try to act calm, because I have to, but what I really want to do is tell her to get back to that girl—the one I knew would make this work. I want to scream at her and shake her, but I can't. I'm desperate now. I have no other choice. I need her.

"I don't want to talk about it, Sabato. I just want to know when you'll let me go. When will you go back to your wife...or Valentina. Whoever."

That's when it dawns on me. "Look at the pictures, Melyssa. Does the woman in them resemble anyone you know?"

She shakes her head, then looks again, then slowly nods. "Me. They look like me."

"Good, then they've served their purpose," I tell her, relieved that she's finally starting to catch on. "My wife will act as my wife in public, she will stand by me when the legal shit storm begins and she will be very wealthy when it ends. But it's a commitment that may take more than a few months."

"Okay, sure. I get that. But why are you telling any of this to me? Why do you have me in—"

She stops and looks at me. I nod down to the photos. She looks again, longer this time.

I watch her eyes widen and see understanding grow as she flips through them, faster and faster. There are pictures at her apartment, pictures at her school, and pictures of walks we supposedly took together. And there were pictures of her at my club.

"Oh, my God. You're crazy," she whispers.

"No," I say. "I'm prepared. Trust me, Melyssa, this can work and be beneficial to both of us."

"No, it can't! Have you ever heard of a thing called *marriage fraud*? This is a joke. What, we just so happened to get married while you're on the run, trying to beat a murder rap?" She looks back down at the pictures. "Why would you do this? *How* would you...? *Who* would do this!?"

Her breathing is quick now and her face is turning red.

I sigh, knowing that the final detail is going to send her running, or screaming, or maybe even both. I brace myself, ready to capture and restrain her if necessary.

I pull a paper from the bottom of the pile and hand it to her.

"This is a state-issued license," I tell her. "It is completely legitimate."

"You are *out of your mind*."

Shaking her head, Melyssa starts laughing. Hysterically laughing. Laughing so hard, she stops breathing completely and tears roll down her face.

I am not fond of tears. They make me uncomfortable and upset. Ever since Luciana.

"Stop." I say, as calmly as I can. When she doesn't stop, I say it louder. "Stop crying, now!"

"Screw you, buddy," she laughs, staggering up off of the bed, holding her stomach, still laughing and crying.

I follow her into the entry, where she fishes her pants out of the bag and pulls them on, then walks over and shoves her feet into her shoes. Next, she moves to the door.

I dart in front of her, stopping her exit. "Where do you think you're going?"

She gasps a few times before answering. "Out. Away. I need air."

"It's dark outside and we are in the woods." I cross my arms in front of my chest.

"Move."

"I don't like your tone."

"I don't care. I need a break," she says and tries to push past me.

Very few people in my life have been stupid enough to put their hands on me, other than my father. I grit my teeth and stand my ground, trying to keep my temper in check.

"Would you move?" she growls, trying to squeeze behind me.

"I don't understand your need to leave this very moment."

"I need to clear my head. I need to breathe. I need to...get away from you."

"Melyssa," I feel suddenly desperate. "This really isn't a lot to ask, considering what you've—"

"I'm telling you, I need out."

"You really have no idea who you're dealing with." In my frustration, I threaten her. Immediately afterward, I realize my mistake.

"And you really have no idea who you're dealing with either," she whispers angrily, into my face.

She faces me defiantly, hands on her hips.

"Please, be reasonable. Let's just discuss the details, Melyssa."

"Let's not, and say we did."

"That makes very little sense, you know." I mimic her stance.

She is looking into my eyes, yet now I have no idea what to expect from her. I can only brace myself for whatever comes next.

Her eyes soften and she looks away first. This gives me confidence that she may be ready to talk. She also looks fucking exhausted.

"Look. I don't know what you want me to say," I begin.

She explodes. "How about, 'I'm a huge dick for getting you involved in this' and follow that up by moving out of the way? I really need to get some air."

"Will you run?"

Her eyebrows turn down and she shakes her head. "I don't know."

Well, at least she is being sincere. "But I'm sure someone like you, who believes this will work, who has enough pull that you've got documentation and a certificate of marriage, that," she pauses and her lip begins to quiver. "You know what? Just let me go. If I run, I'm sure you'll find me, no problem."

"I will give you ten minutes." I step away from the door and she bolts out.

While she is gone, I busy myself by putting everything in order. As Melyssa mentioned, there will more than likely be a lot of disbelief surrounding our story. We will need our story to be believable.

I look at my watch and then out the window where Melyssa is pacing back and forth, wearing a path in the grass. I am pleased she hasn't gone far, but not that she is still sputtering angrily to herself.

She looks back toward the cabin and I move away from the window. After several moments I look out again. She is sitting on a picnic table. I give her fifteen more minutes before walking out to meet her.

"Are you ready to come in and discuss this further? The faster we get on the same page, the sooner I can take you back."

She wipes her eyes. As she turns, I can see the trails left on her cheeks by more tears. I try to remain calm.

"You need to let me process this. You need to, at the very least, give me the illusion that you actually give a damn. That you actually acknowledge this is a lot for me to handle."

"I don't understand why you are viewing this as such a suffering."

"AND," she raises her voice to just below a scream, "I am still trying to sort you out in my head. Unlike you, I don't just jump to conclusions, five seconds after meeting someone—I don't just up and decide, 'Hey, this guy would make a fucking perfect fake husband! Let's do this!'"

I let out a laugh, but immediately regret it when she jumps up and shoves me with both hands. She isn't that strong, but I sway slightly on my injured leg. Then she raises her finger and pokes it into my chest.

"I don't like you and sometimes I think I hate you, but at least I try to understand why you are the way you are."

"Oh?" I puff up my chest, waiting for the next jab.

"I'm pretty smart. I even have a fucking degree to prove it, asshole," she snaps, in a whisper of course, as she turns and stomps to the cabin.

I walk in behind her and she lets out a growl, a fucking growl and every instinct kicks in. I snatch her up, ready to take her insolent little ass over my knee, when the tension completely leaves her body. Suddenly, she is limp in my arms.

I walk into the bedroom and flop her onto the bed and she becomes like a wild animal, desperately trying to escape. I grab her ankle and pull her back towards me, then quickly flip her on her back and position myself on all fours, hovering over her.

Her eyes are wild. She isn't afraid, but anticipating. This is exactly what she likes, I know. She craves my touch. I push my arm under her and lift her as I sit up. Her body is against mine and her nipples are hard as hell. My cock presses into her and she gasps as it grows.

I am an inch from her mouth, ready to take what she refused me before. It was a fucking gift to her. I take no pleasure in kissing. But now, all I want to do is kiss her. I want her to see she can't refuse me—anything.

I take the back of her head and pull her to me. I suck her plump bottom lip between my teeth and pull. She whimpers and I shove my tongue into her open mouth. Her tongue is motionless and I caress it with mine. It tastes good. So fucking good. I pull her hair, bringing her head back, causing her lips to open further.

I feel her hands on my shoulders, pushing me away and I grow more insistent. I lick her harder, as my need increases. Now she is pulling me closer. Her tongue strokes mine and I unwittingly groan into her mouth.

I reluctantly pull away from her mouth. Eyes closed, I keep my head against hers as I pant in rhythm with her.

"Do you like me now?" I growl.

"I like that," she hisses. "You, I'm still not sure about."

I reach between us, pushing my hand inside her pants.

"How about now?"

"It's wrong," her voice quivers. "You're wrong."

I push my finger between her soaked lips and rub her. Satin.

"What about this feels wrong, Melyssa?"

"Almost everything."

"Then why don't you focus on what doesn't feel wrong? Enjoy the pleasure, get out of your fucking head for once and feel."

I lean back on my knees and pull her pants down with no fight.

"Look," her voice is strong, like she is about to make some sort of statement against pleasure. So I lay beside her, on a fucking bed, going against everything I believe in. "This—"

I press my lips against hers again, because I want to shut her up. I also want to taste her again. Lips, mouth, tongue, all of which I have avoided for ten fucking years and all of which I want, right now.

I kiss her until I can't fucking breathe. My heart is pounding when I push myself up and off of her. My body is all tension and as much as I want to fuck her now, I need a fucking moment. I look down at her, sucking in slow, deep breaths. No longer anxious, her face is flushed, her lips swollen and red.

She looks fucking stunning, heartbreaking. I need to walk the fuck away and take a minute to clear my head.

I stand up, grab a bottle of discount store wine off the counter and walk out the door.

Standing on the tiny cabin porch, I unscrew the cap—fucking wine doesn't even have a cork—and take a drink. The sky is clear, but my head is far from it. I sit on the steps with an aching hard-on and drink until the bottle is nearly gone.

I look up when the door opens. Melyssa sits next to me on the steps.

"May I?" she asks, pointing to the bottle. I hand it to her. "Thank you."

"Answer a question for me, Melyssa."

She takes a drink and hands the bottle back to me with a nod.

"Are you going to accept my....."

"Proposal?" shakes her head. "You know how messed up this is, right?"

"I know it will make you rich."

"Please don't treat me like I can't see the big picture here, Sabato. This isn't about me being rich; it's about your freedom."

"I am freer today than I have been all my goddamned life."

"Since your mother passed away?" she asks.

My heartbeat quickens and I look away.

"Look, If I agree to go along with this...this farce, I'm going to do it smart. Which means: if I agree to this, you and I need to be able to get through a Stokes Interview with a big fat A."

"So...you're agreeing?"

"I am *considering* it."

Like she has a choice.

She stands up. "I'm going to make a sandwich for myself. Would you like one?"

"*Per favore. Grazie*, Melyssa."

I finish what is left of the screw-top bottle of wine and sit, staring up at the sky.

"What are you thinking?" she startles me when she hands me a plate full of sandwich squares.

"It's too quiet," I take the plate. "*Grazie.*"

"It is, but...peaceful."

I take a bite and nod.

"It's an illusion." I point up to the stars. "There is a glass ceiling up there waiting to fall down on us, Melyssa. All the twinkling stars will come tumbling down, causing a kind of hell only some people can understand."

"It never goes away, you know."

"What's that?"

"You think it's going to rain glass. You think that, because of what happened to you. You expect it, because it is something that hurt so bad, but—"

"Don't." I try to stand and she grabs my hand, stalling me.

"If this is gonna work, I need to know you, Sabato." She stands, "And you need to get to know me well enough to know that you can trust me with your feelings. Otherwise, there is no need to continue."

She puts her hand on my shoulder. I close my eyes, sighing. Then I feel her lips press to the top of my head.

"Goodnight."

Getting Me

The sun is just coming up, when I wake.

Sabato sits in the chair at the end of the bed with his feet on it—and a gun on his lap. His face is lightly dusted with stubble and he looks...at peace. I wish I had my phone, so I could take a picture of him like this.

I get out of bed quietly and go into the bathroom. Everything he bought is unpacked now and I want a shower. I had a decent night's sleep—considering...everything—and now I want a clean and clear head, to discuss how we can make this work.

I have a plan and I'm going to make sure that if I am going to go against everything I am, breaking the law and completely going against everything I've been taught, I am going to make sure I can walk away at the end of this feeling like there was a greater purpose.

I stand in the shower for a long time, just thinking about yesterday and how I finally lost my 'V card.' All those years of not wanting to just give it away to some boy who rubbed against me, of never getting a guy off and then yesterday I went straight to being fucked. Hard. And yet, he didn't even finish. On some level, I take satisfaction in it. Not that leaving him unsatisfied was my intention, but it makes me feel better.

After throwing on my clothes, I grab some cash out of my pocket. I decide to go to the campsite's little general store and buy some eggs and milk. I will make a decent breakfast, then Sabato and I can sit and discuss this arrangement.

Walking back towards the cabin with my groceries in hand, I consider the fact that I might be a complete idiot.

Is it stupid of me to think we can pull this off? Is it me being led by desire? I look up, when I hear a vehicle come to a skidding stop. Sabato jumps out and I know he's annoyed—panicked actually. I hold up the bag and smile.

He shakes his head as he stalks toward me. I see his eyes dart left and look to see what he is looking at. A family is walking out of their cabin. He grabs the bag from my hand, pulls me toward him and kisses me softly as he whispers, "Don't fucking do that again. Get in the car. Now."

Even though he's practically dragging me behind him, my head is spinning from that kiss. It's like nothing else and the fact that he is doing it in public means to me that maybe, just maybe this will work.

He opens the door for me and I smile. "Thank you."

"Uh huh," he hisses his whisper, before slamming it shut.

Once in the vehicle, I see his chest rising and falling quickly. He is scowling and I am liking the fact that even though he came after me because he clearly thought I had tried to run, well...he actually came after me.

"Did you miss me?" I ask, jokingly.

"*Questo non è divertente*," he growls, as he throws the vehicle in drive.

"Okay, then. I'll take that as a no and also assume that you did not just call me a nasty name," I say in a light tone, hoping to change his mood.

"It's not funny."

"It is, a little. You thought I took off."

"What would make me believe otherwise?"

"Because I said I wouldn't," I state simply. He pulls into the parking lot and turns around, heading back to the cabin.

"*Sei uan rompicoglioni.*"

"English?"

"You're a *pain in my ass.*"

I shrug, scoffing. "Jesus, I just wanted to make breakfast before going over my terms."

"Your terms?" He snaps. "*Sei pazzo.*"

"English?"

He groans, clearly frustrated with me. "You're crazy. *Come è possibile che si desidera sempre....*"

"English?" I laugh.

"Never mind." He throws the car in park and gets out. He looks back at me, impatiently and I decide to start with my list of demands now. After another couple of seconds, he storms over to the door and opens it.

I shove the bag at him. "Thank you for getting the door, Sabato."

He rolls his eyes and forces a fake as hell—yet completely panty-melting smile.

"You have a very nice smile," I say. And then it's gone.

Once inside, I grab a pan and a bowl from the small cabinet. "Do you want to wash these out? Who knows how long they've been in here. There's dish soap in the bag. Do you like scrambled eggs?" I hand him the soap.

"I don't know how to wash dishes," he scoffs.

"Well, you're about to learn." I shrug. "First on my list of demands: equality in this marriage. Turn the water on as hot as you can handle it and make sure you put the stopper thingy in to keep the water from going down the drain. Squirt some soap in the water and viola: you have dishwater."

Sabato lets out a long, slow breath, then walks to the sink and begins. I grab the dish sponge out of the bag and stand next to him. "Use this."

"My hands are very capable," he says, and there is a hint of amusement in his eyes.

"The sponge is the appropriate way to wash dishes. Watch." I stand next to him, but he doesn't budge, so I am forced to lean in front of him. He still doesn't move and I feel his breath against the back of my neck as I rub soapy circles around the small glass bowl.

I hear him take in a deep breath. I am very, very close to losing my train of thought. Also, forgetting how to wash a dish.

I turn my head to look up at him. "See?"

He nods and stares at my lips.

"Do you think you can do the pan?"

He shakes his head, no. "I think you'll have to show me again."

"Okay, but then you'll rinse the soap off and dry."

"Now, why would I want to dry?"

There is a hint of a sexual innuendo in there—I think, but...maybe not. I quickly wash the pan and reach to turn on the faucet to the other basin. I nudge him with my hip a little and he moves, just enough for me to squeeze between him and reach the sink to rinse both dishes.

I do it quickly, because I know where this can lead: me over his shoulder, then on the bed and...damn.

I grab the paper towels and dry everything myself, then I get ready to make scrambled eggs and bacon.

He leans back against the sink, crosses his arms and watches me. I whisk up the eggs and milk and dump everything into the pan. The stove is heating up and I look around for a toaster. There isn't one.

I am extremely uncomfortable, trying to perform even the most basic tasks with him watching me.

"Why don't you sit? It'll be ready soon."

"I'm fine."

"Okay, then why don't you see if there are plates and forks in that cupboard over there?" I point.

"Now, why would there be dishes in the bathroom?"

Flustered, I say, "Then, why don't you look for them...wherever? While you're at it, maybe wash them."

I don't wait to see his reaction. I just go back to attempting to cook while he watches my every move.

Somehow, I get through it. Somehow, he manages to find plates and silverware while still watching my every move. I know he does, because I can feel his eyes penetrating me.

I am fully aware that in order to try to get Sabato to open up, I should probably try to use his fascination with me to get him onboard and work with my demands. My demands...for my marriage. My marriage, that I had no idea about. And yet, somehow, I still ended up losing my virginity to the man that holds a license which says he and I are man and wife.

So...I guess technically that means I got to be a blushing, virgin bride, after all.

I can't help but laugh at the ludicrous truth of it, as I carry the plates to the table.

"What's so amusing?"

"This...this whole situation."

"I don't think it's funny at all." I set Sabato's plate down across from mine.

"Well, from your point of view, you're right—it's very serious. But from mine, it's laughable."

"How so?" He scowls.

"I am supposed to be in class right now, at an Ivy League school." I smirk and shake my head, "for law."

"And I am fighting for my freedom." He sits back and pushes his plate away. "This is not a joke...."

"I never said it was, but answer a question, the one you haven't yet: Why me? I mean, you keep saying you chose me, because of that night at dinner, that you thought I was perfect for this plan...at least, before. So. What makes you look at me and think, 'Hey, she's the one.'?"

He looks confused, but then he shrugs. "You've shown me that you want me."

"Really?" I am not exactly arguing. "So, because I checked you out, because I thought you were...decent to look at...you just assumed—"

"Melyssa," he holds his hand up. "Let's not complicate things with any expectations based on feelings. This can be messy, or it can be very simple. A business arrangement and an investment in your future. One hand washes the other. You help me, I help you."

"But...."

"You want to know 'why you,' because you want me to say I am enchanted with you." He shakes his head. "My God, all of you, like little girls obsessed with a fairy tale. I will admit, this was an issue I didn't expect to encounter with the woman peeking in my window, watching me fuck like an animal and clearly liking it."

Says the man who kissed me stupid for nearly thirty minutes, last night.

I swallow hard, trying to keep the disappointment out of my voice. "Okay, well.... Just make sure that works both ways and we'll be fine." I want to add that I can feel the way he looks at me, but I am still unsure if in fact I am just romanticizing this crazy situation, because he's the man holding my V card.

He looks slightly amused. "Love is a disease, Melyssa. I would prefer to avoid it as much as you seem to want to avoid STDs. And, as you know, I will tempt fate by fucking whoever I wish—with a condom, of course."

I am slightly annoyed by his response, yet I am not surprised.

"That is actually a great place to start. If this is going to work, if I am to agree to this, this...sham of a marriage, you need to know that I am zero percent on board with cheating. So—"

Sabato laughs. "Well, that is just too bad. Sex is a necessary part of my life. Don't worry, I will make sure my indiscretions are not public."

"I warn you," I jab my finger at him. "When this investigation happens—and it will happen, because of who you are and...what's been happening—it will not work unless people think we're crazy about each other. This isn't me talking, not some 'stupid little girl with a fairy tale obsession,' it's the U.S. government. For this to work, it has to be believable. No one will ever believe that I would agree to be in an open marriage."

"Hmm. Interesting point. Would they believe you were a voyeur?"

"I *am not*."

Sabato's head cocks to the side and he rolls his eyes. "Right."

I refuse to dwell on his...accusation. "Moving on. If you are unable to abstain from fucking whoever...*whom*ever you please, this will never work out."

"Oh," his dark eyes glitter, "I'm sure we can work that out."

"Fine, you go right ahead. I mean, it's not like you haven't already banged Valentina, so...." As the words come out, so does the realization that there is just no way I can possibly handle this. "Okay, look. You're right, I mean, you were wrong about me before. I'm not the right person to be your...fake wife. I can't do this. I won't go to jail for you. If I do, every chance I have at becoming a lawyer is shot to hell. So you'd better just, I don't know...figure something else out."

I stand and make my way to the bathroom. I know I'm going to cry. I know how stupid I am being and I know I am probably going to cry. I also know he hates it when I do. Inside the bathroom, I look at myself in the mirror and stand there waiting for tears to flow, when the door opens.

"Come out and finish this conversation," he demands. I push away my tears and I dig down deep to find anger. I can't put what I'm feeling into words though, so I give him the finger.

What happens next is not a surprise. Or, it shouldn't be. The jungle cat appears, lifting me over his shoulder and carrying me to the bedroom.

"Put me down, you...you ass!" He plops me down on the bed and grabs my ankles. When I try to retreat, he flips me back over and surrounds me with his body, caging me in.

"You want me to be monogamous? Fine, then you're going to have to stop being a little fucking tease. In case you haven't noticed, I like to fuck, Melyssa. A lot."

His mouth lingers over mine, breath to breath, reality fighting desire, realization fighting fantasy. Suddenly, the part of me that acts as my voice of reason stops giving a flying fuck. Actually, a flying fuck is starting to sound pretty damn good. I wrap my legs around his hips and using strength I didn't know I possessed, I flip him onto his back.

"I'm *not a tease*," is the first thing that comes out of my mouth.

But I am. *I so am.*

"I'm not a man who enjoys bottom," he says and flips me just as quickly.

"Then I guess we have some things to work out," I say, as his lips come closer to mine. "Don't."

"Why?" he whispers as he edges closer.

"You know why." I squeeze my eyes shut.

"Because you crave what I can give you." His lips are on my neck, followed by his tongue.

"No."

"Add this to my list of demands, while you're at it: No more saying 'no' to me. As far as you are concerned, that fucking word does not exist. If I am going to do this, you'll have to give in, because women *don't tell me no*, Melyssa. They whimper, yes. Scream, always. They beg for my touch."

Subconsciously, I roll my head to the side, giving him more room to play.

"How many have there been?" I gasp out.

"More than you want to know about." He pushes himself off of me. "And how many for you?"

"What?" I try to clear the desire from my head.

"How many men have you been with?"

"Twenty," I say, too quickly, without thinking it through.

He laughs out loud and I raise my eyebrows.

"Were they all hung like a toddler?" He seems very amused.

"Back to the table."

"Why, Melyssa?"

"You know why," I huff and push off the bed.

He walks out behind me, adjusting himself as he shakes his head, "There is no reason we need to do this out here. You're much easier to negotiate with in bed. Much more agreeable."

"Well, this is my life and my future and yours as well. I think business discussions should take place in appropriate places."

"My business *is* pleasure. My boardroom is the bed. And the sex couch and the cross and the whipping post...."

His voice is still down in thick, sexy mode. I silently scold Elsa, for swooning.

"Could you grab the folder? I want to go over it all in detail." I begin clearing the plates. Mine is still full, but his is empty. Deep down, I am happy I cooked him a meal.

Stupid girl.

SABATO
Negotiation

When I walk out with the file, she is at the sink, cleaning the dishes.

So, it seems that she wants to be my partner in this. She needs to be, she says, because apparently she doesn't trust me to make the decisions. This isn't something I am used to, but I will compromise if I must.

And it is clear now that I must.

She understands the fact that I don't do enchantment and love. At least, I think she does. That's a good start.

"Shall we begin?"

"Sure." Melyssa dries her hands on a paper towel and comes over to sit across from me. She reaches for the file.

"You wanted to know why you, if I remember. When I met you, I figured you were going to be perfect for this. Your attraction toward me was evident." I look up, and she is blushing. "Don't be embarrassed, Melyssa, it happens."

"Well to be fair, you seem to be erect all the time," she says petulantly, "so I guess it goes both ways, now doesn't it?"

"You're an attractive woman, Melyssa. So of course, I want to pleasure you." Actually, that's not completely true. At the moment, I just want to fuck her, because she has given me a serious case of blue balls. I clear my throat. "However, I also chose you because of your knowledge of the law, which I think will prove—."

"Assumed knowledge," she corrects. "Remember? I'm only just beginning law school. Well, I was. Who knows, now?" The thought seems to upset her. I feel bad that it upsets her, but I also believe she is not being honest with herself about what she wants.

"It's more than I have. Hell, I am not even from this country."

"Right," she says, as she looks down.

"Moving forward," I pull out the dozens of photos, "There are actual pictures of us from the dinner at my club. I made sure there were many times where we appear to be 'noticing' one another. You seem to be looking at me often and there is clearly an attraction there."

She pulls the pile over and looks through them again. "Huh. You seem to 'appear' the same way."

I hate that she sees it. I am drawn to Melyssa, just as strongly as she is to me, but in a different way. I've always had women want pleasure from me, ever since I was seventeen. Pursuing physical attraction has always been easy, almost an instinct, for me. It's not a challenge. I've never truly had a challenge.

"Intrigued."

"Right."

"These are from the security cameras at the club." I pull another set of pictures out of the envelope. She has yet to see them.

Melyssa moves through the first few, where her car is there in the back parking lot, all date stamped. When she gasps, I look up.

"Is there a problem?"

"Um, yes," she shuffles the photos in a pile and shoves them back in the envelope. "Why do you have these? Cameras in the um, the room?"

"For proof."

"Of what? That you're tying women up and banging them?"

I nod. "That it's not illegal activity, and it's always consensual."

"I don't want these used in proving our relationship," she says. "I don't want anyone to see them. They're...."

"Beautiful."

"No," she shakes her head. "I do *not* want anyone to see those."

I sigh. "All right, I will keep that in mind."

"Sabato...."

"Melyssa." She looks at me, eyes full of concern and anxiety. "I'm not going to promise. If it comes to that, I will use whatever I think is ne—"

"No! No. No. No." She stands, moving away from the table.

"Melyssa, sit. The likelihood of us needing to use them is...slight"

"I *don't want anyone* to see them."

"Fine."

"Fine?"

"Sit please."

She is pacing back and forth now and mumbling to herself.

"Melyssa. I promise, it will be fine. Sit." After a few more paces, she sits down and pulls the chair closer. "This is our apartment in the city. It's close to your school. It is the place you and I go when we aren't at your place. It's a place we planned to live together, after we got married. Do you like it?"

"Of course I like it," she snaps irritably. "It's beautiful."

I watched her look through the pictures of 'our place,' her loving attention to detail contradicting her tone. She actually traces one photo with her finger.

"And this is the car you and I bought together," I continue, pulling out another photo. "It's in your name, Melyssa."

She shakes her head and tries not to smile.

"It's all right to be happy," I tell her. "You see? This will be fine. You will be fine." She looks up at me, closes her eyes, and nods. "There, see, there is very little left to worry about."

Her eyes open and she looks confused. I wish I had not said that last part.

I clear my throat. "You'll be safe there. Regardless of what happens to me."

"What do you mean?" Now she is confused and growing afraid.

"My father...."

"Is dead." Her voice quivers.

"Right. But, that doesn't mean the threat is gone completely."

"Oh," she says, as the truth dawns across her face. "Oh! You're saying...you think there may be...retaliation?"

I haven't allowed myself to give it much thought, until recently, because until now I never cared what happened to me—as long as Salvatore was gone.

"I can't be sure."

"Is that why you killed him? Was he threatening you?"

I nod, even though that's not at all why. I can't open that part of me. Not to her, or to anyone. I can't, and I won't.

"He came after me. He knew I was working with Dominic to bring him and Benito down."

"So...it was self-defense."

"Melyssa, I wanted him dead. I wanted him dead more than anything I have ever wanted anything."

"But...it was self-defense."

"It was provoked," I tell her, getting angry now. "Why does it matter why? I killed him. I fucking killed him."

"Okay, okay I get that. I understand."

Something is breaking inside of me now, fucking breaking wide open. I feel. I feel and I don't like it.

"It's okay," she whispers and reaches for my shoulder. "I understand."

"How?" I move away from her. "How the fuck can you understand?"

"I just...do."

Somehow, I believe that she does. I round the table and take her face in my hands. I'm not sure what I'm going to do next. It doesn't matter. Or maybe it does. Maybe it matters more than anything.

"Then you're in," I tell her. "No bullshit, no teasing, no empty promises, you're in."

I realize I am holding her face a little too tight. My hands are shaking.

"Yes," she whimpers.

I am seconds from fucking her on the table and she is seconds from allowing it. I see it in her eyes, that excitement mixed with fear. I let go. I sit back in my chair and I hear her sigh.

"What's your favorite color?" she asks.

"What?"

"We'll need to know all kinds of things like that, for the interview."

"I like black and white."

She nods. "I like green. Favorite music?"

"Everything."

"I like country."

"*Except* country." I make a face.

She smiles. "Well, marriage is about compromise. So, I guess one of us will have to give in."

"I don't give in," I warn her.

"And *I* don't give up." There is heat in her eyes, but I'm not sure what it means.

"So...color and music. That's it?"

"Oh no, how about, your birthday?"

"May 27th."

She frowns and then nods. "Wow. Coincidence. May 26th for me, so...we should be able to keep those days straight. Do you...have any siblings?"

"No."

"Any other family?"

"No."

I look up and she is frowning again, biting her lip. "And, um, your mother died...."

"When I was seven."

"Who raised you?"

The question is curious. I would have expected her to ask where I was raised, not by whom. I stare at her for a moment and she is looking at me with a deep kind of sadness, one I recognize.

"What do you already know about me, Melyssa?"

"I know that when you were seven, you and your mother...." Her voice breaks and she blinks hard.

"Do you have something in your eye?"

"No." She shakes her head.

"Then, what?"

"I don't want to cry," she says. "I know it upsets you."

"Why would you cry?"

"Because, I feel your pain."

"Your parents are still alive," I remind her. "They are divorced, but still live near one another. Your mother is remarried and your father isn't. You have two half siblings and you seem close to them. Their mother died when they were young. But yours didn't. I don't see how you can 'feel my pain.'"

"She was my mom's best friend. She and my father, they used to fight a lot about the time Mom spent with her dead friend's husband, but by the time my dad noticed, it was too late. They loved each other."

"How did your father feel about that?"

"Angry, of course."

I am asking questions about people's feelings, people I barely know and have no idea why. But she is answering them openly, easily. I am intrigued.

"Do you get along with them?"

"My half-siblings? I do, yeah. I grew up with them. Every other weekend, you know. Typical divorced family situation."

"Why did your father never remarry?"

She smiles and it's a little sad. "Mom says it's for two reasons: one, he's too preoccupied with his indulgences. Hunting, fishing—you know, a sportsman."

"I do know. I spoke to him."

"You *what*?" She is shocked.

"I assumed it would be the right thing to do. To ask his permission to marry his daughter. Is that not how things are done in America?"

"No way." Her eyes are huge.

"You stayed at your father's house, when you went home. He was away on a hunting trip. Apparently he didn't have good cell service, so the fact that he told me 'No fucking way' could easily be dismissed as 'I didn't fucking hear him.'"

This part doesn't seem to have occurred to Melyssa before. "Oh my god, *my parents*."

"Your mother and her family are away on a vacation." I watch her carefully; to gauge the amount of annoyance I cause her in knowing that.

"Right." Instead of annoyance, there is a tinge of hurt in her voice and it bothers me.

I take a deep breath. "The Valentina indiscretion can be easily explained by saying that you took off because I asked your father's permission and you were concerned with his reaction. Because of that, I thought you had broken off our engagement. See? Easy."

"Our engagement? I thought it was a marriage license."

"Well, I can make sure it's properly dated if I have to. But there is a place we can go, if you want to get married for real. A judge who owes a favor. We can have photos taken, more believable ones. You may feel less concerned about it being fraudulent?"

"I really wish you would just tell me the truth and stop the charades."

"Which way do you prefer?"

"Does it matter?"

"Yes, I want you invested in this. Whatever it takes."

"And it will be less suspicious and Valentina won't hate me? Well, she might anyway, but...." She looks down at her lap.

"She has no reason to hate you, Melyssa."

"She likes you."

"She likes to get fucked. She is no more attached to me then I am to her." I notice then that I have my hand resting on the back of her chair and am rubbing her silky blonde hair between my fingers, so I stop. "Okay. Tomorrow we will take a drive back north. We will make this legal. Then we will stay at a nicer hotel, in your name. If the police show up—"

"No, I don't want you to get arrested," she says, quickly. "We stay here. We stay right here and find a way to make sure you're not in any kind of—"

"Hey," I interrupt, because she is panicking. "I need you to stop talking right now. I need a break."

"Okay." She bites her lip. "Um, do you want to go for a walk or something?"

"No."

"Well, then *I* need to take a walk." She tries to push her chair out, but I put my foot behind it to stop her escape.

"Why?"

"I need to clear my head." She looks away.

"Of what?" When she doesn't answer, I stand and hold out my hand to her. "Come. Let me take care of clearing your head." She starts to open her mouth to protest and I pull her up, rather forcefully. "It's part of our agreement. Remember? You aren't allowed to say no. All you can do is tell me how you want it."

I watch her eyes dilate, then she nods. I smile. She wants me.

I grip her hand tightly and pull her back into the bedroom.

"How experienced are you? You say you've been with twenty men, but I don't think that's true at all."

"I've dated twenty men, in four years," she says in that tone she uses when she's pretending to be strong.

"That's nice, Melyssa. But it doesn't answer the question." I swiftly move behind her. One hand is on her stomach, holding her back against me and the other is toying with fucking buttons. "Add jeans to our list of items to negotiate."

I finally get them undone and shove them down.

"Mmkay," she whimpers, as my hand slides into her panties. Plain, cotton, blue.

"These things, too. I like the lacy little shorts you wore at the club, but none of these. I want thongs, or lace. Understand me?" I rip those cotton bitches off and grab her roughly between the legs. I use the palm of my hand to rub against her as I push my finger inside, just enough to heighten her anticipation. "This landing strip is nice Melyssa, but I'm not an airplane. I'm a man. Do you understand?"

"I think, ah!" I shove two fingers inside of her harshly.

"No thinking, Melyssa, just feel."

"Mmkay," she says again.

"I want you naked down there, exposed to me. Add that to the list."

"Yes," she cries out, as I slowly start moving my fingers in and out of her.

"That's a good girl." I use my other hand to grab the hem of her shirt and pull it over her head. "Bras need to match the thong and lacy little covering. You know why?" I ask, as I release her shirt so it's resting behind her neck.

"No!" She cries out as I cup her little tit and squeeze.

"What did I tell you about that word?"

"But I was just answering—ah!" I pinch her and she stops trying to argue.

"When the underwear matches, it means you thought of pleasing me. It means you wanted me, from the moment you woke in the morning, until I finally come between your legs and feel the hot, wet, desire you've been carrying around for me all day. Add that to your list, Melyssa."

"Mmmm-kay," she says, as her head falls back against my shoulder.

"I don't eat pussy," I say, as I fuck her swollen little cunt with my fingers.

"But," she protests.

"You're the exception, so when you are making that list, remember that I am offering you something that is a rare gift."

"Mmkay," her knees begin to give way and her tight little twat squeezes even harder. I pull my fingers out of her. "Sabato!"

"No talking. No thinking. Feel."

"You—" I push her forward until she is bent over the bed.

"Don't move. Don't talk, unless you are asked a direct question."

And she doesn't say a fucking word. This will work out just fine.

I grab my bag and take the blindfold and rope out as she watches. "You can't stay still, Melyssa, this is necessary. You need to tell me with your mouth what your kinks are and what you're adamantly against. I know you like to watch, but you're the one who set the monogamy rule up, so I can't give you a good show with someone else. Not again."

"I don't want that."

"What, then? My bag of tricks here is limited. We can get beads, vibrators, whips, floggers, nipple clamps...." I pull her shirt all the way off, allowing her hands to go free.

She rolls her shoulders and moans.

"I need an answer."

"I don't know how to answer." Her face is red with embarrassment.

"Truthfully." I put the blindfold over her eyes, "This will make it easier. Watching for my reaction tells me you are not allowing yourself to feel."

"I feel embarrassed."

"That's nonsense. The only feeling you need to concentrate on is how your body responds to my stimulation. When we are together like this, there will be no emotional bullshit, because that fucks everything up. As a matter of fact, let's have no emotional bullshit, ever. Pleasure, and planning; that's all you and I need to worry about, Melyssa. It's a win-win. Do you understand?"

"Sort of."

I cup my hand and smack her little round ass.

"I don't like punishment."

"Noted." I pull her up and sit on the edge of the bed, then pull her down over my knee. I raise my hand and strike her ass again. "This isn't a punishment, Melyssa." I do it again. "Feel."

"What am I feeling?" she asks. She is not upset, but curious.

"Does this hurt?" I do it again.

"No."

"The spanking, when done in the right way, causes vibration to ripple through your muscles. It's actually a form of massage." I do it again, but this time I don't stop. "It's a rhythm. It will relax your muscles, while sending the vibration to your pelvis, stimulating you. It causes fresh blood to flow, which makes this," I shove my finger inside her and she cries out, "more sensitive and pleasurable."

"Mmkay," she whimpers.

"So is this punishment?"

"Nooooo," she moans, when I curl my fingers up inside her.

"Mmkay," I say, with a smirk. "Now tell me Melyssa, what else is on your list of hard limits?"

I spit in my hand and rub it between her ass cheeks.

"No um," before she has a chance to finish, I smack her ass in rhythm again, over and over. With each strike, I watch her ass shake. She really has a beautiful, round ass. I use my hand to spread her cheeks and she tenses up. "No, not that."

"You'd enjoy it."

"No."

"How about 'not now?' Keep an open mind."

"Not now."

"What else, Melyssa?"

I rub her back and squeeze her ass, while she thinks about it.

"I think that's it."

I know better, of course, but I will table that discussion and enjoy this moment, this feeling of giving pleasure to her. Teaching her, touching her. Watching her lose her mind and come until she can't move.

She may have a strong mind, but she is weak when it comes to touch and desire. I will use that to my advantage.

"Give me your wrists. I remember how much you move around. You need to be tied up. You like that."

"Mmkay."

BOUND

"Are you comfortable?" He asks in his rough, husky voice and tugs on the rope.

"Yes."

"That word Melyssa, that's my favorite."

I am secretly smiling inside. I like to make him happy. I like letting him make me happy. And, oh my god, do I like to be spanked and tied up.

I'm also suspecting that I may really like to be spanked, tied up, kidnapped, threatened at gunpoint and forced to marry a man.

Should I be ashamed of myself? Yes, definitely.

But there is no time for shame, not when he won't give me time to think. I trust him with my body. I also know his warning about feelings and I know I can handle it. I have to. I have a plan. It's the only thing that will make this arrangement work for me.

My eyes are covered and my body is bare—except the rope tied around my wrists. He lifts me and drops me on the bed, face down. I feel the cool air from the ceiling fan blow across my back. Then my hands are pulled up above my head and I feel a tug. I hear ropes being tied.

He isn't touching me, not like I want him to, but he is tying me up. I secretly wish I was suspended and—

My ankles are whisked apart, and I feel the prickle of the rope wrapping around them as I am spread wide.

"You look amazing, Melyssa," Sabato says. "Your ass is beautiful, perfect, actually. I want to do things to it, things I know you'll love. But I am not going to push you too hard today."

"Mmkay," I whisper. I swear I hear a chuckle in his throat.

I want to scream, 'Do it! Push me!' But I don't know exactly what that means.

Whack! I jump at the sound and the sting.

Whack, whack, whack, whack, he spanks me and then I feel his hands kneading my butt, both of his hands. He pushes up and my back arches under the pressure and then back down. My crotch rubs against the bedding and I am quivering. *Whack, whack, whack, whack*. I feel my ass rise up of its own accord, accepting each blow. Then his hands, I know they are coming and I meet them by arching my back. When his hands don't touch me again, I am confused.

Whack, whack, whack, whack, and then cool air blowing across my skin. My butt rises up again, when I feel the air directly between my legs. No touch.

Gawwww!

Stupid butt. I'm catching on now. Butt up, means no touch. I ready myself by gripping the ropes and curling my toes tight.

Whack, whack, whack, whack. It hurts a little more this time.

I wince. His hands are on my ass then, rubbing up and down, up and down. Squeezing, kneading, *ooooohhh*, kissing. My ass lifts in the air in response and his hands grip my hips and push them down to the mattress. Then I get teeth.

"Ouch," and a hand smack. *Whack!* "Mmm."

"*Siete impossible.*" He groans.

I don't say anything then and he doesn't do anything. I wiggle my butt a little, hoping for a reaction or some more action.

I hear a rip, a groan, then the bed buckles and his arm is under my waist, pulling me up.

"Knees." The rope loosens and I am plopped down on them.

His hands grab my cheeks, he spreads, he squeezes and I feel something between my legs. His mouth.

"Oh god," I cry out, as he sucks on my lips.

He squeezes my ass and I know he wants me to be quiet, but...how?

His tongue circles my clit.

"Oh god, I'm gonna—"

He smacks my ass, squeezes my cheeks and sucks.

"Aaahhhh," I cry. He grumbles something, but doesn't stop, doesn't spank, doesn't— "Stop! Oh god, stop!" I cry out, as my knees shake and he pushes my hips up. "No, don't. Don't stop! Don't!"

He pulls me back down hard on his face. I am not thinking. I am feeling, feeling...I am feeling. Lightning.

"Oh...no...." He pulls me tighter, sucks, nips and I am shaking. He pushes a finger inside me, and I can no longer hold back. I fall apart then, and it is beautiful. My butt raises and I hear the sound of plastic ripping.

One hand is on my hip, and I feel him rub against me.

"Please, not like this."

"Melyssa," he hisses my name.

"I just, I want to see you." I realize I am begging, but he pulls the blindfold off, appeasing me. I crawl forward and roll onto my back. "Like this."

He looks at me, then his jaw tenses and he shakes his head.

"This isn't how I—"

"Please, just this," I stop talking when he is over me. Eyes angry, breaths rapid, he pulls my leg up with one hand, bracing himself with the other beside my shoulder.

"No more demands," he says. In his eyes, there is something different.

I nod and he slams fully into to me. I cry out and he stops. I open my eyes to see that his are blazing. I pull my hips back, trying to alleviate the pressure, just a little.

His jaw is clenched, nostrils flared.

"Damn it," he growls.

I push against him and squeeze my eyes shut.

"Open your fucking eyes, Melyssa."

I open them and when I look up at him I can't hide the pain. He looks concerned, as he slowly pushes into me again, then stills and rotates his hips. I let out a breath and he pulls out, slowly. In and out, he pushes further each time and I can feel myself beginning to relax. He drops my leg to his side, grips my hips and pulls me close as he leans back, never breaking the connection.

He gyrates his hips and bends down, kissing me as he pushes further in.

He pulls me to him more tightly and suddenly I am not touching the bed. I am suspended. After a moment, my shoulders ache. I look down, as his thumb begins to rub my clit and I feel it again. The warmth, the heat, and then the burn. He isn't looking at me, he is watching us. His pace speeds and he pushes in further. The bed creaks and he looks up and into my eyes.

Concern and then it's gone, as he leans forward, allowing my back to touch the mattress again. I let out a sound that concerns him.

He quickly reaches up, unties the ropes and pulls me up, bringing me down on him fully. I cry out and my arms are lowered over his head, slowly. I moan, because it feels good to have my arms in a different position. He looks into my eyes as he moves me up and down on his hard cock.

I tremble and cry out. I lean in, seeking his mouth as I come. He pushes his forehead against mine, keeping me at a distance as his thrusts hasten and I swear he grows thicker. His teeth bare and he growls as he twitches inside me, still looking into my eyes.

I lean against his shoulder and he cradles my ass as he leans forward, depositing me on the bed. He is still inside me when he ducks his head out from under my hands. He covers me with all his weight. His body is so hard, everywhere. He unties my wrists and I try to touch him. He takes my hand, quickly stopping it. He bends down, kisses it and pulls out of me.

"Rest." He gets off the bed quickly and unties my ankles. "Stay there and rest."

He walks out the door and his ass flexes with each movement, until I can't see its perfection anymore. I roll onto my side, pull a pillow down into a hug and hold it tight. I shudder and try not to think, just to feel.

My body is coming down from the most unbelievable high.

..*

I wake up feeling a bit disoriented and sore. Very, very sore. My shoulder, my wrists and everything between my legs.

I roll to my back and look at my wrists. They're red and I can imagine I'm a little red 'down there,' too. I force myself to sit up and even my bottom is sore.

I hear Sabato talking in the other room and immediately I am concerned. I jump up and grab the shirt I was wearing and throw it on. I can't find my panties, so I grab his shorts.

When I walk out, he is on the phone, *a phone!*

I stop before he notices me and I hear him speaking in Italian. The only word I understand is, *Valentina.*

I try not to think, to focus on how I feel. I *feel* stupid. I *feel* sick to my stomach. I *feel* angry.

I walk past him, shove my feet in my shoes and head to the door.

"Melyssa," he snaps. "Melyssa, where are you going?"

I lift my hand up, give him the finger and then I am gone.

I walk fast down the path, holding onto the shorts that are falling down.

I am not stupid, I am not.

I hear footsteps and I am assuming they are him, so I speed up. I need to think and he had damn well better allow me the time to do it.

Sabato's hand grabs my elbow, but I yank it away and turn to face him. I put my hands on my hips and the shorts start slipping. I grab them to stop them.

I scowl at him, he scowls back.

"You need to come back to the cabin. Now," he says, between clenched teeth.

"No."

"So help me god, Melyssa, you are making a scene."

"You're the one chasing after me, buddy. Go back and talk to your *lover* and leave me the hell alone."

He shakes his head, rolls his eyes and grabs my wrist. I wince and he lets go. When he looks down, I expect to see concern or regret but no. His lips curves a bit and then, back to emotionless.

"Walk, or I will carry you."

"I'm walking." I turn back around in a huff, grabbing the shorts that are once again falling off—although half of me would love to bare my ass to him right now. But, I'm sure it's red too and the asshole would find that just as amusing.

He is at my side as I walk. "You're not seriously going to go around...in public...like that."

"Screw you, I'm taking a walk. *You're* the one causing a scene Mr. Shirtless."

"I apologize for not putting on the proper clothing," he growls. "However, I had to catch a fucking wild animal."

"Sorry to interrupt your little phone date. Won't happen again. Maybe you should marry *her*, while you're at it." I pause, when it strikes me. "Oh, that's right! Valentina can't give you a green card, now can she? How stupid am I?"

"You're fucking ridiculous, is what you are," he snaps in a whisper. "You were told not to feel anything but pleasure, Melyssa, and you're fucking that up within an hour."

"Pleasure? I woke up sore and honestly," I trip on a rock and he catches me by the elbow. Once I regain my footing, I quickly pull away. He grabs the shorts I had completely forgot about in that moment, which are now about plumber height.

"Your hair is fucking crazy, your shirt is inside out and your ass has been half bared a couple of times already. There are people watching us, Melyssa. Come with me now, or I will throw you over my shoulder and carry you. Though, to be honest, my fucking leg is sore and I would prefer to save my energy and take this out on you later, while you are tied up."

The leg injury gets to me and I'm not gonna pretend it doesn't. "Fine."

"Good."

"Don't mock me," I warn him.

He reaches over, grabs my hand, pulls me against his side and rasps in my ear, "Mmkay."

"Fuck you," I whisper.

"Mmkay." He smirks.

"Don't—"

"Mmkay."

"I'm serious, Sabato!"

"Mmkay."

I smack him in the stomach and he chuckles. I want to smile, but I won't.

Because I keep reminding myself. "If you feel the need to have Valentina come up here, just warn me and I'll—"

"She won't. She is doing me a favor."

"I bet she is," I retort.

"I am concerned about getting an infection in my leg. Tomorrow, when we are back in New York, she is going to get some medication to you. Today, she is calling the doctor and pretending she is you, to say that she lost the prescription and she needs it refilled. We'll both then have something we need."

"Well, I'm sure that makes her happy."

"Melyssa, for the last time, sex is sex. You and I know this, correct? Monogamy is part of our agreement, only because it is not in your...public character...to have an open marriage."

I nod, because in fact we did have that agreement. But now, after doing 'it,' I felt differently about things than I know I should. I am sure I will get over it soon, just not right after.

Not this soon.

"Good." He gives my hand a squeeze. "She is also helping me try to pull off a little get together and contact a justice of the peace for tomorrow. She even offered to get you a dress."

"I will get my own dress, thanks." I try not to sound bitchy, but I know I do.

"It's already taken care of." I snap my head around and look at him. "I mean, I already took care of it. I understand that you're concerned that it will come out and mess up this interview that may occur. We both have the same goal here. This will be beneficial to you, Melyssa. When we get back inside, I will explain more."

I feel my stomach knot and have to remind myself that his intent is not to feel, or even to protect my feelings, but to make this arrangement work. I also have to remind myself that I am trying to help him and those are the only feelings I can allow to enter into this. I just have to find a way to not confuse the feelings I'm having with the feelings I am not allowed to be having.

Back inside, he immediately lets go of my hand and I feel the distance growing between us.

"Let's continue our 'business' chat." He pulls out the chair at the little table and I sit. He moves the chair to the other side, away from mine and pushes the folder across to me.

"As I said, I own several clubs in Italy, which are being—"

"Like the one here? Steelettos?"

"Much nicer, but yes. They all went up for sale when Salvatore and Benito were arrested. All but one of them sold within hours." He seems proud. "The last has not sold."

He pauses and I feel like he is waiting for me to say something.

"You must be...happy?"

"That I am forced to sell something that I worked hard at creating? No."

Again, he is waiting. "I'm sorry, that must be hard."

He gives a quick nod. "There are harder things, Melyssa. The money has been moved into an account in the Caymans, under our names."

"Ours?"

"Mine and yours. As soon as our contract is legal, it all goes into your name." He leans forward. "This is where I am trusting you. There is eight point four million American dollars in the account."

I am sure my jaw is about to come unhinged. Sabato looks pleased with this.

"You name your price and commit to whatever amount of time we must keep this partnership going and I will agree. This will be a gentleman's agreement, just a handshake, Melyssa. A prenuptial agreement will obviously look suspicious."

"Ok. Okay, yeah, I guess that's true."

He looks at me impatiently. "A number?"

As in, how much money do I want, when all this is over? "I have no idea. This is a lot to take in. I...."

"If I may make a suggestion, how about we go by the time period during which we are legally married."

I nod.

"The penthouse in the City and the vehicle are yours to keep. Consider them gifts. If I am able to go back to Italy, those remain yours without question."

"Uh....Thank you?"

"Well, that's a polite thing to say."

"I don't know." Then it strikes me. "Wait. Why can't you go back to Italy now? Do you really think the *Cosa Nostra*...the family... the mafia, do you think they'll be after you?"

"I'm not afraid to die, Melyssa. I am not going back because I could be facing charges there. My businesses were run legally. However, my father used them to launder illegal funds and I knew it. Therefore, I can be arrested. I'd rather die than spend time in Italian jail, with so many of my father's ex-employees."

That made sense. But it also did not make me feel any better. Not one bit.

SABATO
Engaged

She honestly looks so confused right now.

It's sexy. I want to fuck her again. She is...well, she is definitely different from what I'm used to, but teaching her control is going to be a new challenge and a very, very pleasurable one.

I try to clear my head of those thoughts and continue.

"But, you think someday you'll go back?"

"I made an agreement with a long-time rival of mine that I would allow the Italian police to sell the business fronts Salvatore owned and use the money as they saw fit. When my father's empire has crumbled and my name is finally cleared, I will consider returning."

"Why would you sign away what is rightfully yours?"

"I want nothing to do with his money."

"But...to give it to an enemy?"

"He hates—hated—my father just as much as I do. He's a good man, deep down I'm sure, but he's also an asshole."

"Why does he hate your father?"

"His father was a police officer that died. He blames my father. I don't understand why it's his fault and honestly I really don't give a shit. But I'm sure Thorello will do the absolute best he can with the money, just to spite me."

I can see her trying to work through my complicated past and failing to make the connections. "Okay, but....why does he hate you? Is it your father's fault, that his dad died?"

My chest tightens. I am annoyed that she asks, but I can't tell her to fuck off and I certainly won't tell her most everything is his fault.

"I told you, he's an ass."

"Right...." The way she says it leads me to believe she is going to pry. If not now, then soon.

"Okay." She looks up from her hands and gives me a weak smile.

"I need a dollar amount."

"I don't know, Sabato. I don't want to take your money. I just want you to be okay."

"This is a business arrangement. I need a dollar amount."

"I trust you, so...you just do whatever you planned to." She starts rubbing her shoulders. I know I was a little rough with her… I would apologize, but why? She is just as much to blame as I am. She knew what she was getting into. Didn't she?

"Favorite sport?" she asks, snapping me back to the here and now.

"Not really a sports fan."

"How do you keep in such great shape?"

I smirk and shake my head.

"Oh, oh."

"That's for cardio. I also enjoy the freedom of running. I also lift and beat the shit out of a bag every now and then."

"Boxing?"

"I don't box, I pretend the bag is my father and I beat the hell out of it. Yours?"

She clears her throat, delicately. "I like to watch baseball, but not on television. I do like to run, I guess. So it's something we can do together, maybe." She shrugs. "For show, of course."

"Your parents and brothers names, remind me?"

"Grace and Melvin are my parents. Lou is my stepfather, Lewis and Johnny are my brothers."

"Younger, right?"

"Much," she smiles. "My last name is—"

"Chance."

She smiles and nods. "My middle name is Ann. What's yours?"

"Salvatore."

"Ouch," she cringes.

"Exactly."

I look at my watch. "We should pack up and get going soon."

"First we should take pictures. They may want to see pictures that we took. From our 'vacation,' or 'honeymoon,' or whatever. I mean, people do that, you know."

"Selfies? They're lame."

She laughs. "But something people actually do."

"One other thing people do is exchange rings."

"True."

"Wait here."

I walk into the bedroom area and grab my bag, pull the box out and open it to make sure it's still there. This shouldn't feel like it matters. No, it doesn't. I won't let it. I've learned what love does. This isn't love, it's a way to finally be free from what love has always done to my life: destroyed it.

I walk out, open the box and hand it to her.

Her eyes widen. "Wow, that's—that's beautiful."

"Well in order to pull this off, it's necessary."

"But this is...way above and beyond necessary. Did you pick this out or...." She stops and shakes her head. "It's beautiful."

"I chose it."

"You have great taste."

"Yes, I do."

She holds her hand out. I assume it's for me to put it on her.

"Is that necessary?"

"Play along, Sabato. When you're finished with me, I'll be a divorced, twenty-something woman with no future. I'm sure not many men will be lining up to ask me to marry them."

"Melyssa—"

"Non-negotiable." She pushes her hand closer to me.

"You interrupted," I scold her.

"Mmmkay." She wiggles her fingers.

"Melyssa Chance, will you allow me to be your fake, first husband?" She laughs. "I'm sure in the future, there will be others who are much more deserving, but I do come with millions of dollars and infinite amounts of orgasms."

"Well, how could I possibly say no?" She laughs again, and it makes me smile. "And a gun and a getaway car and—"

"Just say yes."

"What if I say no?"

That is confusing to me.

"Why would you?"

"Fine. Yes, Sabato. I would love to marry you for all your millions and promise of, well, you know."

I push the ring on her finger and for a brief moment, I think about Mama. What does she think, if she is looking down on us right now? But I quickly push the question out of my head. Why would my mother care about some sham wedding?

"Alright," Melyssa says, with a smile. "Let's do pictures."

"Let's do lunch." I look at my watch. "Or, early supper."

"How long did I sleep?" She grabs my wrist and looks at my watch. "Wow."

"You were tired."

She looks up at me and I can't help but smirk.

"Let's go somewhere decent."

"And chance getting caught?"

"I've been taking chances all week. I think it's probably—" She puts her hand over my mouth and I am shocked for a moment.

"Don't tempt fate."

"Don't tempt me." I nip at her hand and she pulls it back. "Be careful Melyssa, I bite."

..*

After stopping at that disgusting discount store again to purchase a camera, we end up at a little Italian restaurant—at least, that's what it claims to be.

Melyssa seems to love it, though. I can tell by all her delicate little moans of pleasure as she eats. I am sure she would have an orgasm if she ate at some of the places I frequented in Sicily and I tell her so, in front of the wait staff. She burns bright red and I can't help but laugh. It is actually very enjoyable, taunting her.

She tells me she's afraid I've offended the people who run the place. I let her know that she should probably get used to me offending people and I tell her to use the language barrier as an excuse, if she needs one.

We take a couple of pictures, which is harder than you'd think. Selfies would be much easier. Our waiter offers to take a few. Even insists on her sitting on my lap.

"Ah, *bella*! *Che* lovers!" he says, in the worst Italian impression I have ever heard.

Melyssa grabs my face and turns it to hers, giving me the loudest kiss I have ever heard or felt in my life. In a whisper, she tells me she hopes it makes me uncomfortable. Without whispering, I tell her it makes me hard. And yes, I make sure the waiter can hear me.

When we are finished eating, I give him a good tip, shake his hand firmly and whisper, "Guarda mia moglie cosi di nuovo, e lei pagherà."

"What did you say to him?" she asks, as we walk out.

"Thank you."

"Uh huh, right." She shakes her head.

"Prove otherwise," I say, as I open the door for her.

* * *

Once back at the cabin, she makes me pose for photos on the porch. I hate it. It reminds me of being a boy, when Mama used to slick back my hair and make me pose by the *fiore* outside of the house, before taking me to school. Except, unlike Mama, Melyssa runs her fingers through my hair, making it messier and laughing while she does it.

When I insist on her doing the same, she mimics my sulking, but it's more a pout. I want to give her a real reason to pout. I want to make her beg to come.

She walks inside and comes back out with a bottle of wine.

"To a perfectly posed engagement." She takes a drink from the bottle and hands it to me. "Did you get the ring in any of the pictures?"

"I'm sure I did."

"Good," she says and holds it out, looking at it as she sits on the porch step. "I like it here."

"You do?" I almost laugh, but she looks up at me and sure enough, her face is gravely serious.

I hand her back the bottle and lean against the railing.

"You look bored."

"I'm not used to relaxation."

"Right, me either. College was very busy."

"With those twenty boys?"

She shakes her head, no. "With classes."

"Sure," I say in jest and she blushes. "I'd like to know about them. The men, not the classes. You know, for the interview."

I sit down next to her and wait.

"Not much to tell. I dated a lot but...you know."

"No, I don't know. That's why I'm asking."

She lets out a deep breath, "I wanted to like them. But the fascination quickly dwindled."

"Fuck 'em and leave 'em?" I say as a joke, but I honestly I want to know. I don't like that I want to know.

"Yeah, something like that."

"Seriously, I should know these things—for the interview, Melyssa." I want to let it go, but I can't seem to. It's not that I'm jealous. Just curious.

"Okay," she takes another drink—and by drink, I mean she downs a quarter of the bottle. "Well, I would decide to be attracted to someone. I would do the three-date-rule thing and most of the time I wouldn't let them get past feeling me up before I was bored with them, or figured out I was forcing an attraction."

She takes another drink.

"Three dates and you wouldn't let them fuck you?"

"Nope," she laughs.

"Wow, you know what they call that?"

"A tease." She says solemnly and takes another drink.

"Well, maybe they just didn't know what you liked. Many men don't."

"You do," she says quietly.

There is something in her eyes that doesn't sit well with me.

"Well, you were not very subtle about what you wanted from me. Our first meeting, you watched me the entire time. I knew you wanted me. Our second meeting, you watched me do a suspension scene and your fucking eyes were glued. The third meeting alone, you were bound to a cross. Luckily, I knew what you needed, or I wouldn't have made it to four, huh?"

She is looking at my lips. Fuck, I'm looking at hers. I look away.

"I know women, Melyssa. In fact, I know people. So if we face an interview, let me lead."

"Of course."

"Longest relationship?"

"Four years." She answers.

It takes me a minute to comprehend, "Four fucking years?"

"Yep, all through high school."

"What ended it?"

"Me. I just always knew he was my friend. I loved him as a friend; there was never really anything stronger between us. We still talk once in a while."

"What's his name?" comes out immediately.

She looks up and laughs. "Ryan. Why?"

"Well, anyone who knows me would know that if our marriage was real, I wouldn't be all right with my wife talking to a past lover."

"We haven't even been together in four years, Sabato." She giggles, as if I am joking.

"Put that on the list, non-negotiable."

Her jaw drops. "Wow, you're serious."

"For the sake of this, this...marriage, I certainly am."

"Fine. Have you ever had a serious relationship?"

"That really isn't any of your concern."

"It sure is. Spill it." She crosses her arms in front of her.

"One. But...I won't be talking to her ever again, so there is nothing to discuss."

"Did you love her?"

"You're pushing."

"I have just told you everything about my tragic past of crappy relationships."

"She's dead." Saying it out loud hurts. It hurts like hell.

"The car accident?" she says, very quietly. "Was she the passenger?"

"How do you know about that?" I snap at her.

She looks suddenly uncomfortable. "I Googled you. Sabato, I'm so sorry. I really am."

It isn't her fault, but I don't fucking care. "I'm done for the day."

I go to stand and she puts her hand on my knee, stopping me.

"I understand. I'm sorry. Sabato, I want to be your friend. Whatever you tell me, I will never tell anyone."

I nod. "Can we go in now?"

"I am going to enjoy the quiet for a little while longer."

"Fine." I settle back down.

"You don't have to stay."

"Yes, Melyssa, I do. By involving you in this, there is a risk."

"Right. Of course." Her eyes dart around and she stands, then stumbles.

I grab her elbow to stop her from stumbling down the stairs.

"No more drinking, either."

Drunk & Stupid

"I'm sorry."

"It's fine."

But it's not. It's not fine at all. Sabato just went from fun, even flirty and relaxed, to frigid.

"I'm ready to go inside." I hold the railing as I walk up the stairs, because I feel a bit tipsy.

Inside the cabin, I look around, just now realizing that things are going to change, for me—for us—as soon as we go back.

"What happens if they arrest you?"

"Then I go to jail," Sabato shrugs, "and you stay at the apartment. Not that old place—the new one. It's your home now. But I doubt I will be in jail very long."

"You're sure it was self-defense?"

I regret as soon as I ask it.

"I assure you that it looks that way, but I wanted him dead."

"So, you...."

"Made sure he died exactly how he should. Like a dog, bleeding in a ditch."

"Sabato, I know it's hard to talk about, but I need to know. Please give me that. I need you to respect me with the truth, even if you can't.... I need that. This situation is crazy, and I am even crazier to agree to it, even knowing—"

"Why did you, then?" He snaps at me.

"Because, I like you."

"You like the way I fuck you."

"No...."

"You are calling for respect, fine. Then give it to me back. Respect me enough to own up to that much."

Honesty. Painful, scary, dangerous.

"Okay," I lick my lips. "The first time, I saw you on Dominic's IG and I—"

"IG?"

"Instagram. There was a picture of you, and even though it was just a picture, I saw something in your eyes that...." I try to think of how to say it. "Was deep, and attractive, and...this is incredibly embarrassing and hard to say, but I am being honest. I promise to be honest, as long as you do the same. That night, I saw you at the steakhouse and there was...an intensity and, well, I thought you were perfect. It titillated me, that after four years of trying to force myself to be attracted to someone I saw you and right away—bam!"

"Titillated," he says, with a hint of humor in his voice.

"Oh shut up!" I glare drunkenly at him.

"Mmmkay."

I laugh and so does he.

"Now, it's your turn."

He paces a bit, sputters a bit and finally he stops in front of me.

"All right, but I don't want to discuss this, ever again."

I nod.

He takes my face in my hands. "When I'm done, I want to forget it."

I nod again.

"After we're done here, you'll go in the bedroom and present for me. You'll deny me nothing. Nothing."

I place my hand over his.

"Mmmkay," I say, in attempt to make him smile. He doesn't.

"When I was six years old, my mother tried to leave that son-of-a-bitch, Salvatore. We had a tiny little apartment in Florence. For a few happy months, we didn't see him. I knew, even then, how awful he was to her. I saw it, heard it and was happy when she decided to run." He stops, swallows. "On my birthday, we visited The Uffizi Gallery. We were looking at the pictures when an explosion went off. My mother covered me with her body, as glass rained down on her."

My heart squeezes so tight, it physically hurts. A soft sob escapes my mouth and he closes his eyes, tight.

"I couldn't save her."

"You were seven, Sabato," I whisper.

"Less than two months ago, I overheard him, Salvatore. He was talking to Benito, about what he would do to me if I tried to leave his service. He said he would do to me, what he had done to my mother."

He starts trembling, with sadness or rage, I can't tell. Maybe both.

I gasp in shock. "He was the one? He planned it?"

His eyes fly open, his jaw tense. "Yes and you know the rest. I am finished discussing this. Present, Melyssa."

"Sabato, I'm so, so sorr—"

"PRESENT!"

"Okay." My body is shaking as I scamper into the bedroom. I throw my clothes off, but then I can't decide where he might want me—the bed, the chair, the floor? I can't stop trembling. I want to cry, hell, I am crying. He doesn't like me to cry. He doesn't like it and—

I look up and he is standing above me. Quickly, I wipe my tears away knowing he sees them and wishing he doesn't.

"Bed."

"Right."

I am on the bed and he is taking his clothes off. He folds them neatly and puts them over the arm of the chair. He is calm and I am a wreck. I don't know how he can be calm.

He stands in front of me and reaches out, but stops before he touches me. I spread my legs wider and arch my back. When he still doesn't touch me, I look up, questioning.

His hands are at his sides and he shakes his head. "I can't do this."

"You can," I say, sniffling.

"No Melyssa. I can't fucking do this. Not with you. Not with—"

"Not negotiable," I say. "Only with me."

"Everyone who gets too close ends up dead!" he snaps, literally. "Do you understand, that is what I bring to the fucking table?! Everyone I let in dies. So no, I will not give you what you want. Not that. The apartment, the car, the fucking ring are yours, those I can give. I will even give you money enough to get through school, I will give you more than you deserve, but I will not—"

I move off the bed and take his hands. He tries to pull away and I don't allow it.

"You think the girl, Luciana, died because...because you loved her?"

"Don't, damn it," he hisses at me.

"It wasn't your fault."

"Yes it was! I couldn't fucking save them! You don't know shit! I couldn't—"

"You were young, you—"

"Failed the only people I loved. I am no good. I can fuck you, but I can't protect you."

"He's gone, Sabato. Your father is gone, because you killed him. You made sure he was no longer going to hurt anyone. He is gone, finally gone, so now you can live. You have already protected the people you let in now, let them in, damn it!"

He looks so broken, so unhinged, so lost and angry, like he doesn't even know how to breathe anymore.

I pull him against me, as hard as I can. He is stone, everywhere. I kiss his neck and he stiffens even more. I reach down and grab him, through his pants. Silk and stone. It feels so good in my hand and I no longer care that I am still sore from the morning.

I kiss his chest, as I continue stroking him. I kiss down him and I am on my knees before him. I have never really done this but I want to do this for him, to him.

He hisses when my tongue circles his tip and thrusts forward with his hips. I look up and he is looking down, eyes raging with an intensity I have never seen. I work my mouth and hand in rhythm, up and down and he growls. I reach around him with one hand to grab his ass. I push him forward, causing his tip to hit the back of my throat. I almost gag, but I don't, I swallow.

He lets out a sound that is pure, raw emotion. I continue pumping him, forcing him further and further into my mouth. I love the noises, the sounds he makes, the scent of his skin, the heat of his cock, the soreness in my throat and between my legs.

I am all sensation, and his reaction is pure temptation, driving me further and further into an unexplainable state of ecstasy. I thrust my body closer wrapping my leg around his, hoping for contact to ease my own burn. I suck him and rub myself against his leg until I am groaning too. I am turned on by doing this to him, for him, with him. He pushes his leg forward, nudging me. I come undone as he pulls out, grabs my hair, yanks my head back and pumps his cock until he comes all over my chest, groaning my name over and over.

I wrap my body around his leg, panting, shaking, and holding onto him for dear life. Fearing if I let go, he'll walk away and that will be it.

The only man I've ever wanted will have ruined me, because he thinks it will save me.

His hand is still fisted in my hair as he breathes in, heavy, deep breaths. I feel more vulnerable than I did as a virgin tied to the cross, the first night Sabato Efisto ever touched me.

"Up." He whispers. His grip loosens and his fingertips gently massage my scalp.

"No."

"Melyssa, up." His voice is gruffer now, but still I hear the pain in it.

"Don't walk away and leave me like this."

"I'm right here."

His hands are under my arms then, lifting me. I pick my shirt up off the ground and use it to wipe his cum off my throat.

"Get in bed."

"Sleep next to me this time." I put myself out there further. "Non-negotiable."

I silently beg for the response I desire. If he says yes, I will know he means it.

"Get in bed." He pulls back the covers. "This is the last night you'll sleep on discount store sheets."

I lie down and watch him walk out, hoping he won't disappear. He returns with a warm cloth and he cleans me, gently, tenderly, and—I may only be imagining this—reverently.

He throws the cloth into the pile of clothes and climbs in next to me. I scoot back against him, needing contact. He places one hand on my hip.

"Goodnight, Melyssa."

"Goodnight, Sabato."

SABATO
Mess

I wake up and the sun is blazing.

It's much later than I should be waking up, I know, but I really don't give a fuck right now.

Melyssa is draped over me, clinging on to me for dear life. After last night, I know things are much more complicated than I anticipated. She touched me, tasted me, stroked me throughout the entire night...and I gave her nothing back. I would have, but she wouldn't allow it.

Two things I am not: a taker and someone who allows others to tell me what to do. Last night, I allowed both. One thing I definitely am not: submissive. Last night, in some small way, I submitted to her.

Knowing that disturbing fact, I don't want to face her today. But I don't want to let go, either. I am in a hole and can't even dig myself out of it. She has messed up my mind, tilted it, spun it, shaken it and fucked it.

I try to remain still, try to let her sleep, but when I look down she stirs and looks up at me.

Green. Green is the color of jealousy, money, greed and her eyes.

"You woke me up," she says, as she stretches. In doing so, she rubs her body against mine.

"I was trying not to."

"Well, your heart woke me up. It was beating against my ear, like a little alarm clock."

"I see. Good thing the new apartment has three bedrooms," I say, watching to see how that fact hits her.

It only takes her a minute, before she smiles in that familiar, petulant way. "I've decided what I want out of this arrangement."

"Let's hear your latest demands."

Good, now we're getting back on track.

"I want to sleep in the same bed. It feels good, I feel safer and you are very, very comfortable. Hard, but—"

"Hard, because you can't keep your mouth or hand off of it." I raise my eyebrows.

"That's the other thing. I like touching you. As a matter of fact, I love touching you."

"Melyssa," I begin.

She places her finger over my mouth, quieting me. "I'm not asking to tie you to a cross, just maybe a bed now and—"

I bite her finger. "Fuck, no! You must be—"

"You've created a monster, Sabato." She sits up. "All that perfection...." She runs her finger down the separation in the center of my abs. "I want to drink wine out of this area."

"Not until I have drunk it from your pussy."

She swallows hard and tries to be courageous. "Are you...thirsty now?"

I stare her down. My mouth is suddenly dry.

Then she laughs and gets up. "I'm going to shower, oh and that was non-negotiable, too."

I sit up as she walks out the door. I may have let her have last night—hell, admittedly, I needed last night. But that is where I will draw the line.

She's already in the tiny little shower when I walk into the bathroom, condom already on. I pull back the plastic curtain and she jumps and turns towards me. I turn her back around.

"Hands on the wall and hang on." I lift her, without asking. "Legs around me."

"How?" I grab on and wrap them behind me. "Oh, I see."

"No more talking," I line myself up and slam into her. This time there is no stalling, no reprieve. I fuck her with wild abandon. This is a reminder of who is in charge.

I grab her tits and squeeze, I pinch and pull her nipples, hard. She cries out, but I slam into her fast and hard, pounding her tight little pussy. I want her bruised, battered, sore, as a reminder that I am no fucking prize to be won.

Her face is pressed against the shower wall. Her hands are beside her head, holding on as best they can. She is crying out my name in pleasure and I want her to remember this moment the next time she decides to poke the sleeping bear.

"Who's in control here, Melyssa?" I hiss against her ear.

"You, oh god! You!"

"Do you like it like this?"

I expect a no.

"Yes, yes, yes!" Her pussy contracts, milking my cock as she comes.

"Son-of-a-bitch," I groan and my release follows hers, not far behind.

I grab the shampoo, cock still buried deep in her, lather up my hair, rinse, then finally pull out. She leans against the shower wall and I step out of the shower.

When she leaves the bathroom, she looks at me like she's going to say something, but then decides against it. I feel some control coming back after an uncontrollable night.

She comes out of the bedroom dressed in one of my shirts tied on the side and a pair of shorts. I don't like how much I enjoy seeing her in my clothes. But I don't hate it, either. Although, I know it would be smarter if I did.

"We should pack the car," I say, as I look away from her.

She stops dead in her tracks and looks at me. "Do we have to?"

I nod. "I've convinced you to play along. So it's time."

"I could use more convincing, you know."

And the balance of control teeters again.

"You'd better think twice about that."

She smiles and starts packing up. After a moment, she giggles.

"I've thought like, ten times about that and I've decided that I'm game."

"I think I've spoiled you," I grumble.

"Meaning?" She shoves some clothes into a bag.

"I've allowed too much freedom."

"Is that so?" She looks up at me, still bent over.

"Yes, that is so."

"What's too much freedom between friends?" She grabs the keys off the counter, pats me on the back and carries two bags outside.

..*

We drive silently as I think about what too much freedom might look like.

Anarchy, knowing her.

Part of me thinks I may have asked for too much from her—no demanded it. And yet, she has taken it all. I can't help it. I like this girl.

I would definitely consider her a friend. I only had a few of those, but she could easily be considered one...if it wasn't for the fact that I had fucked her. Then again, Valentina was something of a friend and I had fucked her too. I'd even told Melyssa that it meant nothing. So who was I lying to, her or myself?

The age old question pressed: can a male and female be friends? I never even considered the issue, until now. I've always liked women, loved to please them, to control them. I was not disrespectful, I never played a game—in fact, I was the game. When I chose a woman for an evening of play, she knew what she was getting. A few hours of fun, with a man who could satisfy her completely—physically, of course.

My employees never had preconceived notions and were never given any false promise of becoming mine, or of me becoming theirs.

I am unattainable. I choose to be so. I am better this way.

I look over at Melyssa and she is asleep. She has no reason to trust me, but she does. She now knows my greatest secret and still I trust her.

She is perfect and yet I will ruin her.

She opens her eyes, covers her mouth and yawns. Then she smiles a sleepy smile.

"Want me to drive?"

"No, I drive." I am angry and I have no idea why.

"Okay." She sits back. She says nothing more. I've upset her and I don't want to. But I can't be a friend.

After a few moments, she reaches up and points to the radio.

"Do you mind if I listen to some music?"

"It's your car," I say.

She rolls her eyes. "Right."

"It isn't?"

"For now, I guess it is."

Melyssa hits the search, until a song comes on that she seems to like. She leans back and begins to bop her head to the music. I look at the radio and the display reads 'Budapest' by George Ezra. She starts tapping her foot and I hear her singing quietly.

"We need a song, to make this believable," she says, after the song changes.

She looks at the radio display and laughs.

I look, too. 'Dear Future Husband,' by Meghan Trainor. I shake my head, but I am curious. I listen to the lyrics and look out of the corner of my eye as she sings along. She sees me watching, but doesn't stop. The song keeps playing and she keeps singing, only she gets louder.

"Is there anything we should be discussing?"

"Are you feeling better?" She leans up and turns down the radio.

"What do you mean?"

"Well, I thought we had an understanding. Our negotiated list. I can't wear jeans or discount panties, I can't talk to my ex, I live with you and...?"

"I can only have sex with you."

"Is that a bad thing?" she asks, quietly.

"Well it certainly...limits things."

She looks out the window and I know I have hurt her feelings. I don't mean to.

"Melyssa," I begin.

"No. You know what, I don't care. You're right. You should do what you want. Just understand that I'm going to do the same."

"Fine." I spit out, even though no, it's not fucking fine.

"Also, I want my student loans paid off—all of them. And I want ten grand when you leave."

"When I leave?"

"When you go back to Italy. When you go back to running your club, when you decide that our crap marriage is worth about as much as the fake paper it's printed on." she pauses, and she is angry. "My legal fees, too."

"Fine."

"Good."

I feel like I should push one more point. "I can't be your friend."

"Obviously."

"What does that mean?"

"Look, Sabato. I can't change your past. But he is dead. The man who hurt you, tormented you, crushed you, he's dead. You can't go back and save your mother, even though I know if you could, you would and hell, I would help you do it. But until you allow yourself to accept that you are not making your life any better after he's gone, well then...you may as well have let him live."

The rage that overwhelms me then, it's almost blinding. How dare she? *How dare she?*

"Fuck you!"

"You have."

"You're infuriating."

"*You're* giving up."

"You have no idea what my life has been."

"And that's where the problem lies, Sabato. You're too focused on what your life *has been like*, before now. Until you can forgive and move on—."

"He *doesn't deserve* forgiveness."

"It's not for him. It's for you. Forgive yourself, because you didn't do a damn thing. A seven year old boy cannot control what an evil, grown-ass man does. You had nothing to do with that bomb, or anything you did after that, when you went to live with an evil man who you thought was your father. I'm sure on some level, you thought you owed him—"

"Enough!"

"Alright, then. I'll stop talking. I'll stop caring."

My blood boils. "Just because you were allowed to touch me, doesn't mean I have allowed you inside, Melyssa. Please don't fool yourself. You are just like the rest. There are *hundreds* of you out there. I barely remember most of your names."

"I want you to pull over, now."

"We're on a highway," I argue.

"Tough shit. Find a place."

"For what?" I snap.

"Because I said so!" she yells at me, really yells. "Now!"

I see a rest stop ahead and decide I want her out as much as she wants to be out. The vehicle isn't even in park, when she is out the door and running to the bathroom.

How dare she! How dare she think that we are friends, that she knows me or my life, that she can speak to me this way.

I want to walk away, fuck, I want to leave her there and drive off. I feel a sharp squeeze in my chest and I hate that she can make me feel this. She is no different than the countless others, except she saw me at a weak point. Once. That mistake will not happen again. Never again. I gave her what she needed. I didn't need that. There was no need to be friends. I sure as fuck wouldn't touch her again and hell would freeze over before I allowed her to touch me.

Suddenly, I need to know exactly how long I will be forced to live in this hell. I need to know because I am now thinking prison would be less of a hardship than living with a woman who actually thinks they can tell me what to do. For twenty years, I have managed to take care of myself. I have managed alone.

Alone is better than this, this, fucking...feeling shit.

Feelings.

The need to get off, the need to get someone else off, hate, lust, desire, orgasm; these are the only feelings that do not betray or get taken away by bastards who want you dead, who want to ruin your life.

The other shit, I have no room for in my life.

I look at the clock and five minutes has passed.

Ten minutes.

Twelve minutes.

I start to get concerned.

Did she run?

I'm so angry, my skin feels like it's steaming. *That bitch better not have run.*

Seventeen minutes.

Is she hurt?

Why should I care, if she is? If I do, it's only because she is my key to freedom.

Twenty minutes.

Is she safe?

I open the door and get out. Three vehicles are parked in the parking lot that weren't here before. I feel panic strike.

I walk around, checking out the area. No woods, just pavement and a building. It's just a rest area.

I walk inside and push my sunglasses up to rest on my head. There are couples looking at maps, children running off extra energy from being in a car too long and older couples, all seemingly happy.

But no Melyssa, happy or otherwise.

I spend a few more minutes pacing outside the women's restroom. My instinct tells me to go in, but that isn't possible right now. Too many people would see.

I try to blend, but there are too many eyes on me. I don't blend. I would never be caught dead in the travel clothes some people wore.

A red-haired woman walks out with a chubby miniature in tow. She looks at me, then shakes her head and walks away. Her daughter turns around as they make their way to the door and does the same look. I scowl at her and she sticks her tongue out at me.

"*Bambino viziato.*"

Another younger woman walks out and another. Finally I ask the last, "Is there a blonde woman in there?"

"A crying—"

"Are there others?"

"No, but she seems pissed."

Ignoring their judgmental glares, I walk in to find Melyssa with a wet paper towel over her face. I immediately feel relieved.

When she pulls it off, she jumps. "What are you doing?"

"You've been gone a long time." I try to hide the fact that I am angry, relieved and angry all over again, all in the space of a half-second.

"Well, I had a lot to consider." She looks past me. I take a good look at her face. It's red and puffy.

She smiles and I know it's not at me.

"Sorry," she apologizes and walks around me, out the door.

When I turn I see two women, both young, both nice looking, both giggling.

They're looking at me, not at Melyssa. I shake my head and follow her outside.

BROKEN

I wait at the vehicle for Sabato to come out.

He takes a few minutes; I assume he is using the bathroom.

I lean against the vehicle, taking comfort in its warmth. I am over this. Completely and totally over this. Who cares if it is what's best for me financially, education wise? Future-wise?

I look up when he finally comes walking up. Black, messy hair, aviator sunglasses covering his very expressive, deep brown eyes. Chiseled face, perfect lips; his strong, solid, muscular upper body is clothed in a plaid button down with a tank top underneath. He has on khaki shorts and brown leather sandals.

These clothes are clearly his attempt to 'blend in.' But he could never blend in. Well maybe one of those reality TV model programs, but not in everyday situations. I think it's amusing that he thinks he does.

I stand facing the car, with my hand on the handle, waiting for him to hit the unlock on the key fob. But he doesn't.

Instead he hands me a bottle of water and reaches in front of me to open the door.

I almost laugh at the forced chivalry of this infuriating man. But I don't really feel like laughing.

"Thanks."

He gets in and looks at me, then at the bottle of water, "Do you need me to—"

I open the bottle, already knowing what he's going to say.

"Who did you live with on breaks from school and holidays?" I ask.

"I don't care to discuss—"

"I'm not asking as a friend. That delusion is gone now. Also, if you want to get fucked, just be discreet and don't get caught. I've decided against that. I will never—"

"Hold on!"

"No, fuck you. I will not ever let a man—or anyone else talk to me the way you just did. I have turned off any hope of being friends, or of making this...this situation, anything more than what it is. I have no desire to force," I pause, "anyone to like me."

My eyes are filling again; I feel the burn, the lump building in my throat, so I squash it.

"You said—"

"Well, I've said a lot of things. So have you. If you want, I can pretend to like you."

"Pretend?" he gasps.

"Don't look at me like that. Tell me, Sabato, does it make you feel better to make others feel worse?"

He scoffs. "I apologize for whatever I said that made you flip like a fucking switch."

"Unbelievable. We are, what? Three hours from pulling off this bogus wedding? And you pick this time to try to make me hate you? Well, good job, bud. No worry about feelings on my part. I keep forgetting that's not part of the deal. But I demand respect."

"Demand?" He laughs maliciously.

"Look at me and tell me you can't at least respect me for doing this for you, Sabato. If the answer is no, then I walk. I don't want your money, your ring, your car, or your stupid, perfect house. All I want is my future. Mine, alone. Pay my tuition for my courses, that's it. Courses, which I pray to God I am still enrolled in, after this, this... foray, whatever the hell it is and we are even. Be rude to me again and I walk. I didn't ask for this. You did."

He starts the car without saying a word and backs out of the parking space.

After about twenty minutes, he says. "I spent holidays and breaks at the housing units at my different schools."

"Since you were seven, you never went to Salvatore's homes?"

"Not once."

My heart burned.

"Briefly after high school. Two weeks, but he wasn't there. Now," he says, his voice tight. "Share, why are you going to law school?"

"I can do more good this way."

And it doesn't fucking hurt as much, I think to myself.

"More money," he says, without expression.

"No, I can *do more* to change things."

He doesn't ask for an explanation and I don't offer one. He has made it clear that he doesn't want to be friends and I have to try my best to try to stop wanting to save a man who doesn't want to be saved. No matter how much I want to. Pushing him didn't break him open, like I expected; it made his hardened exterior even stronger.

Last night was insane and perfect and for a few naive hours, I thought I had gotten through to him. Shown him what it's like to feel cared for. But no, I was sadly mistaken.

"So. You're a voyeur. Would you like to discuss that?"

I am ready to crawl under the seat at this point, but I decide to not let this intimidation tactic work on me.

"I've watched porn online." I shrug. "Always just streaming, casual. Never rented a movie, never that pay-per-click stuff. It was to settle my curiosity."

"Did you get yourself off?"

"No."

"Why not?"

"I told you, it was curiosity. My friends don't know. No one does."

"Are you ashamed?"

I shrug. "I suppose."

"Have you watched your previous partners fuck other women for pleasure, or just me?"

"Again, you were a curiosity. And no, I wouldn't enjoy that."

"Then why?"

"As I have told you before, I don't find many people who are able to hold my interest," I lie.

God I am such a liar. Even as I sit here talking to him, trying to be as cold as he is, I am lying to myself. The problem is, he's way better at it than me.

"Did it make you as hot as—"

"Sabato, please no more questions."

"Fine."

"Good."

We are more than halfway home, when he pulls off the highway. "I'm hungry."

I'm not, I want to say, but why bother? It's not like he'll listen. I wish I had something to distract me, but my phone is still in my car. Not that I could use it, even if I had it, but—hold up, he's been using a phone.

"Can I use your phone?" I ask, and he looks at me confused.

"For?"

"Never mind." I cross my arms and look away.

"Where would you like to eat?"

"I'm not hungry."

"You haven't eaten all day."

"I'm not, *hungry*." I enunciate hungry and his eyebrows shoot up.

"Fine."

He pulls into a parking lot and goes towards a drive thru.

He orders burgers, fries, some of those chicken nuggets and sodas. He orders a lot of them. When he pays, I catch the drive through attendant flirting with him and he smiles. I lean forward in my seat, so she can see me. I even hold up my ring finger. I am like a fucking child hidden in an adult body when it comes to him.

Even worse, Sabato snaps his head around and catches me doing it. I swear he smirks before he looks away. Like he's pleased with himself. Fucking head-trip.

He hands me a drink, which I choose to take, only because I am thirsty.

"We haven't eaten today Melyssa, eat, please."

"I don't feel well. I'm not hungry. I do have to use the bathroom, though. So if you don't mind pulling over up over here?"

"Will you be gone long?"

"Does it matter?"

"Will you start trouble with the girl?"

"Excuse me?"

"The girl who was working in there. You obviously had a problem with the way she and I interacted."

I roll my eyes. "That had nothing to do with you, Sabato."

"On the contrary, I think it had everything to do—"

He pulls over and I jump out, not letting him finish.

Girl code, that's the problem. Some bitches don't seem to care.

I walk into the restaurant to use the bathroom. When I come out, the fry chick is standing beside the car, talking to Sabato.

He is smiling and I am immediately pissed off.

Fuck him, fuck her and fuck this.

I walk up and tap her on the back she spins around, "You want him? He's yours, bitch. But do me a favor and make your little arrangements when I'm not around, you fucking low-rent skank."

"Fuck you bitch," she says, already reaching for her hoop earrings. "You wanna throw down?"

"Melyssa, that is enough!"

Sabato opens the door and gets out.

"I'm not afraid of either of you! Perfect fucking pair, if you ask me."

I jump into the driver's seat and lock the door. He tries to open it, then beats on the window when he can't.

I roll it down a little. "My fucking ride, pal. I'm driving. You can choose to ride bitch or stay here with McSleazy. Either way, I'm going home."

"Oh no you didn't," she sputters.

"Oh fucking yes I did, whore!"

Sabato is in the passenger seat slamming the door behind him, before I can think up worse names to call her.

"You are out of control!"

"Go fuck yourself." I don't even try to hide that I am furious. Why would I? He doesn't bother to.

I peel out, leaving McSlutbag in a cloud of dust.

"Don't you ever act like that again! I am humiliated! She was only being—"

"I'm out, I mean it." My hands are shaking angrily on the wheel. "You are cruel, heartless and downright mean."

The floodgates open and this time my tears turn to pure, unadulterated meanness. "I would *never* be friends with someone like you, let alone marry you. You are trash, Sabato, plain and simple. You can dress as nice as you want and drive the most expensive cars, but you clearly have no idea how to be a gentleman, or treat a woman. So," I pull over at the side of the road. "You can either behave like the criminal you are and kill me, or accept that I cannot help you."

His face is almost purple with rage. "Can't help me? Or won't?"

"Both!" I get out and he is around the vehicle before I can walk even five feet away.

"Get in the vehicle now." He sneers.

"No."

"You get in there or," His eyes are cold, his face dangerous. "So help me God, Melyssa. If you cross me now, I am going to make you sorry."

"I'm already fucking sorry! I thought you were messed up, but no more than the rest of us. I was wrong. You are cruel, mean, evil!" I am sobbing and spewing the most hateful things I can think of. "In a matter of days, you are making me question who I am. I don't even recognize myself. Back there, that white trash showdown? That wasn't me! I don't even like who I am now. And that's on you! So yes, I am going back on the deal. I want you to do whatever it is you need to do and then leave me alone, just leave me alone!"

"Get. In. The. Vehicle."

He grabs my arm and pushes me to the passenger side, opens the door and pushes me towards it. I give up and climb in with the attitude that I don't give a shit what happens.

For a long moment, there is silence. Then he walks around the car, gets in, takes his cell phone out and dials. "I need one more day," he snaps into the phone. "Yes, Valentina, just one."

"No he doesn't," I yell.

His jaw nearly hits the floor and he looks at me in a way he never has before, disgusted. I try to get out and he yanks me back, pulling me to him.

I'm so full of rage, but kind of impressed at the same time.

I yank my arm, but he only grips it harder.

"You sit, YOUR ASS STILL!"

Putting the car into drive, he peels out.

His chest rises and falls quickly, he's growling words, he's hitting the dash and I am crying into the oversized shirt that I am now hiding in.

The car is jerking around wildly and then suddenly he slams on the brakes. I feel his arm in front of me, stopping me from hitting the dash. Then he grabs my arms and forces me to turn towards him.

"LOOK AT ME!" he screams.

"No!"

He pulls the shirt away from my face and grabs my jaw, lifting it so I am looking at him. I snap my eyes shut.

"What the fuck do you want from me!?"

I don't answer, I can't answer.

"I trusted you!"

"And then you crushed me! Then you made me feel insignificant and, and used!"

"You're crazy!"

"Yeah, only took me twenty three years to become a sensible, responsible adult, but look how quickly it crumbles!" I poke him in the chest, "You should be proud of yourself, that's fast fucking work! Are you happy now? Are you happy?!"

"No! I'm not fucking happy! Of course I'm not fucking happy!"

He stares at me, breathing hard, as he realizes the truth of what he's saying. He's not happy. Maybe he never has been. Maybe he wouldn't recognize it, even if he felt it.

I grit my teeth and look away. *I will not feel sorry for him.* I will not do that to myself, not again.

"Fine." He lets go of my face and his voice sounds defeated. "Fine, I will take you home and I will do what I should have done to begin with."

"What's that?" I choke out.

"It's none of your concern, not anymore."

"That's not true! I am concerned. I don't want to be, but I am! You made this my concern, my problem! You," I sob again. "Oh, god! I don't just want to go home! I want to go back, *I want to go back*!"

Sore

"**B**ack where?!" I yell at her, trying to force her into making sense.

She makes about as much sense as all these feelings inside of me right now.

"To...before I met you, before I saw you. I was fine! I was fine and happy and I was going to be fine. I was going to be happy. I was getting there, I was—"

"You are making no sense right now, Melyssa!"

She is covering her face again. Good, at least I can't see her cry.

I'm starting to feel a little unhinged, too. "I hate this, the crying. I hate to make women unhappy. I like to make them come, not feel giddy and crazy and emotionally drained. I like to tie them up and fuck them. Then, I like to untie them and let them go. Not keep them, because obviously, that's what ruins them."

"What?" she squeaks out.

I have no idea what she is talking about, or what I am talking about, anymore.

"What do you mean, *what*?"

"You just said, 'I hate to make women unhappy.' Then you said a bunch of other things. Like how you like to tie them up and fu—"

"No, I didn't." I look away.

Did I say those things out loud? Fuck!

"Yes, you did. In plain English. But that's not the lifestyle you promised. That's not what bondage is."

"So, now you have become an expert!?"

"Based on my internet research...well, yeah. With you, I expected to be free from my shame, free from choices and free from trying to force feelings."

"I gave you pleasure and offered you a different kind of freedom."

"No, see, that's where you're wrong! You gave me *you!* You gave me a *lover*, someone to obsess over and think about and want, constantly. From day one, you pretended to care what I wanted. Listened, when I said stop. Then the past two days, you have pushed me away, yes, but at least you did it in a way that I still trusted you! You promised me monogamy and I believed I would be safe and have a friend, at least until you were done with me, when this was over. You trusted me with your pain and then you just...you took it all back! You stole it all back and made me feel like an idiot for thinking I ever had it. But I am *not crazy!* I had it, I felt it, I know I did."

"I never gave you a lover, Melyssa. I was never gentle. I never used words of love to get you under me. Think about the biggest difference between me and all those other men. They offered love, I offered only release."

"You," she whimpers, and her lip quivers, "You are lying to yourself. You care about me, I know you do."

"No," I shake my head. "That's not what I offered. I said I would care for you—financially, and physically—I never said I would care about you. Not like that."

She laughs, hysterically. "So, I'm not just crazy, I'm stupid! And you aren't cruel, you're just...it's just a language barrier problem, is that it? You hurt me, and it's my fault for misunderstanding. ...No, I take it back, you're still cruel."

"How am I cruel?!"

"Because it's not just what you say. That girl back there, you were flirting with her. Why would you do that—act that way in front of me? Because burger girl was just too hard to resist? No fucking way! You did it because of me! To hurt me!"

"You went to the bathroom. I didn't invite her over. You then instigated that...ridiculousness. Then you acted like a wild animal and not just then, either. You screamed when I was on the phone to Valentina—"

"Well....That was just poor timing on *your* end. Can't blame me for that one bit, you loved seeing me jealous! Just as much as you love the idea that I am a sobbing mess right now."

"No," I say, dryly. "I would prefer this not to happen."

Melyssa looks away. She breathes deeply, trying to stop herself from crying. Her body shakes with each intake of breath and her lips purse as she lets each one out slowly. She lifts her shirt, wipes her eyes and sits back.

"Take me home now, please."

"No." It comes out before I can even think about what I am saying.

"Then shoot me. I'm not a game to be played, over and over, until you beat your high score. You've cracked me, you've won. Now leave me alone and maybe someday I can relocate my dignity, my sanity and my," she pauses, "nope, that one's gone forever. Just take me home."

"I'm sorry."

"I'm sure," she laughs bitterly, wiping away more tears. I reach over and help her. "I'm sorry I hurt you."

She shrugs. "It was bound to happen."

"Right."

My thumb catches the next tear on her lips and slides across. Tears have always bothered me, but not these. They're soft, they're hot, they're...hers.

"Please, don't." More tears fall and I am engrossed in them. The way they keep coming, the heat of them, the clarity. They are emotions. Each one causes me to soften.

"I'm sorry I hurt you," I repeat. "I don't want to take you home."

"Jesus! Tell me what you want from me, Sabato? I'm so tired of letting you confuse me."

"I don't want that, either. I don't know what I want. But I know what I don't want."

"Then tell me."

"I don't want to make you feel used, but I realize now that's what I am doing. I don't want you to feel like I was trying to make you jealous, but maybe...I probably was. I don't want to find someone else to be my wife, because honestly I don't want a wife. But if I had to be stuck with one, you're a good choice. The best choice. I don't want to wake up in the morning next to anyone, but if I have to, I would rather it be you. I don't want to share my feelings, but when you share yours...I like that. I don't want you to have feelings for me. I don't want to have feelings for you. I don't want make you cry. And I really, really don't want to trust you, but...somehow, I fucking do."

She covers her face with her hands.

"I don't want you to feel ashamed, because you have nothing to be ashamed of. And I don't regret that I was the first man to tie you up and make you come. ...And I know as soon as you open up those green eyes, I am going to regret that I didn't just let you go, but because I am incredibly selfish, I don't want to believe that this was all a mistake."

Her tears are rolling down her face now and I want to taste them.

I have always been a marked man. Marked by sadness and misery. Everyone I touch is destroyed in front of me, and as much as I want to give her what she asks for, I can't give her that burden. Because, in the end, she will realize that's all I am: a damned, cursed burden.

I lean in and kiss her tears, expecting her to pull away from me, even wanting her to, for her own good.

"Call her back," she whispers against my face.

"We can wait," I say, between kissing her tears.

"No, tomorrow you may piss me off again and that will be like the third strike."

I can't help but chuckle, relieved and full of regret. "It's bound to happen."

"Just call your girlfriend."

"Don't do that. She's not anything."

"At the very least, she's your friend."

"No...."

"Sabato," she pushes her forehead against mine, nudging me away. "Don't pretend no one cares about you. And don't pretend you don't care, because you care harder than anyone I've ever met."

"Oh?" The way she says it, I feel as if she's about to taunt me. I start to pull away and she grabs my face between her hands, stopping me.

"If you didn't care, you wouldn't try so hard to be a gigantic douche bag, just to push people away. For whatever reason, you think you deserve to be alone, that it's safer that way. But you don't and it's not."

I frown, but she's not entirely wrong.

Her thumb drags across my lip. "Don't push me in a corner and disregard how brilliant I really am. When I am not playing an infatuated teenager, I am really pretty damn smart."

"Infatuated?"

She nods. "Just watch. I'm gonna prove to you I'm right."

"About?"

"You."

She presses her lips against mine and I feel warm and lit up inside.

"Do you want to feel something profound?" I ask. As she kisses me, I pull her hand to my erection.

She laughs against my mouth. "Okay, I like you again, for now. But I have places to be. You need to make a phone call, before I change my mouth."

I raise an eyebrow. "Mind?"

"Mmmkay."

Then her hands are unleashing me from my pants and I am scrambling for the phone. I send a text to Valentina, but I don't call her. I've learned my lesson.

"Drive." Melyssa leans over and kisses my neck and slowly makes her way down. And down.

"Damn," I hiss, as she sucks on my tip. "I think making you angry might have turned out to be a good id—" She bites down, not very gently. "Fuck, okay, bad fucking idea!"

..*

I have the stamina of twenty men.

I smile, knowing that her smart mouth will be so sore after this, the only thing she'll be able to say for the rest of the day, is 'I do.'

After almost twenty minutes has gone by, Melyssa looks up at me in frustration. "Am I doing this wrong?"

I smile wider and shake my head, no. She looks insecure, which is a turn on, but I've done enough damage.

"No, *bella*, it feels so good I don't want it to stop." She looks pleased and I push her head down. "*Dammi di più.*"

After another minute, I set the car on cruise control, steer with my knee, grab the base of my cock in one hand and the back of her head with the other and finally take my pleasure.

She sits up when I let go of her head and immediately grabs her drink from the cup holder. She sucks that straw just as furiously as she did my cock. There is perspiration on her forehead and a sweet little smile on her lips.

"That was very good," I praise her. "I want it again, in an hour."

"Really?" she gasps.

"Really."

I don't tell her why and I am not so much of a 'douche bag' that I really want her mouth so sore she can't talk. It's because of the dress hanging in the back.

I reach over after she has settled in her seat and take her hand. "I want to be your friend."

She laughs and it's contagious.

"It's because of the blow job, isn't it?"

I kiss her hand. "No. Well...maybe."

She is quiet for a minute, then, "Sabato?"

"Yes?"

"I'm sorry I was, well crazy. That's not me."

"It's understandable."

"No, I am usually way cooler than that."

"Okay."

"If I hurt your feelings, with some of the things I said...I'm sorry."

I nod, once. "If I had feelings, I would accept your apology."

"Sabato, don't joke. We need to—"

"Melyssa, I pushed you. I know that. I am man enough to accept my responsibility in what happened, but not so much that I can promise not to push you in the future. I do, however, promise that I won't try to make you jealous or hurt you emotionally."

I think about what I have just said, knowing it's too late to take it back. I wonder if I can give her that. I wonder, because I have never tried before. I kept my promise to Luciana for a very short time, only a few weeks. God must have known I couldn't keep a promise for much longer.

She sits up and looks over at me, then looks down. I point to the clock. I didn't even bother to put my cock back in my shorts. Why bother? She leans over, seeking a kiss. I give her one, then another.

"Tic toc," I say and point down.

"I hope you know that was the first time I have ever, you know...in a car."

"Given head?" I am shocked.

"Well, I mean at the club sort of, and last night, but I've never...."

"Swallowed?"

"You're clean, right?"

"Yes Melyssa," I answer with certainty, because I am certain. "I am."

When she bends over the console and takes me in her hand, I am sure this time won't take as long. There is something sexy as hell about being a woman's first. Maybe I wasn't cursed as much as I thought. Luciana was a virgin and Melyssa's mouth was unclaimed, before me.

When she finishes this time, it's all on her own.

After she takes a drink, she sits back again and this time I seek her hand and pull her toward me. "Rest."

She nods, already closing her eyes. "No Melyssa here."

She leans against my shoulder and I like this.

As I drive, I think of Luciana. I also think of my mother and for the first time in my life, I pray that my selfishness doesn't get taken out on her. But as she pointed out, the Devil himself is dead. I have proof of his death and I have taken measures to prove that it was self-defense on my part, so he cannot drag me to hell with him.

"Melyssa?"

"Yes?"

"What do your friends call you?"

"Mel," she answers, with a little smile in her voice.

"Okay."

A New Day

I wake to him turning off the car. I don't want to open my eyes, because I worry that Sabato will be in a mood again.

I know I should expect it by now, instead of constantly being surprised by it. Sabato spent his life alone. Everyone he cared for died and he recently found out his father killed his mother. Almost killed him in the process. A fact I can't even begin to process, let alone understand.

My heart breaks for him. But it also breaks for me. I am a sad excuse for a feminist. A sorry reflection of who I once was—who I want to be again, someday. He was my first and I have fallen for him. Only he doesn't know he's my first.

Aside from the blow job part.

Other than the fact that I've fallen for him, I only know one thing for sure: Sabato will ruin me. Actually, two things: I will go, like a willing lamb, to his slaughter.

But even though I believe this, with every part of me, deep down there is still hope. Hope that whatever love I can show him will help him grow. Hope that he can somehow see himself as the good man I know he can someday be. Hope that he might break the cycle of hate and abuse he has suffered his whole life. Above all, hope that maybe, just maybe he might love me. Someday.

The song Believe by Mumford and Sons is playing. I decide it's ours.

"*Dea*," I hear him whisper. "We have to change fast. They are all waiting."

My eyes fly open. "What? Who?" I look around wildly. "Where?"

He grabs my hand, "*Where is the ring??*"

"What? Oh. ...*Oh!*" I push my hand into my pocket and pull it out. "I was pissed at you."

"I know." Sabato takes the ring from me and shoves it roughly on my finger. "It doesn't come off again."

I nod. "Who's waiting?"

"The witnesses. *Andiamo, andiamo!*" he says as he gets out.

We are in front of the Ritz Carlton and a valet takes the keys from Sabato as he grabs a bag and a garment bag from the back of the car. "*Dea, andiamo.*"

He holds his hand out to me.

"Okay, I understand nothing you are saying to me and I just woke up and you expect me to—" I stop when he takes my hand, pulls me flush to his body and kisses me. "Wow, it's show time, huh?"

"*Dea*, goddess," he explains with a smile, "*Andiamo* is kind of like hurry up."

He half laughs as he pulls me behind him.

Before I know it, we are at the desk and the he is talking to the pretty concierge. I am very aware she is smitten with him and I am equally aware that it is pissing me off. Sabato looks at me and shakes his head. "My wife gets jealous, but she has no reason."

Holy shit! I feel myself panicking, now that I'm awake enough to realize what's happening. Holy shit, he is fucking crazy. Holy shit, *I am crazy*. And super excited. I feel him tug my arm then and I follow him. I practically run to keep up. We are in the elevator and he looks at me, "You are never at a loss for words. Is your mouth sore?"

"My head is spinning, I feel like I just went through relationship boot camp in the span of two days and I am scared—really, really scared, that you are going to start getting pissy within the next—I don't know, any second, and that I am going to follow suit and act like an insane person. And I am not insane. I really am not, except for when it comes to you," I take a quick breath, before continuing, "and I don't even know where to begin with that, and—"

The door opens and I stop talking. The concierge is still with us. I am babbling like a crazy person. I might actually be a crazy person.

"Mr. Efisto, Mrs. Efisto, this way." We follow the concierge to our suite and I nearly die when the door opens. "Your guests are in the bar waiting. As soon as you're ready, we will call them up and dinner will be served here."

"*Grazie*, ten minutes and we will be ready." As soon as she leaves, Sabato looks at me with an intensity that makes me remember the first time I saw him. And yes, the effect is still insane. "*Voglio baciarti. Ma poi ho intenzione di scoparti. Non c'è tempo. Ma io farò si rilascia dopo.*"

Whatever he said speaks to Elsa in the recently redecorated Arendelle. I just nod.

"We have to change now. Come."

Oh I wish, I think to myself.

The dress is white and silk. It's not the typical wedding dress—of course it's not, it's not a typical wedding, after all. Strapless and form-fitting, its skirt hits the knees and is a little poufy. It's simple and beautiful. Sabato pulls out a baggie from inside the garment bag and hands it to me.

"Hold this." As soon as I take it, he starts pulling my shorts down and my panties.

"There isn't time," I whimper.

He seems to take this as a challenge. He grabs the bag he just gave me and throws it on the ground. Then he lifts me up.

"Legs."

I wrap them around him, without questioning. I hear the rip of a packet, he rolls the condom on. Within seconds, my back hits the wall and he is slamming into me. His finger rubs my clit as he thrusts in and out of me.

"Oh, God," I moan.

"*Shhh*, our guests will be here soon." He pinches my clit and I cry out again. "What will they think if they hear you calling for God, Dea, hmm?"

"That I'm a lucky," he slams into me, "yet bruised, girl."

"Should I be gentler?" He thrusts hard again.

"No!"

"Good, hang on."

As soon as I come he does too, then he pulls out of me quickly.

"The baggy has your underclothes. I would have dressed you, however...."

"You need to change, too."

"How about you use the bathroom? I hear our guests. I can change fast. Go *Dea*, hurry." He gives me the intense stare again, when I don't move right away. "Melyssa?"

"What if I need help zipping?" I have no idea why I said that, but I did.

"You want me to wait?" He looks at me curiously.

"No. I'll be fine." I make my way to the bathroom, dress and baggy in hand. It's huge, the bathroom is huge. It's the size of the cabin, maybe bigger. I look at the shower, then throw my clothes the rest of the way off and quickly jump in. I can take two minutes to shower, I decide. It is my wedding day, after all.

The water is hot and the soaps—all three kinds—smell like heaven. I pick the one that smells like vanilla and scrub my body. The important parts get extra attention. I find a razor and decide to rid myself of the 'landing strip.' A few quick swipes of the blade and it's gone. I am bare, just like he said he wanted. I don't have time to wash my hair, so I don't.

Next, I dry off and grab the baggy. White lacey boy shorts and a matching bustier fall out. I fasten the bustier around me, then spin it front-ways. This is when I notice that there are no cups. I feel ridiculous, but when I look in the mirror, I don't feel ridiculous anymore—I feel sexy. I notice then that the counter has been lined with cosmetics and hair products. Everything is perfect.

This is the most beautifully messed up fairytale, and I am living it.

Quickly, I let my hair out of the clip and blow-dry my hair. I roll the back into something like a French twist and fasten it with bobby pins from the counter. I tease the top and smooth it. Somehow it looks elegant, despite the rush job.

I take some mascara and swipe my lashes three times, then use the liner to line just the top lid. I apply just a touch of lip-gloss and powder my nose. I look at the dress and shake my head. It's stunning and I will be wearing it. I grab the deodorant off the counter and apply it, then turn back to the dress.

Once dressed, I walk out of the bedroom and find a pair of shoes. I don't have to look at the label to know they are expensive. That's it, I officially feel like Cinderella. Although I know this wedding is just for show, I am going to enjoy it and allow myself to believe it's real.

I look up and walk to the mirror, turning slowly checking myself out. I hope Sabato thinks I'm beautiful. I hope he wants to cut the night short, because he is so hard he can't wait to be inside me. That's almost as good as love, I suppose.

I look up as the door opens and it's Valentina slipping in.

"Wow, you look amazing," she says with a smile as she comes towards me. "I brought a bag full of things, in case Sabato forgot something. But...looks like he remembered everything, except a necklace and earrings. I also have this." She shakes my bottle of medication. "And this." She holds up birth control pills and smiles.

"I don't know what to say to you," I say, honestly.

"You're doing a good thing." She smiles. It irritates me.

"I'm doing it because it's what he wants."

"And needs." She counters.

"Tell me Valentina, why are *you* doing this for him?"

She looks shocked.

"Probably for the same reason you are." There is a bit of a bite to her delivery.

"Just so you know, he won't be banging you in the bathroom again. While he and I are married, I'll be the only one bent over the counter."

"Is that so?" She half laughs, half looks at me as if she feels sorry for me, like I'm slow or stupid.

"Yes, it is." I nod. "Thanks for everything, but I assure you, I have it from here."

"Melyssa, I am not your enemy." She shakes her head. "On the contrary, I may be the only one in you and Sabato's corner, when all is said and done tonight."

"He's the only person I need in my corner," I say, with wavering conviction at best.

"I don't want him. He's a great fuck." Her words slap me in the face and I close my eyes. "But he is not my end-all-be-all Mel and he's not yours."

The door opens and Sabato comes in. "Are you ready?" I nod, without looking into his eyes.

"*Che diavolo gli hai detto?*" He speaks to Valentina. I don't know what he is saying, but he seems angry.

"*Solo la verita,*" she says back, obviously in Italian.

"*La verità di chi Valentina? Tu non sai la mia verità!*"

He walks up to me and I see her look at him, then at me and back and forth again. She laughs. "*Sei innamorato.*"

"Valentina," he snaps.

She grabs my face and smiles. "*Non so come hai fatto.*"

"*Fuori di qui, ora!*" he snaps at her.

She smiles at me again, kisses my cheeks, and whispers in my ear, "Enjoy that counter. You look beautiful."

As soon as she leaves, Sabato and I look at each other.

"What did she say?" comes out of both of us, at the same time.

"Okay, I feel like I'm in the 'Twilight Zone' here. Speak English, please."

"Let's go. Our guests are waiting."

We walk out hand in hand and Nikki and Paige are there. They both look to be in total shock and I am in shock because a: I didn't expect this b: I definitely didn't expect this! If anyone could see through me, it was them.

My stomach skips, as I realize this is going to be a mistake.

I feel Sabato's hand squeeze mine and then he casually walks us up to a man I don't recognize.

The man immediately starts talking and of course I have no clue what he is saying. But I am standing in front of him, face to face with Sabato and he is holding my hands.

Behind us, I hear Paige whisper, "What the hell is going on? Is Mel gonna be part of the entertainment?"

Oh, of course they don't know why they're here. I can't help but laugh. I look at her and wink.

"Holy shit," she whispers, much too loudly. "I know that look, you gave it up!"

My jaw drops and I feel my face turn a million different shades of pink.

Sabato's grip on my hands tightens, but I refuse to look up from the floor.

"*Grazie per Essere Venuti a sostenere l'Unione di Sabato e Melyssa.*" The man in front of us is talking to everyone now and I giggle inside and look up, just a peek. His face is stone, so clearly he must not speak English.

"*Sono incaricato dallo sposo per mantenerlo breve e semplice, proprio come il loro corteggiamento,*" he continues.

I hear a man's booming laugh from near the doorway. He's attractive, tall dark and handsome—just like the rest of the men in the room. He has a blonde girl snuggled up against him and he is whispering in her ear as she giggles.

"Zandor Steel," Sabato whispers to me, "A friend."

"What the hell is going on here, Sabato?" Now it's Abe's voice interrupting the poor, serious Italian guy.

The officiant interrupts, "Sabato vuoi accogliere Melyssa come tua sposa nel Signore*?*"

"*E 'il mio onore e apparentemente mio privilegio,*" Sabato says, looking at me sternly. "I do."

'I do.' I can't help but smile at the words. I hear all sorts of gasps and then Nikki and Paige's voices arguing quietly. But I pay no attention to what they say. 'I do' is all I can hear, or think, or feel. He does.

"Melyssa vuoi accogliere Sabato come tuo sposo nel Signore?"

Sabato squeezes my hands when I don't reply, then he nods toward the man I now recognize as some kind of officiant. "English for her, please."

"Do you take this man to be your husband, to honor, respect and love?"

Sabato's jaw tightens and twitches at the 'L' word and my stomach squeezes.

Suddenly, the whispers are all I can hear. The room seems cavernous and stifling at the same time. I feel like I'm on display, naked and cold. My throat instantly turns as dry as the Sahara.

"I do." Somehow, I squeeze out the words. When I do, a warm feeling of relief rushes through me—or maybe it's something else, stronger than relief.

Sabato pulls two wedding bands from his suit pocket and pushes one on my finger. He hands me his and I do the same.

"*Puoi baciare la sposa.* Kiss her!" Finally, the officiant's solemn face breaks and he laughs.

The room is half laughs, half roars. I am all smiles as Sabato's arms surround me and he lifts me. We are eye to eye when he whispers, "Thank you," so that only I can hear. Then he kisses me, as if I am the only other one in the room.

When I am dizzy and Elsa is cranking up the AC in Arendelle, he sets me on my feet.

"You prepared for the inquisition?"

"Bring it on."

"*Signore e signori, il signor e la signora Sabato Efisto.*"

SABATO
Uncharted Territory

I release one of her hands and look at the waiter. "Serve dinner now, please."

The officiate walks over and sets the papers on a table. "Who is signing as a witness?"

"Zandor, will you do me the honor?"

"Hell yes I will," he says. He comes up and pats me on the back, very hard. "You didn't just drink the water, man, you fell into it. When you come up for a breath, the four of us need to do some traveling."

I smile to be polite, but I'm pretty sure Melyssa and I won't be traveling anywhere for a while yet.

I look at Melyssa, who is gesturing excitedly to her friends. Abe's girl seems angry, but the other girl—Paige—only seems to be wildly amused.

"Pick one of them to sign, as a witness."

"What?" Melyssa gasps.

"One of your friends needs to sign," I say again, as I watch them both approach.

"Oh boy," she mumbles.

"Pick Paige," I whisper in her ear. "She seems less angry."

This makes her laugh. It also makes her look at my lips. For the sake of the show, I kiss her. For the sake of how good her lips taste, I do it again.

"Get a room," Zandor chuckles.

"You're in my room, Steel." I attempt to joke back.

"Which one of you wants to be my witness?" Melyssa asks in a sweet little voice.

"Witness to what exactly, Mel? Do you care to explain how two of your best friends since childhood had no idea you were dating anyone? And now we just witnessed you marry into the fucking mob?" Nikki snaps at her.

"I'm not in the mob," I snarl back.

"Easy Sabato," Abe warns. "You don't want to talk to her like that. Trust me."

I laugh, because it's funny shit, but Melyssa gives me a pleading look.

"Noted, O'Donnell," I look at Nikki. "But how about you also keep that same respect in mind, when you speak to my wife."

"A minute, Melyssa?" Nikki points over her shoulder.

I look at Paige and then the paper. She brushes past me and whispers, "You hurt her and a dead horse in a bed will seem like nothing compared to what I do to your dick."

Then she grabs the pen and signs.

Nikki turns on her immediately. "Are you fucking stupid, Paige?"

"Hold on there, chick," she laughs.

"No you hold on, *Chick*," Nikki snarls at her.

"*Chick* says butt out. She's an adult, sober, seems pretty damn in love.... I mean, think about her dating past. Can you say *train wreck*?"

"Okay, both of you!" Melyssa takes the pen and signs the paper, then hands it over her shoulder to me. "I'm married. Look, nothing anyone can do to take that away now, so—"

"He's wanted for questioning for his father's murder," Nikki points out.

"Well, good fucking riddance to the asshole," Melyssa snaps back.

"Okay ladies," Zandor steps in then. "And Abe—"

"Fuck you, Steel." Abe rounds on him and I try to hide my amusement.

"Am I late?" I look behind me to see Signora Josephina Steel barge into the room.

"No Momma Joe, just in time." Zandor goes over and gives her a kiss on each cheek.

She laughs. "So what problem can I help solve?"

"Just in time," Valentina greets her with a kiss.

"Zandor causing problems?" Joe asks.

"No Sabato and Melyssa are married. Abe and the girls think it's a hoax.*"*

"*Is that so?*" Josephina laughs and walks over to me. "*Complimenti. Trattare il suo bene e noi non saremo in grado di dire che l'avevo detto.*"

"*Of course.*"

"I really need to learn Italian," Melyssa grumbles.

"I prefer if you don't."

Signora Steel laughs, then she gives Melyssa a hug. "Congratulations."

"Thank you."

"Mel, now!" Nikki is still waiting.

"Can we wait for another day, ladies? This is her wedding day," Signora Steel says, as she sits down at the table. "*Mangiamo*, let's eat."

Zandor sits next to her and I see her show him something on her phone. "This can't be put off much longer. D'Angelo wants to speak to him."

I sign the paperwork and hand it back to the officiant. "See that this gets filed immediately."

We all sit at the table. Melyssa, myself, and our six guests settle in to pretend we're happily celebrating together. *Cozze grattugiate* is served, along with Champagne.

Melyssa looks at it, but doesn't touch it.

"Is everything all right?"

"She's allergic to shellfish," Nikki tells me, in a condescending tone.

"Something we haven't discussed. I apologize," I say, looking at Melyssa, not Nikki.

"She gets sick every spring with allergies and ends up with bronchitis. You'd never know she is even sick, because she doesn't want to bother anyone. She doesn't like peas and she doesn't know why. She loves music and dancing, but—"

"It isn't a big deal, Nikki," Melyssa interrupts.

"It *is* a big deal." I tell her. *Not a big deal?* It could have killed her.

"I wouldn't have eaten it." She pushes back from the table. "Nikki, Paige, let's go."

"Melyssa," I stand to follow, but she shakes her head, no. "One moment, please."

I take her hand and pull her behind me.

"I'm here," I whisper. "I'm the one in your corner. Or, on your *counter*. You don't have to—"

She covers her face. "Dear God, what else did you hear?"

"Bent over the bathroom counter and I plan to—"

She laughs and pushes me. "It's a really nice counter."

"Better than the cabin?" I ask.

"I think...maybe."

"Did you think the toilet was clean enough?" I push her hair away from her face.

"Pretty sure," she says, as her body arches towards me.

"Is there something of importance you failed to tell me?" I throw the question in, hoping she'll confirm what I should have already suspected.

"I'm allergic to shellfish. I don't eat fish at all, actually."

"Anything else?"

"Nope."

"Hmm."

"Leave it alone," she says and begins walking away.

I grab her arm and pull her back. "Don't you think you should kiss me? You know, for show."

"Mmmkay."

I watch her walk towards the master bedroom and feel like I am sending her off to the slaughter.

After everyone is finished with the first course, I have the wait staff clear the table and tell them to hold off on the seafood feast.

"Chicken and beef please, whatever is quickest."

I sit back down at the table and look over at Abe, who is clearly pissed and then Zandor who is amused and lastly at Valentina and Signora Steel, who both look at me in a softer way than they ever have before.

"Detective D'Angelo has been looking for you for almost a week." Abe crosses his arms.

"Huh, if you hear from him, let him know I am going to be busy with my wife for a while. Honeymoon, you know."

"Will you be taking her back to Italy?" His tone pisses me off.

"No, I think we will be sticking around here."

"Because you'll be in some trouble if—"

"Abe, he fucking helped us out." Zandor tries to placate him.

"And he's using one of Nikkolette's best friends."

"Is that so? What exactly am I using Melyssa for? I need no money and there is no lack of ass to be had—"

"Bro, my Mom." Zandor says, trying to hold a serious tone and failing.

"Abraham, how long did you know Nikkolette before you knew she was the one for you?" Signora Steel asks.

"With all due respect Momma Joe, Nikkolette and I are engaged and taking our time."

"To each their own." She smiles, raises her glass and turns to me. "Now, what will you do with that *club*?"

"I haven't thought about it yet."

"And Melyssa, what do you think she'll want you to do with it?"

"I'm sure she'll be fine with whatever I decide." Zandor laughs and I look at him. "What?"

"Nothing, man." He holds up his hands and when I look around the table, everyone seems to be amused. It annoys me.

I stand up again. "Please excuse me."

I go to the room, where Melyssa and her friends have been hiding. I don't like that she has disappeared. I open the door and walk in, without knocking. They aren't in there. I look toward the bathroom next and the door is cracked open.

I can hear talking. I can also hear crying. I don't want anyone to make her cry.

"You're sure?" It's her friend, Nikki, who asks.

"What choice do I have?" Melyssa's tone frightens me.

"You have plenty of choices," Nikki says.

"No, I don't," Melyssa grumbles.

"What happened with Ryan's family isn't your fault," Paige says.

"I know that. This isn't the same thing."

"He needs you. You feel obligated," Nikki interjects.

"No, I don't feel obligated. I just...feel. I don't know how to explain it. I won't even try to explain it to you, but I know that I want. I want him."

"And what if this is just a convenience for him?" Nikki again.

"It's not."

"How do you know?" Nikki is pushing her. I don't like her. At least her friend Paige had the common decency to tell me to my face how she felt.

"That's between him and me, Nikki. I won't betray him."

"How would it be betraying him? Come on Mel, give me something."

"Fine, he doesn't want to hurt me. He doesn't want me to cry, he doesn't want me to wear cheap panties or get STD's."

Her friend Paige starts laughing and then so does Mel. "And he has mad skills."

I have to bite my tongue, because she is amusing.

"Like the stage thing?" Paige asks.

"Paige, really?" Nikki scoffs.

"That was nothing." Mel giggles.

"You were a virgin, for fuck's sake," Nikki says.

"Was," Mel says. "I am sooo not a virgin anymore."

The three of them laugh. Mel laughs the hardest, "Even my mouth is not a virgin."

They laugh more loudly.

"And I'm pretty sure that later, I'm gonna get a little ana—"

"Enough!" Wow, that was Paige. "Don't even."

"I haven't but," Mel and Nikki laugh. "Pun intended."

"You two bitches are sick."

"Are not," Melyssa laughs.

"Is that what got you the proposal? Did you say, 'Oh, hot, Italian, scary mafia dude, I am a sexy little virgin and I want to know how—"

"He doesn't know. And for the last time, he is not involved in his father's business."

"How does he not know you're a virgin? And how do you know he's not, Mel? Come on!"

"Cause I'm pretty sure my cherry got popped by a crop."

They all start laughing again.

"True story, though. Don't go looking for action if you can't handle the—"

I knock on the door then, having heard enough. I really need to have a conversation with my wife. I don't wait for permission before going into the bathroom.

They are sitting on the counter and they all jump up when they see me.

"Shellfish-free dinner is being served."

They scamper to the door.

"You," I grab Mel. "Need to give me just a moment."

"I saw dental floss on the counter," Paige laughs. "Don't tie it too tight."

"Go away!" Melyssa laughs.

When they are gone, she is looking down.

"Look at me."

"Nope." She shakes her head.

"That other thing that you needed to tell me?"

"Nope."

"This is a topic that needs to be discussed."

"Yet, can never be revisited," she shakes her head. "Let's just skip over that, shall we?"

SKIPPING THE GOOD PARTS

"I wish you had told me." Sabato is growling, practically roaring at me.

"Why? Would you have been gentler?"

"No," he answers, and I look up, surprised. "What? That's not what you wanted."

"So, you would have just rammed it in there?" I almost laugh.

"Yes. Only I wouldn't have stopped when you freaked out. I would have kept going and you would have liked it. Let us assume that your first time...that it counted...with the crop."

"Let's not assume, let's just go with it," I yawn.

His face is hard now. "Am I boring you?"

"No, I'm just tired. I've been feeling pretty crappy these past few days. But the good news is, Valentina brought my medicine."

"Have you taken it?"

"Well, no. I've been a little busy." I look down at my ring.

"Really?"

"Did you pick these out?"

"Of course I picked them out. Who else could possibly—?" he stops, gets it, and then takes a deep breath. "I picked them out. No one else."

I smile, because I like that answer. He leans forward, corralling me against the counter's edge.

"I still want to fuck you, sick or otherwise. You smell delicious, look stunning and—"

"We have guests," I grab hold of his lapel and pull him forward. "But after they leave, you can fuck me."

"Mmmkay," he winks.

He grabs the bag of medicine off the bed as we pass—including the birth control. "You'll take these before you eat."

"You will, too."

"You are extra sassy tonight." He pulls me toward him.

"You can blame it on the girls. They bring it out in me."

"Actually, *you* should thank them. That may win you some extra spanks to that ass of yours."

I smile a big cheesy smile and he rolls his eyes. "*Sei impossibile.*"

"Me?" I ask. "You just told me I was impossible right?"

He nods. "I did."

"You'd better watch it bud, I am catching on."

After we sit at the table, Sabato opens the bag and pulls out the pills. I scrunch my eyes shut when I see him looking at the oral contraceptive packet.

"No kids in the near future, huh?" Zandor jokes and everyone laughs.

After he hands me the antibiotic, Sabato starts to close the bottle, "You too."

He shakes his head.

"I'm serious, if that thing gets infected, you'll be the one hurting...boy."

"Boy?" His head tilts to the side.

"Okay, man."

"Much better." He squeezes my knee under the table and pulls it towards him, spreading me.

As the plates are being set in front of us, his hand travels up my thigh slowly, inch by inch. I attempt to close my legs and he makes a very quiet tsk-ing sound.

His fingers stroke the skin of my inner thigh, slowly driving me crazy. Up and down, up and down. I take his hand to stop him. He pulls our hands up, kisses mine, then hooks his foot around my ankle and pulls my leg apart. He sets my hand on the table and then his hand is quickly between my legs again, but higher up this time. He is barely touching me, but when he applies pressure, he does it exactly in the right spot.

I am writhing under Sabato's touch and he is acting like nothing at all is going on. He knows exactly what he is doing, what I can handle, and how much I can take.

Concurrent with the assault to my lacy shorts, conversation is flowing. Nikki and Paige are no longer giving Sabato snarky looks and I am happy they aren't.

Whenever the conversation shifts from me, he starts again.

After a few minutes, he leans over and whispers, "Are you still tired?"

I shake my head, no, as he begins rubbing me again.

When the plates are being cleared and I am ready to just give up and ride his finger, Zandor gets a call. He excuses himself and when he returns, he looks at his mother and then Sabato.

"Please excuse me for a minute." Sabato stands, pats my shoulder and walks away, leaving me sitting in a pool of my own dirty desire.

"We need to do a toast," Paige says. She reaches out her hand, pulls me up and grabs a bottle of ridiculously expensive champagne.

Nikki and Valentina join us and we all sit together on the couch.

"Where did Abe go?" I ask Nikki.

"Apparently there is an all-male conspiracy."

"All male and Aunt Joe," Valentina giggles, as she hands us all glasses and fills them up. I look at her warily as I take the glass.

"Mel, we bury this. I like you."

"Bury what?" Paige asks, as she takes a drink.

Oh great, I think. Paige doesn't let anything go.

"I've *been with* Sabato." Valentina says it like it's no big deal, but both Nikki and Paige's heads whip around to look at me.

"It's in the past. I'm sure she doesn't want her brother to know." I shrug. *Ooooo, good one, me!* I silently pat myself on the back. "So let's let sleeping dogs lie, shall we? Plus, Laney would probably be upset thinking I'm upset and well, Laney doesn't need to be upset." I drink the glass up and then hold it out to Valentina, "More please."

She smiles and fills it up. "Of course."

"So Nikki, when will you and Abe get married?"

"When we have time. We are both on the go nonstop and when we do have downtime, well, we like to spend it together."

"You should just do it, like Sabato and Mel," Paige says and takes another drink, "This stuff is good."

"Be careful, you'll get a headache," Valentina says.

"Listen *Chick*," Paige jokes. "Fill this bitch up and keep it coming. We are celebrating."

"All right then, *Chick*," Valentina laughs, "How about you, Mel?"

"Please."

By the time the men and Momma Joe come back, we have drunk an entire bottle and almost finished a second. I am tipsy and will not look into the eyes of my husband.

I giggle out loud, thinking: *husband*. I'm married, and my parents are gonna be pissed. I tip my glass to finish it off and it gets snatched from my hand.

"How much have you had to drink?"

"Well, less than I intended now that—"

"How much has she had to drink?" He snaps, and Nikki and Paige laugh.

"Nikkolette?" Abe's voice mimics Sabato's level of annoyed, which is just enough to make the girls and me giggle like school children.

"You two are in so much trouble," Paige laughs. "Spankings all around and grounded, you're both—"

"Okay, let's get you two out of here," Abe says, as he takes Nikki's hand and gives it a sharp tug up.

Her eyes meet mine and we both have the same look. Yep, no doubt about it. We are both getting spanked.

"I hope you know what you've signed up for," she says, as she bends down and kisses my cheek. Then she whispers, "I want to compare notes."

"Nikkolette," Abe growls.

"Abraham O'Donnell," she growls back, then laughs. She bends again and gives me another sloppy kiss on the cheek. "Congratulations. I love you girl. Call me when you're not too...tied up."

"Miss Bassett."

She looks up at him and smiles. "Mr. O'Donnell, you may want to start working out a time to change that last name."

"Oh?" He seems mildly amused.

"Indeed." Nikki says. "Let's go, Paige."

Paige gives me a hug, then gives Valentina a hug, to my surprise. "Thanks for getting me here."

"You're welcome," she says.

"Melyssa, change of plans: you and I are going home for the night." Sabato seems irritated, but I don't understand why.

"Home?"

"Home. Do you think you can manage to walk out of here?"

"If I can't, then I suppose you'll have to carry me, hot stuff."

"Jesus Christ, how much did you drink?"

"It's not my fault, not my fault at all."

"Well, whose fault is it?"

"Elsa."

He looks around and then back at me and shrugs.

"It's a shame we don't get to use this suite, it sure is beautiful."

"Valentina," he says, as he pulls me up. "Feel free to stay here tonight. And thank you for all your help."

"My pleasure," she says, with that sexy accent that probably makes him wonder how the hell he ended up with the sloppy drunk American girl.

Now that I am on my feet, though, I decide I have had way too much.

"Congratulations." I hear them all say as we walk—and I stagger—out the door. "Franco," he says as we walk out. "Valentina is staying here tonight, feel free to do the same."

I look up into the angry bodyguard's eyes, the same guy that Sabato was scrapping with just a few days ago.

"If she stays, I do," he snarls.

"I'm well aware of that."

Huh. That's...interesting.

Once in the elevator, I look around.

"Different elevator," I shrug. "See? I'm not that loaded."

"It's the service elevator. We are using it because the New Jersey police detective that wants to question me is on his way here."

"*Here*, here?" His eyes narrow, and he nods, "Wow, then we better make a run for it."

"Now how will you run, when you can't even stand?"

I lean in and whisper, "They got nothing on me, so if they get close, just leave me behind, okay? I got your back."

"You have my back?" He shakes his head, rolls his eyes and says something in Italian. "No more drinking, Melyssa."

"Right, got it, noted."

"Melyssa."

"Mmkay?"

He shakes his head. "This is serious."

"Sure is." I nod and lean back against the wall of the elevator.

Sabato takes off his jacket, folds it over his arm and loosens his tie.

I close my eyes and lift my arms up above my head. *I am sexy. I am sexy and married to the sexiest man in the world. Even if it's only—*

"Melyssa, what the hell are you doing?"

"Waiting for you to take me."

The elevator comes to a stop and he takes my hand, gives it a tug.

"Oh, I'm taking you. Home, to sleep it off. Let's go."

SABATO
Going Home

I hail a cab as I half hold up my wife, who has further made me realize how wrong I was about her, when I first decided she was the answer to my problems.

When a cab stops in front of us, she laughs. "Taxi cab confessions?"

"Excuse me?"

"It's a show. Maybe this is one of those cabs." She climbs in and her dress rides up so I see the lace of her little panties. I want to redden that ass, but she's drunk.

Once in the cab, she sits facing me, smiling and chewing on her lip.

"Thirty Park Place," I instruct the cab driver.

"Are we playing Monopoly?" She asks, with a bigger, goofier smile. When I don't answer, she sits back and pouts.

"You're angry with me."

"Melyssa, I really would like you to just be quiet for a while all right?" Her bottom lip puffs out and I know this sign. "Come here."

She scoots over and snuggles up to me the way I imagine a kitten would.

"I could behave, if it wasn't for Elsa."

"Excuse me?" *Who the fuck is Elsa?*

"Well you see, when I first saw you, there was a giant thaw in Arendelle. She is the queen down there and well it was frozen. And she didn't have anyone to play with, except for Olaf and well, he's probably dead now because it's summer."

"Melyssa, you are making absolutely no sense."

"I made perfectly good sense, until Elsa wouldn't shut up and that's your fault. Well now, Arendelle is completely gone."

"Okay. I'm sorry about this, but can you wait to go crazy after we get to our destination?"

"I'm making perfectly good sense. Arendelle was frozen, now it's melted. Elsa is not a princess of anything, anymore. Arendelle, melted, she got picked up by the Navy or something. Now she is a whore floating around on the USS Ronald Regan, just waiting for you with one of those flag things that landing people use. She's just hanging out, waiting for you all naughty like, 'Oh, Sabato, look at me! I'm Elsa, your dirty little whore!' all waving that freak flag. Actually, I think she has a flag in each hand."

"Right. You're making perfectly good sense. Melyssa, shut up. Just, for Christ's sake, be quiet."

The cab driver laughs and I am immediately annoyed.

"Frozen," he laughs.

"Apparently not."

"The movie."

"See? He knows!" Melyssa laughs.

"My kid watches it," he laughs again. "'Let it go.'"

"Yeah see, I'm not crazy. Tell him, I'm not crazy."

"Melyssa," I snap in her ear.

She shrugs. "Not crazy."

She leans back again, seemingly content, but I am still just as fucking confused.

When we pull up in front of our new place, I pay the cab driver and she, whoever the hell she is, has fallen asleep.

I carry her in and the doorman smiles when he opens the door.

"Good evening, sir."

"Started out that way," I nod, as he pushes the elevator button.

"Hope it ends that way too, sir."

"Thank you, Alfred."

"Congratulations." The way he says it makes me laugh. Yes, apparently now, I laugh when I am horrified.

We are in the elevator when she opens her eyes. "I don't feel very well."

"You don't say?"

"You're mad."

"Yes, but I'm not sure which one of you to be mad at. You, or this Elsa."

"Neither, she really likes—" She covers her mouth as the elevator door opens. I snatch her up and set her in front of the trashcan in the hall. She throws up, three times.

"Let's go." I take her arm and walk across the hall, then I punch in the code to open the door.

"I feel better now."

Her eyes close and I lift her up and walk into the apartment.

"You certainly don't smell better."

"I suck." Her eyes widen and she looks around. "Where is the safest place for me to be right now?"

"You're safe." I kick the door shut behind me.

"I mean if I get sick?"

"Probably the bathroom."

"It's lovely here. Beautiful."

"You match its beauty Melyssa-Elsa."

She giggles and hiccups. "To the bathroom?"

"Good idea."

I walk through the foyer and down the hall, to the master bedroom.

"What do you think? Is this better than the cabin?"

"Mmm-hmmm."

"Will you be comfortable here?"

I set her down on the bathroom counter and she smiles sickly. "As long as you're here."

She is nodding off and I am just as exhausted. "How do you feel about a bath?"

"Probably best."

I unzip her dress and she stands. It falls to the ground and I am left to see her tits sticking out of the corset I bought for her. She is fucking stunning.

I start the bath and watch her reflection as she pulls the pins from her hair. Strand by strand, her hair falls down past her shoulders. She cocks her head to the side and runs her fingers through it, shaking it loose.

She is lost in thought, but when I watch her cup her breasts, I am no longer able to hold back. I walk quickly over to her as I pull the condom from my pocket and hold it in my mouth. I quickly unbutton my white shirt and shrug it off. I unbuckle my pants and then the zipper. I allow them to fall to the floor as I roll the condom over my cock.

I look up and she is watching me. "Bend."

She does and I decide I will take it easy on her tonight, because she is ill. I rub my cock up and down her already slick entrance. "Do you want my cock, Melyssa?"

"Yes."

"Say please."

I push just inside of her.

"Please," she whimpers.

"How does it feel?"

"Hard. I want you, please."

She braces for impact and I feed her just a little more.

"Yes," she moans.

"How bad do you want me?"

"So bad," she begs. "I want you so, so bad."

I push in a little more and I can already feel her pussy clench. "I'm gonna fuck you nice tonight, like I should have the first time." I push in further. "Tell me Melyssa, why should I have been informed about how special this pussy was?"

"I don't know."

I am ready to bust her in half, but I hold back.

"Whose cock was the first inside this tight little pussy?"

"Oh, God."

"Try again," I hold her hips still.

"Yours. Your cock was in me."

"No one else's?"

"No one!" I slam into her.

I am all sensation, high on the fact that I was her first.

"Whose pussy is this?" I slam into her, again and again.

"Yours!" she cries out. "Just yours."

"Whose cock is inside you?"

"Sabato," she screams out, as I ram it in again. "Oh yes!"

"What do you want me to do to this pussy?"

"Fuck me!" she cries, as I fill her again.

I run my thumb down around my cock, getting it wet from her juices and then I push against her ass. "Who is going to fuck this first?"

"You!" She whimpers as I apply more pressure.

"I'm not going to fuck it tonight, but when I say I'm going to, you're going to let me, because I own your firsts. I own your body. Do you understand that?"

"Yes," she cries. "Yes, yes, oh yes!"

With that, she crumbles around me.

I don't try to hold back. I come and I come hard.

..*

When she is asleep, I get up, make my way to the foyer and open the closet door. I pull out her handbag and look inside for her phone. I take it and walk to the fourth bedroom, the room I have decided will work as my office and her study. I look around and am pleased that everything is as it should be. I open the drawer to her desk and pull out her docking station and set it up. Her phone will be charged in the morning. From what I have learned, she talks to her parents once a week. I wonder if that's normal.

As I pass through the living area, I hope that she likes it and immediately feel regretful that I wonder. She is a complex creature and little by little I am seeing more and more of her. Not just her body. Before, I was sure that along with the defined sexual need and awareness she exuded, her body was what drew me to her. Now I think I was mistaken.

She is not unlike Luciana was, in her youthful and far too innocent ways, but she didn't come off that way at first. Trickery. Back then, I was so angry that I was so easily manipulated by her. Now I know it wasn't manipulation. She truly didn't know what she was asking for.

Melyssa is very childlike in her ideals and manners, as I have come to find out. What I didn't expect was that I would be so wildly attracted to the freedom she has in acting that way. Tonight with her friends, she showed a carefree and fun-loving side of her, yet she was still adamant that she wanted me. Cared for me. Even stuck up for me.

I feel guilty that I want this and I feel even more guilt because I am selfishly accepting this kindness from a young woman who doesn't deserve my darkness clouding her life. I am the son of an evil man and the son of a saint. Both are now dead, because of me and yet here I am. Still living, still cursing those around me.

I stare at my phone, waiting for it to charge enough to receive and make a call. It shouldn't be long before I know what lies ahead. While waiting, I wake the computer from sleep and Google search this Elsa from Arendelle, hoping that she can shed some more light on the complex creature lying in my bed.

To say I am shocked is an understatement. It's a fucking cartoon. From what little I know about Walt Disney, I am sure he would roll in his cartoon-like grave at what Melyssa said last night in that cab. And what the fuck is that song? Five million views on YouTube? How have I never heard of this before now?

Lost in amusement, I laugh out loud.

But as fate has it, that amusement is taken quickly by the message that appears on my screen.

I am outside your building. Buzz me in… N. D'Angelo.

..*

I open the door and he isn't alone, just like Zandor said. He is with another cop. Surprisingly, Zandor is behind him.

"Come in gentlemen, but please try to keep it down. My wife is sleeping."

I lead them in through the kitchen to the family room and the lights come up. I watch them look around at the walls that are adorned with pictures of Melyssa. Their eyes fix on the painting of her on the cross.

"She's beautiful, isn't she?" I say, as I sit and motion for them to do the same.

It makes them all uncomfortable and I like that.

"We have some questions about the night your father was killed," Detective D'Angelo says, taking out a voice recorder and a pen and paper.

"Where were you?"

"I was there." I don't say anything more.

"When you left, was he alive?"

"When I shot in the air, attempting to get away, it was hard to tell. I was forced to run, because I was being shot at."

"Was he alive?"

"I assume yes, I heard him say something like, 'Forget him, get me out of here.' I did look back and saw he was impaled by shards of glass." I try to hide the fact that I am pleased by the memory. By Zandor's look, I'm not sure I pull it off. Oh, well.

"Do you know what that looks like to us?"

"I really don't give a shit. To me, it looks like you lost officers due to the fact that you underestimated the devil himself. I warned you that he couldn't be caged. You got cocky, thought that you Americans could handle a man who was born of hate and bred to think he has to answer to no one, not even God himself. So please humor me and tell me what it looks like to you, Detective D'Angelo? Feel free to follow it up with a 'thank you' to me for accidentally taking care of a situation that you and an army of men failed to take care of."

"Sabato," Zandor warns.

"No. Those men died because you didn't listen to me. Let's get right to the point, shall we? Did I kill Salvatore Efisto? Yes. I caused glass to rain down on his soulless body. I caused his death. I have no remorse and would do it again if need be."

"He died the same way your mother died, in an explosion when you were seven years old."

I feel my hands tremble. "He did."

"Do you think he was behind—"

"I was seven years old, Detective. I had no idea what was going on in his sick and twisted mind."

"If you're not here to arrest my husband, I am going to have to ask you to leave." I look up and Melyssa is tightening the robe from the bathroom around her waist.

"I can handle this. Go back to bed." I stand up, but she comes closer and sits down.

"No. This is our first day as a married couple. Unless they are going to falsely arrest a man for self-defense, they need to leave."

"Melyssa, Detective D'Angelo is just trying to close a case," Zandor says, in a gentle tone.

"Your visa expires in just a few weeks. Will you be heading back to Sicily then?" D'Angelo asks.

"I am pretty sure I am staying right here."

The detective stands, Zandor and he walk out and I follow them.

"If you have any more questions, feel free to contact me." I say, as they walk out the door.

"There are surveillance cameras in your club."

"Feel free to watch the tapes."

Zandor looks at me. "You good?"

"I'm fine. Thank you, Zandor."

As soon as the door closes behind him, I look back. Melyssa is carrying the painting of her on the cross. She growls at me when she walks by.

"Where do you think you're going?"

"To hide this!"

"I happen to love that painting."

"Pervert!" She tries to hide a laugh.

"How does the saying go, isn't that the 'pot calling the kettle black,' Melyssa of Arendelle?"

"Don't you—"

I am in front of her, snatching the painting. "Just, Let it Go."

She shakes her head. "The next time my husband invites NJPD over, could he let me know?"

"Next time my wife decides to get so intoxicated that she tells a New York City cab driver a naughty little tale, do you think she could just keep her mouth shut when asked?"

"I don't care to talk about that again."

"Oh," I laugh. "We certainly will be."

I hang the picture back where it belongs.

"Is it to your liking, Princess Elsa?" I take a pseudo bow.

"Do you think you'll get arrested?" Melyssa is no longer playful. She is concerned. *Fucking whiplash.*

"No, I don't."

"You're sure?"

"Yes."

"Okay." she reaches out for my hand. "Now show me—"

"Arendelle?"

"Okay, that's quite enough of that business."

"My wife is a conundrum of naughty and nice. Innocent, yet has such sexually corrupt desires. She likes to be spanked for pleasure, yet names her pussy after a—"

"You are one lucky man." She pulls on my hand. "Now, give me a tour."

ARENDELLE

"**D**emanding little *pazza*," he murmurs under his breath.

"Speak English, please."

"You'll learn." He yanks my hand. "We're in the entry. To our right," he walks as fast as he talks, "The pantry and kitchen. Through here, the den."

"Family room." I pause when he looks at me like I'm crazy. "For the interview."

"Of course. Now through here, the living room and dining room."

I pause to look around. "It's beautiful."

"It's no cabin in the woods, but it should suffice. Back this way is the fourth bedroom, but I have it set up as an office, for you and me."

Sabato points but doesn't let me go in. He keeps moving. "Foyer again, bedrooms three and two and then back to the master suite." He lets go of my hand. "Now, if you prefer not to share a room, there is another set up that—"

"Not negotiable."

"Right." He looks like he may smile, but he doesn't. "Your clothes are in the closet we passed by when we walked in here. All of your things can be delivered, so there is no need to go back there."

I nod and he sighs and it's sexy.

"I'm exhausted. I get 'pissy' when I haven't slept in a few days, so I really would like you to climb in bed and go to sleep, so I can do the same."

I climb in and he is right behind me. "Sabato?"

"Yes?" He plumps his pillow.

"Are you okay? I mean, are you sure you'll be okay?"

"I'm not in jail. If they had anything, I would be. This apartment is very secure, so yes, I am honestly better than I have been in a very, very long time. Just tired."

My heart melts a little bit more for him. "Good."

When he lies back, I look at him. "Do you need to be fucked before you go to sleep?"

"No."

I am almost offended, almost.

"Good, then lay down and promise me I won't wake up and find you gone."

"I will be here. Where else would I be?"

"Good." I lie back. "Sabato?"

"Yes, Melyssa?" He yawns.

"Promise me, when I wake up, you won't act like you did this morning."

"Things are not the same as they were this morning. They have changed. I have a piece of paper saying you're my wife."

"Do you trust me?"

It takes him a minute and another yawn, before he responds.

"More than I have anyone in a very long time."

"I want it to be more than anyone, ever." I yawn in response to his.

"Goodnight, wife."

"Goodnight, husband."

..*

When I wake, he has a hand loosely tangled in my hair. I wonder if that's how he planned to stop me if, I had tried to escape. It should freak me out, but nothing does anymore.

I say my affirmations for the first time in a long time, before getting out of bed.

They are different today than ever before:

I will make him smile. I will let him see me—the real me, every facet, every flaw. I will not drink. I silently scold myself for that one. I will be a blessing to someone who, in the strangest of occurrences, has blessed me by making me feel like I may be crazy. But it's okay. I'm crazy for him.

I pull away from his hand and his grip doesn't tighten. His nearly silent snores tell me he is in a very deep sleep. I won't wake him. I slide like a snake off the bed and tiptoe to the bathroom, where I close the door very quietly and look around. Everything in this place is so elegant and I cannot wait to explore. I will try my best to wait for him to do so, but I can't promise anything.

After a very long shower with water pressure that could rival the massage in Ft. Lauderdale with my girls, I finally pull myself out of it.

I wrap myself in the exquisite softness of the plushest white towels I have ever felt and wrap my hair in a smaller version. When I walk out of the bathroom, he is still asleep. His hand is now griping the pillow my head was on as he lies on his back, with his other hand covering his eyes. He is covered with a sheet, but only enough to cover his manhood and...even that is visibly plumping up the sheet. His chest is, *gawww*, his abs are *hell yes*, that V is *lickable* and I am ...*wet*.

My mouth is watering and Elsa is eagerly stretching in her little slutty bikini, flag in each hand, just egging me on.

I defeat temptation and walk away, toward the closet where my belongings are promised to be.

When I open the door, the light automatically comes on and it makes me giggle inside. I can see myself opening and shutting the door repeatedly, just to see that happen. And then I finally see the closet. It's huge and organized by color and I am pretty sure these are not my clothes—well, maybe a third of them but, not *all* of them. I see his things on one side and mine on the other. The room is divided by shelves. The upper part is drawers and the lower is shoes. *Shoes. Lots of shoes. Holy hell.*

I open a drawer and as I suspected, the panties are all matched perfectly with bras. One drawer is all white, there is another with all black and one with red. *For you Elsa*, I laugh, then scold myself. One more drawer is for other colors and I am smiling so wide now, my face hurts. He must have joined the 'panty of the month' club and got the first year in advance.

I grab red, because I am feeling awfully naughty today and decide it's allowed because I am married to the man who is naked in my bed. I shake my imaginary fist at hell and Elsa flips it the bird. We high five and then I do a little dance that starts with dropping the towel and shaking my ass and ends with a very loud clearing of the throat.

I freeze, knowing that I am not imagining things.

"Good morning, Melyssa."

"Good morning, Sabato," I say as I shimmy my panties up to cover my ass.

I quickly put my bra over my arms and clip it in the front. He has yet to say anything else, so I break the silence. "Hungry?"

"Famished," he growls.

"Great, I'll make you breakfast in that big, nice kitchen of ours."

I go to grab a shirt and suddenly he is standing in front of me, naked and erect.

"Yours." He nudges me with his cock.

"Mine?" I nod. "But I want to feed my man first. So, if you'll excuse me—"

"I like pussy for breakfast." He lifts me up and I grab hold of him as he walks us out the door.

"Just like that, huh?" I joke as I scratch my nails up his neck and into his sexy, messy hair.

"Just like that." He reaches up and unhooks my hands, then drops me on the edge of the bed and pushes me back. "Don't move, or I swear I'll tie you up."

"Don't you threaten me with a good time." I laugh, as he yanks my red, lacy panties down.

"Well, look here," he says and then licks my bare flesh.

"Wedding gift," I gasp, as my hands fist in his hair.

"Mmm." His mouth vibrates against my skin and I clasp my knees tightly around his face. He pulls away and looks up at me sternly. "No. Moving."

"How is that even poss—" He stands and grabs me up, walks to the door and down the hall to one of the bedrooms.

When he opens the door, I see the St. Andrews cross against the bare wall. I know it's supposed to be a threat. But it's not, not at all. He sets me down and I make my way to the cross.

"Face front or back?"

He doesn't answer so I look back at him. He looks totally lost, like he just realized Christmas is cancelled, forever.

"This is supposed to...intimidate."

"Is it?"

He shakes his head.

"Look, I got the ring now, so I am gonna just roll with the punches, Sabato. I'm not going to pretend anymore. I am who I am, right?" I shrug and he stares at me. "I don't have to hide from you, not like I have everyone else."

"Hide what, exactly?" He looks at me with concern. Probably thinks I am crazy all over again and that's okay—because maybe I am, a little.

"The V card," I hold my hands beside me, palms up like scales. "Blessing or curse? I've thought maybe both, at times. But now, I can honestly say that if I was waiting for my prince, I am sure I found him."

"I'm no prince, Melyssa."

"You are so much more than you'll allow yourself to believe. I see you, Sabato. I see past the tragic circumstances you have faced all your life. I. See. You. And you are my prince. I will tell you the truth and I will pray you don't run, but I know what I feel. I won't try to push it away anymore. It makes me crazy when I try. All I know is that I am falling for a man who says I can't and it feels really good, so I'm not going to stop. I just hope," I pause. "No, I pray that in a year, I can still be carried into this room and punished the way I—"

"Melyssa, don't do that. Don't ask me to—"

"But I'm asking. How do you feel about me?" I shrug. "I can take it. It won't change what I promised you I would do. I guess...I don't even really need the answer, just maybe for you to think about it." I stand looking at him, naked in every possible way and he stands staring, just searching for something to say. So, I change the subject.

"Front or back?"

"Back to me," he demands. "Now."

The threat in his voice awakens every lust-filled cell in my body.

I feel the palm of his hand on my back, pushing me against the smooth wood surface. I raise my hands and he wraps each wrist in leather cuffs attached to chains. My ankles are next and then he is beside me. He pushes the top of the cross and it rotates, then clicks and stops when I am lying face down.

I look to him, but his eyes carry no expression.

"Are you in the zone?" His jaw tightens and his left nostril twitches a bit. "Okay then."

I hear him behind me and don't bother to look back, I just wait.

My eyes are covered with a blindfold, and he hisses, "Not a word."

I nod once and I feel the sting of a flogger against my skin. As quick as it's there, it is gone. I feel it again. It's faster than before, less of a reprieve, but it feels good. He strikes between my legs now and my back arches, pushing my ass up as he hits me again and again and again.

"This is what I bring, Melyssa." He hits my ass a little harder this time. It still feels good. He does it again in the same spot and it stings this time. He stops when I start to feel tender.

"Like a wound that begs to be bled, to alleviate the pressure of the blood rising in it. When it breaks, you feel good, because you don't know the difference between good and bad. You only know me and I am bad."

"No you're not. No—ouch!"

"No words, Melyssa, just feel. Feel what I have to offer."

Again, I feel the sting, again and again. It's a rhythm of pain, but I still can't feel the bad in it. It feels good, somewhat painful, but good. Again he hits me and again. I am now anticipating the strikes, anticipating his touch. He stops. I hear movement behind me. I feel my left nipple being pinched tightly, then the right. I want him to suck them. I love when he sucks them. When I hear him behind me again, I realize it isn't him pinching my nipples, but clamps.

Whack! Whack! Whack!

"Does this feel nice, Melyssa? This pain? No, it doesn't. It's the sensitivity aroused in you, the anticipation of the orgasm."

Whack! Whack! Whack!

I am now sore and I don't know how much I can take without him touching me. The clamps are removed and I feel so much better that I arch my back in anticipation. I am waiting for him to taste me, suck me, and pleasure me. I feel a snap of leather under my armpit, then the flogger slaps between my legs.

"Oh, god."

Again he alternates strikes: armpit, pussy, armpit, pussy. With rapid fire quickness and repetition, he beats my pussy like a drum and I am almost *there*, I just need a couple more hits to put me over.

He stops and I wait. I hear a door close and I realize I am alone.

Tears threaten to fall, not because I am in pain, but because I am in need. I need the release. I need him to give it to me.

I need him.

SABATO

I'm going to hurt her.

I have hurt her.

I am not in control when I am with her and I am not able to tolerate that. I go to the kitchen and get a glass of water. If she had just not said anything, I would have been all right. *She* would have been all right.

"FUCK!" I throw the glass against the wall and it smashes into a thousand pieces. I walk into the bedroom, take some clothes out of the closet and get dressed. I kick the door open and her body tenses.

"This is what you ask for, Melyssa! Disappointment!"

"No, I ask for you. Every piece of you!"

"Well, that may never come. I hope you enjoy that fucking position and anticipation as much as I anticipate watching you falling apart because of me. That's not what I wanted. I didn't want to give a shit about you. You fucking tricked me!"

"I am falling in love with you. It's not a choice!"

"Then you hang there, until you fall right the fuck out!"

I slam the door behind me and hear her begin to cry.

I tell myself it doesn't matter. That I don't care. I lie, over and over.

I leave the apartment and get into the elevator. I hit the lobby button and begin descending.

The door opens and I step out. My hands are shaking and I have no idea where I am going. But I know I need to stay away from her. I need to stay away from her, or I will ruin her. It's best she knows this now.

What she doesn't know is that it isn't because I am unfeeling. Because I don't care. I do care and that is the problem. Hell she does know. She's the one that pointed it out. I don't want her to know. I will prove her wrong.

"*Chiedo scusa*," I look up when I hear the woman's voice.

I stumble back, so distracted that I don't notice how strange it is, that the stranger automatically addressed me in my native language. "*Sti bene?*"

"*Sì, certo, mi scuso.*" I walk around her and head for the door. Then I stop. Freeze.

"Do you know her?" the doorman asks.

"No," I answer.

"She's here to see you."

I look back as she gets in the elevator and the doors close.

"And you let her pass?"

"I'm sorry sir, she said she was here with a wedding gift, that she missed the wedding, that—"

I turn and run for the elevator. I hit the button several times, but it's already on the fourth floor. I yell back at the doorman, "Can you stop it!"

"No sir, but I can slow it down."

"Do it now! Or so help me God, you'll pay."

I run for the stairway and start to ascend. After a few seconds, I hear footsteps chasing me. I don't stop, but I turn. Thorello Archangello is behind me.

"Was that Maria??"

"Yes, go!" he yells.

I don't wait for him to catch up. "How did she get into this country?"

"Maria's resources go beyond the Italian police. Go!"

"My wife is in the apartment."

I run faster.

"I know that too."

I push through the stairwell exit, then run to the apartment door and punch in the code. I throw the door open, yelling over my shoulder for Thor to follow and help me search. "Check-in that direction."

I run straight into the second bedroom and pull the straps from Melyssa's arms and ankles as fast as I can.

"You came back," she sobs, throwing her arms around me.

"I always will." I hold her, grateful that she is all right.

"I'm sorry, I love you," she starts, as I pull my shirt over my head and use it to cover her.

"Don't be. Please, don't be. Listen to me, Melyssa. There is a woman here in this building. I think she's coming after you."

"Why?"

"I told you, I carry a curse. That's why I can't say I love you, ever. I won't put you in that kind of danger."

"You're scared."

"No, but you are not going to get hurt on my watch."

"Sabato?"

"What?"

"Tell me you care."

"How could I not?"

"She isn't here." Thor says from the doorway. As if to punctuate his statement, there is the sound of a gunshot. He falls forward to the ground.

I shove Melyssa behind me, as Maria walks through the door. I can't believe I didn't recognize her before.

"Sabato, how are you, son?"

"Put the gun down, Maria," I say, as she pulls back on the hammer and chambers a round.

"You don't get to be happy, Sabato. Your whore of a mother, your slut of a girlfriend, they were just collateral damage. You were the cause. It was always you. You caused a strong man to fear you, because you were invincible, because you refused to die. No matter how many times we tried to end your miserable life, here you are, married. And the man I loved, who would have loved me, if you had just died when you were supposed to, he is the one who is gone. You killed him, you son-of-a-whore. Now your new whore will die, just like your brother, who lies dying on the floor."

Maria reaches forward with her toe and nudges Thor's body, but I am too shocked and appalled to make the connections of what she is saying.

"Everyone dies, Sabato, because you refuse to."

Then it clicks, even though it doesn't matter, or it won't soon enough. "He is not my brother, you bitch!"

I start to stand.

"Sabato, don't!"

"Listen to the girl, Sabato. Don't push me," she pulls the trigger and I feel a hot slap as the bullet hits me in the shoulder. The force knocks me back and I fall against Melyssa, taking her to the ground. "As you bleed out slowly, I will fill her full of holes, so you can watch her die."

I try to put myself in front of Melyssa again. Another bullet hits my shoulder and I fall back.

"Oh God, Sabato," Melyssa cries, as she pulls me into her arms with no regard for her own safety. "I love you," she whispers, as her tears fall on my face. "I love you."

I hear the gun click back again, as the darkness moves in around me. All my life, I've been waiting for death to welcome me into its embrace. But now, I don't want it. I can't let it. It's too soon.

"Say goodbye to love, Sabato Archangello." Maria aims at Melyssa and rage and adrenalin course through me. I jump up, in front of Maria. Another bullet hits my side, as I turn the gun and force back the barrel, struggling as I fight to lift it to her chest.

"Die, bitch!"

I pull the trigger and watch her eyes widen. I don't wait, because I learned my lesson last time. I fire again, and again. She falls back on the floor and I shoot her one last time, before I fall to my knees.

Melyssa kicks the gun away and grabs me.

"Don't you leave me, don't you leave me here alone."

I feel hope, even as the bits of knowledge scatter with the blood leaving my body. Salvatore is not my father. I have a brother. I finally saved a life, someone I loved.

Finally, I was someone's *eroe*.

The world blurs and I feel afraid.

"*Dea*...." My goddess. My lips move silently, uselessly.

I feel despair next, because I will never be able to tell her I love her. Then I feel nothing.

..*

I am floating, weightless, when I see them.

"Mama!"

Emotions swell in my heart and in my eyes. Mama is with a man. She is happy, he is smiling. He loves her, I can tell. As I move closer, I see him. I've seen him before. He was the police man with the sad face who seemed to fear my father after Mama was killed.

She loves him, she always loved him, I can feel that, too. He is Thor's father and my real father. He looks like me, but happy like Mama.

"Eroe, come to me."

I do. I run to her arms, happily. "You are grown."

"No Mama, I am still your boy. But now, now I am...."

"A man. My Eroe. I am proud of you. We," she looks to her side. "Your father and I are proud of you."

My chest swells with pride, even as my heart squeezes. I don't know what I did to make her proud of me. But whatever it is, I want to do it again.

"Be happy, son. Be happy."

Blackness comes toward me again.

When light returns to my eyes, I see her. Luciana is in a white dress and her long, black hair is longer than I remember. She is holding the hand of a child and they walk towards me.

"Sabato."

"Luciana." I don't mean to cry, but tears come anyway and I hug her tight. "I am so sorry I couldn't save you."

"Don't say that, my love. Had I not found you, I would never have known love." She kneels down in front of me. "This is Eroe, my son—our son. He is the reason my eternity without you is still filled with love."

She turns to the boy. "*Di ciao a tuo padre.*"

"*Ciao, padre.*"

"*Ciao*, beautiful one."

I hold them both and weep for the life I never knew, the life I could have had. Such great happiness, snatched away in a moment. I spent so many years punishing myself for her loss, not knowing the extent of it. And yet, I feel lighter, more at peace, knowing she is not alone.

After a long embrace, she pulls back. "We will never stop loving you."

They turn and walk away and I want to follow them. I want to stay with them. But I can't move. "Where are you going?"

They turn, blow kisses and smile.

Sono felici.

There is nothing worse in the world than sitting in the front of an ambulance, watching through the window as the paramedics try and seem to fail, at saving the person you love most.

Sabato has flat lined three times in the matter of ten minutes.

When the paramedics arrived at the apartment, Maria was pronounced dead. I was running back and forth between Sabato and Thor, trying to perform CPR on both of them, trying to keep their hearts beating long enough for help to arrive. I'm pretty sure I was in shock by that point, because it didn't even occur to me to check and see if Maria was still breathing. Or maybe I just didn't care. Maybe I wanted her to die, for killing the man I love.

Not killing, I correct myself, for the thousandth time. Trying to kill. Because he's not dead. He can't be dead.

My hands are covered in blood, as I pace outside the ER, wearing nothing but Sabato's dress shirt and the jacket one of the paramedics gave me. I can't breathe, but I have to. At least for a little longer. If Sabato dies because he saved me, then I don't want to go on. I now know this is how he has felt for the last twenty years. I know it, because there wasn't anything I could do but pump his chest and pray as I cried, trying to get him to breathe again.

My arms are sore, my whole body is sore and shivering, but none of that matters. I don't care how I feel, as long as I'm breathing. As long as he is. I look up when I hear my name, and I see Valentina, and her bodyguard running towards me.

"No, no, no," I cry as she hugs me and I finally fall apart.

Ironically, she's the one person I think understands—in some tiny way—how I feel.

"He's strong, he'll be okay. He'll be okay because he loves you, Mel. It's okay." She is holding me, rocking me back and forth while Franco stands at the desk. I hear him ask about Sabato, but they won't tell him anything.

Why won't they tell anyone anything?

After a while, I have no idea how long, a nurse comes out and asks us to follow her. I jump up and follow, refusing to let myself think about what I'm going to find when we get to wherever she's leading us. When we reach a room just inside the doors, she tells us it's for privacy. We need to stay there, and when they know something, they will tells us. I want to scream at her, but I don't.

I know it's because I am crying, and I'm hysterical, and probably scaring everyone in the waiting room. But I can't help it.

Valentina says something to Franco in Italian and he leaves us alone. I sit in the corner, hugging my chest and praying for Sabato, asking God to take me instead. I want Sabato to live long enough to see that he is a good person. I want him to understand that none of this was his fault. I want him to live, because he never really has before.

When I look up at the clock, I'm shocked to see that it has been three hours. Three hours and still, I know nothing.

I stand up, ready to walk out and tear the place apart, but Valentina stops me.

"Mel, put these on." She hands me sweatpants and a sweatshirt. "There is a shower in there. Go. Clean yourself up."

"No, if they come in here—"

"When they come in and they tell you he's ready for you, you'll be clean. You'll feel better."

I look at Valentina's kind, pretty, calm face and hate her all over again. I don't want her here, and I know I shouldn't feel that way. I feel guilty that I don't want him to be surrounded by people who care for him. I also know that I am being a total bitch to someone who is showing me kindness.

"Thank you."

She visibly relaxes. "You're welcome."

I take the fastest shower I can. I throw on the sweatpants and sweatshirt. Then push my feet into some flip-flops.

When I walk out of the bathroom, Nikki, Abe, Paige and Zandor are all packed into the tiny room.

I swallow hard and promise myself I won't cry. But when the girls hug me, I can't help myself.

The doctor walks in behind them. "I have an update on Thorello Archangello. Who here is related?"

I step forward. "I'm his sister in-law."

"Great." He ushers me into the doorway, pretending that he doesn't notice everyone else listening in. "He's had a transfusion and the bullet was removed. He is expected to make a full recovery, no organ damage. But he lost a lot of blood. When he is about ready to wake up, I will come and get you. They are sewing him up now, should only be a couple hours."

"Thank you. And Sabato?"

"He's still in surgery." He looks down. "We are doing everything we can."

"Do that and then some," Zandor Steel says.

"We will try." When the doctor leaves, all eyes are on me.

Oh, right. They probably have no idea what just happened. "Thor is his brother. The woman, Maria, told him. Salvatore was not his father."

"Unbelievable."

"Fuck! He needs to wake up, he has a family!" I say out loud, without meaning to.

..*

Two hours later, we get word that they are *still* 'doing everything they can' for Sabato. They are trying to remove bullets that are in danger of rupturing his heart. Thor is in recovery, but still sleeping.

"He needs someone there when he wakes up."

A nurse comes in and asks for Melyssa Chance.

"That's my maiden name."

"Your parents are here," she tells me.

I look at Nikki, and she smiles wanly. "I called them."

"Dear God." I suddenly have to sit down.

When they walk in, they look awful. Both stressed and confused.

"Hi," I say.

"You okay?" My dad sits next to me.

"When he wakes up, I will be."

"He...meaning....?"

"My husband, the man I love." Suddenly, I'm irritated all over again. "And no, I won't apologize for getting swept up. I won't apologize because then I am lessening how much he means to me, so please, don't expect me to do that."

I can't believe the words that just came out of my mouth or the strength behind them.

"Okay," Dad says.

Mom is quiet, but that's okay, better silent than angry.

"Mrs. Efisto?"

"Yes?"

"Your brother in law is waking up. Come with me."

I don't bother saying anything else to my parents, I just follow the nurse.

When the elevator stops, I immediately ask if Sabato is on the same floor and they tell me yes.

"When he comes out of surgery," I tell her, "they should be in the same room."

She gives me a look as if I am some disillusioned girl.

"He *will* wake up. If he doesn't, someone will pay."

I walk through the curtain in the post-op room and look at the man who is supposedly Sabato's brother. I see the resemblance immediately.

"How are you?"

Thorello shakes his head weakly. "How is Sabato?"

"Still in surgery." I hold out my hand. "I'm Melyssa."

"I know this," he holds up his hand, which is attached to an IV.

Thankfully, the doctor told Thor, the bullet just missed his spleen.

"I need to get back to my home, as soon as possible." He tells me. His accent is very thick compared to Sabato's, but their first impressions are not much different. Except, Thor doesn't have that implacable, sensual pull. At least, not for me.

As I sit next to him, I feel that he is very intimidating, but I won't leave him alone. He is family.

"So...you're a police officer."

"Yes, very different from your husband," he says, in a condescending tone.

"Well, maybe not as much as you'd think."

"You do not know him."

"I know enough. Look Thor, I think you might be surprised if you saw how much he—"

"It is none of my concern," he interrupts.

"Okay, but...."

"I don't wish to discuss him any further. I am tired, and need to rest."

"Well, okay. I'll be here until he wakes up. So you go ahead and rest, because you and your brother have years of catching up to do."

"*Ragazza testarda.*"

"*Ragazza testarda?*" I fold my arms. "Okay, I'll add that to the list of things to Google. How does one say 'family' in Italian?"

"*Una rompicoglioni,*" he says, as he leans back and closes his eyes.

"*Una rompicoglioni*...is a good thing?"

I notice a smirk and then it is gone.

I go out to the nurses' station when I know he is asleep. "I need an update on Sabato Efisto."

"We'll let you know soon."

I nod, even though I'm not happy. "Thank you."

For more countless hours, I sit and wait and pray and fight tears.

Each passing second feels like an eternity. I weather them silently, stubbornly watching over Sabato's sleeping brother, like somehow that will bring me closer to him.

"Pain in the ass." I look up, startled when I hear Thor's voice. "*Una rompicoglioni,* means pain in the ass. Is he awake yet?"

I shake my head, no.

He looks at the ceiling blankly for a while and then he says, "*Famiglia.*"

"*Famiglia.*"

"You should rest. I will make sure to wake you when they come in."

A Dream

"**H**e is very handsome."

"When he wakes up and he smiles, you'll think you've seen an angel."

"He's okay." I hear a man's voice. "I don't know why you'd pick a man with holes in him to fall in love with."

"Dad, those aren't holes, they are love bites."

"I don't wanna hear that from my kid."

"One for each of the women who were allowed to love him."

"Allowed, huh?" I hear a woman's voice.

"It's definitely a privilege."

"It's been four days. You should prepare yourself, Melyssa."

Melyssa. I hear Melyssa.

"We have unfinished business, him and I. So yes, he will wake up. He has everything to live for now."

"When he heals, I'm gonna kick his ass."

"You'll have to go through me first," I hear her laugh and then feel her lips on my forehead.

"Man to man, I owe him, he knows that."

"Why? At least he called you."

Melyssa.... I want to say her name, but I can't.

"He called, all right. 'I am marrying your daughter,' he told, not asked me. And he sounded like Count Dracula. Now, how can my little southern Mel fall in love with Count Dracula?"

She laughs. "Southern Mel, Dad? I'm too old for that."

"It still fits you," the woman says, her mother I believe.

"I'm going to grab some coffee, anyone want some?"

"Yes," they both say.

"When he wakes up, you'll see how perfect he is, Mom. His eyes are so expressive, and I promise he doesn't sound like Count Dracula."

"It's okay if he does, I just want to meet the man my daughter loves."

I slowly open my eyes. They weigh more than usual. The light stings, but when I see her, I don't want to look away.

"I wish I had taken at least one of those bullets. Just one and maybe he'd be awake."

"He's breathing on his own now. That's a good sign, honey."

Melyssa's mother looks at me, my eyes lock with hers and she smiles in relief. "Well. the eyes *are* a very nice shade of brown."

"I know and they are so—"

"Open. Honey, they are so open." Her smile broadens. Melyssa has her smile.

My wife turns quickly to look at me, but she doesn't say a word. She only closes her eyes and mouths 'thank you.'

Then she smiles. "Hi."

"Hello, Melyssa." I croak out.

"Get him a drink," she says to her mother, as she reaches for me.

"Thor?"

"Awake and in the room next door. He gets released tomorrow. I'm letting him stay at our place."

"Maria?"

"Dead, the rotten bitch."

"Melyssa," her mother scolds, as she hands me a drink.

"Thank you." I reach for it, but Melyssa takes the cup and holds the straw for me to drink.

"Toothbrush?"

"I'll get the nurse." Her mother pushes the call bell.

"Sit here?" I move over and she tells me not to. Once she sits, I whisper, "*Mi sei mancato.*"

The nurse walks in, pushing Thor in a wheelchair. "You're awake."

"I am."

"Good. You going to stay that way?" He asks.

"I plan on it, yes."

"Good." He scowls. "Your wife seems to think you and I need to move forward. She has also offered a place for me to stay while I stick around for a while for physical therapy. You okay with that?"

"Yes, if she is."

"Good. I will see you again soon."

"Glad you're all right."

"You too."

The nurse begins poking and prodding me and then things become incredibly busy with people in and out of the room.

When things finally slow down, her father comes in with coffee. Her father is a big man. Like a bear. He looks at me with intent to intimidate, but with all I have survived, I can't really be intimidated.

"You married my daughter."

"I did, as I said I would."

"I suppose."

"If you hurt her, I will tear you apart."

"Dad," Melyssa gasps.

"Understood." I nod.

At the end of the day, everyone has come and gone. When I say everyone, I mean everyone: Valentina, Zandor, the rest of the Steel family, Abe, Melyssa's friends, even the owner of the apartment building, who would not stop apologizing that the doorman let in a would-be assassin.

I feel ready for another four days of sleep, but I also feel ready to be alone with Melyssa.

"Come," I pat the bed.

"Okay but you need sleep. I want you home."

"Will you be going home tonight?"

"No, I haven't been there since, well since...."

"Where have you stayed?"

"Here, of course." She looks at me like it's the simplest answer ever, easier than two plus two.

I look at her and really take in her eyes. "I have so much I need to say to you and so many reasons that I should not."

"Sabato...."

"No, listen."

She smiles and braces herself, as if she is waiting for her world to fall apart, yet she is not afraid.

"*Sono così innamorata di te, Melyssa. Penso che volevo esserlo quando ti ho incontrata. Credo che avevo paura di ammetterlo. La mia speranza per il futuro è più forte della mia paura del passato Ma l'amore é più forte della paura e della speranza. Io vorrò sempre stare con te, niente di più, niente di meno.*"

She looks at me and nods, "I have no idea what you just said, but okay."

"Okay?"

"I love you, so whatever you need, whatever you want...okay."

"Just like that."

She nods. "Just like that."

I decide to tell her in English, even though it's incredibly hard to do so. Hiding behind a language she doesn't know is enough for her, but I want to give her...more.

"I said, I'm so in love with you, Melyssa. I think I wanted to be when I saw you. I think I was afraid to admit it.

My hope for the future is stronger than my fear of the past. But stronger than fear and hope is the love. I'll always want to be with you, nothing more, and nothing less. "

"I just fell harder," she whispers.

* * *

The visa application is in review and an immigration officer is on his way to our house. Melyssa has flowers sitting on almost every flat surface in the house. On the kitchen table, there is coffee, tea and pastries.

"It's a civil servant, not the Queen, correct?"

"Hush," she laughs at me, the way she always laughs. Joyfully and without apology.

I roll my eyes as I watch her carry the painting through the house again.

"I love that painting," I remind her, as I have every time she hides it, which tends to piss me off. She isn't afraid when I am 'pissy,' though. She thinks it's adorable, she says so often.

This time, Melyssa comes out with another panting, one I haven't seen. Of course I follow her. What else do I have to do? I am a 'man of leisure' now, which is a cool way to say 'unemployed.' Of course, I'm still rich and that doesn't hurt.

I watch as she stands on her little step stool and hangs the painting.

To say I am shocked is an understatement.

She steps down and turns to me.

"When I was cleaning a few days ago, I saw an old folded up paper with a picture of this painting. You must have had it for a long time."

I nod, unable to form words.

"I wasn't sure why, but I think I know. That woman Maria, she mentioned that you tried to end your life many times. Now I think I get it. When I thought I may lose you, I decided I wanted to die. That life without you," she stops and swallows hard, "would be unbearable. That one love, even one that was unspoken, would never be able to be replicated."

She looks back at the photo.

"I'm so glad that you're still here," she whispers.

"Me too."

"I looked into the picture's meaning and well, its art and art is subjective so this is what I see when I see this. I see three women, the Graces, the girls that were at your club when...well, before." She smiles sadly at me. "They adore you, and I know if they spent so much time with you, they were able to see into you deeper than most. The angel represents many, the loves you have lost. Your mother, Luciana and your father. But the woman right there is me, and the man lying there just needed to open his eyes. He was hurt, not dead. And as soon as he opens his eyes, he will see how loved he is, by so many. I can't change your past, I can't pretend I was your first love, or your first sexual partner. But I know on some level that you love me. I feel it every time you look at me. I don't want to push your past in your face, but I know that it made you the man you are. The man who makes me dizzy with lust, full of love and so incredibly aware of just how lucky I am."

"Thank you."

"Can we keep it?"

"Of course."

..*

We are sitting at the table as the man pulls his notepad and a folder out of his briefcase.

I have my hand on Melyssa's leg under the table to hold it still. She is fidgeting like crazy and I don't want her to stress about a thing.

"We have your application, so the basics are covered. My job is to find out if this marriage is real. The questions I ask will reveal that. Please answer them completely so that I can make my decision without having to fill in the blanks myself."

We both nod.

He looks at me, "When did you fall in love with Melyssa Chance?"

"The first time I saw her." He rolls his eyes slightly, which pisses me off. "I didn't know it then, but it's true."

"Of course," he says as if he's heard that a thousand times. "When did you first have sex with her?"

"Excuse me?" I snap and Melyssa squeezes my hand.

"When did you first have intercourse with Melyssa?"

"A few days before our wedding."

"I see." He starts writing.

"You see what?" Melyssa gives my hand another squeeze.

"Typically, sex between people who are in such a hurry to get married is immediate, unless they wait for the wedding night."

"Well, we fucked around before we had sex, isn't that typical?"

"Sure."

"I would have fucked her the first time we were alone, but she said no."

"Sabato," Melyssa tries to stop me but the fucker is rubbing me the wrong way.

"When you say 'fucked around,' what does that mean?"

"It means—"

"Could you explain the relevance of these questions to getting approved?" Melissa interrupts me.

"The validity of your relationship, Mrs. Efisto."

"Well, as you can see, we live together and have been for a few weeks now. The only time we weren't in our residence is when he was hospitalized, because of a mad woman being allowed into this country, who was issued entrance by the very government who allows you to question our marriage."

"That has nothing to do with this." He gives her a look like he's annoyed with her.

"Watch how you speak to my wife."

"I'm fine, Sabato."

"Is this an intimidation tactic, Sabato Efisto, who has mafia connections and—"

"Those connections have been severed." I glare at him.

He points his stubby little finger at me. "I am not intimidated by you mister...Pacino, of the Pacino Pacinos, so you *listen to me*, Dom Perignon, your threats don't scare me, Tony Soprano."

"Wow, that was...a lot of references."

I look over at Melyssa and she is shaking because she is trying not to laugh. This little comb-over, briefcase-toting bastard is obviously confused, or racist against Italians, or just fucking crazy.

"Scarface doesn't intimidate me, you don't intimidate me, you *can't* make me an offer I can't refuse," his fake Italian accent is horrible, and I am trying really hard to be angry at this little fuck, but Melyssa is right—it's actually very funny.

"I'm not afraid to be swimming with the fishes, no sir, I am not! So you stow that gun, I'll take the cannoli."

Melyssa laughs out loud then and I can't help but laugh too.

His face is red as he stands and grabs a handful of pastries, none of which are cannolis and basically runs to the fucking door. "I'll be back!"

As soon as the door shuts behind him, Melyssa and I are laughing so hard tears are rolling down her cheeks. She stands up and walks to the counter, where her phone sits. "I'll call and ask for someone else."

"Will they do that?" I try to stop laughing so she can make the damn call.

"I don't know, do you know?" She uses the Godfather voice and then falls into a fit of laughter.

God, she is beautiful.

And she is mine.

~The End~

Epilogue

No more law school for me.

Sabato was right, of course. We had a conversation that started in the hospital, when he asked when I would go back. I told him I would figure it out when he was one hundred percent better. He didn't push.

When we got home, he pushed.

"You don't want that anyway," he looks deep into my eyes, my soul. "You tell me why you decided not to continue with social work, and then you tell me why you want to practice law."

"I followed on a case, one that changed my mind." I say, not wanting to appear weak or wanting to hurt him. It would open a wound and he was just beginning to heal.

"I see." He sits up on the bed and reaches into the nightstand drawer and grabs the blindfold.

"What are you doing?" I laugh as he covers my eyes.

"Sometimes it's easier for people—well, you and I—to open up when we feel most free. You feel freest when you're not trying to gauge my reactions to you."

"Maybe when we, well...when...." I reach up and try to remove the blindfold. But his quick, jungle cat-like instincts kick in and he grabs my hands.

"Don't." He whispers into my ear in his silky smooth voice and then pushes his face against mine.

"A case I followed closely. It was clearly abuse, but the child was adamant at the hospital that she fell down the stairs. The mother and father's stories matched. The home visit was perfect. Beautiful home, too." I feel sick to my stomach. "You can always hope your gut is wrong. But," I swallow hard because I know I am going to cry and he pulls me tighter to him. "The mother, Rachel, killed herself. She left a note saying she couldn't stop him, that he threatened to hurt her, to kill her and their daughter. It said she has died a little every day since the abuse began and felt like she had been a horrible mother. That maybe ending her life would help shed some light on the situation, on Chloe."

I try not to focus on the darkest details. Instead, I focus on the warmth of his skin, on how tightly he holds me as the tears fall.

"Chloe, is Ryan's niece."

"Your ex?"

"Yeah."

"I'm sorry."

"That's why we remained friends. She opened up to me when she was with Ryan, while I was home over the summer. We took her to the police and she told them everything. She is so brave. Her father was arrested. He got two years, Sabato. Only two years, that's it. Ryan has custody."

"Is he good to her?"

"Yeah, the best he can be. I mean, he's doing it alone. His parents help."

"And you?"

"I talked to them on the phone."

"And you wanted to be a lawyer because the system failed her?"

"There is a terrible injustice in our legal system. Chloe has to visit him once a month and write him a letter once a week. She is a ten year old little girl, who was abused, severely abused, by this man. And she was ordered by a judge to do this, because it will 'help her father heal.'"

A sob escapes. I don't mean it to, but it does. I've known Chloe since she was three. I used to babysit her with Ryan once in a while.

Sabato pulls the blindfold off and wipes my tears away with his thumb.

"What about her healing? What about the fact that she has lived her life being abused and they are forcing her to...to...."

"Okay," he pulls me into another hug and I feel him tremble.

"I didn't want you to know, Sabato. I didn't, because—"

"I know and I'm fine. I'm stronger because of it."

"You shouldn't have had to be stronger. Someone should have protected you."

"But I am." He pulls back and looks into my eyes. "How can we help?"

Overwhelmed by emotion, I wrap my arms around him and hug him so tight that my muscles ache. "I don't know. The only thing I could think to do was become a lawyer and fight against a very broken system."

"Have you considered the fact that you are now a wealthy woman? With money comes power, Melyssa, and responsibility. I will help you. But I'm afraid my previous lifestyle and affiliations might—"

"Be a very good reason to want to help. It could also give a child like Chloe, hope."

"And how will Ryan feel about accepting help from me?"

"He loves that little girl. He'd do anything for her. He already has changed so much."

"Do you think you and he—"

"Don't be ridiculous."

"It's a valid question."

"I love you. That won't change. Nothing would ever change that."

"I will see to it that it never does."

I can't help the smile from spreading. It starts in my heart, travels through my soul and lands on my face. "How did I get so lucky?"

"Well, you came peeking in my windows, then came back because you wanted to be fucked."

I giggle, and he smiles.

"The moment I saw you at the restaurant, there was such a draw to you, Melyssa. I tried not to flirt with it, but I did."

"You flirted? That was *flirting*?"

He smiles, "I flirted with the idea."

"I would like to see you flirt."

"It was dangerous. Careless, actually. I knew if I showed an interest in a woman for anything other than physical need, I could be putting her at risk. It never bothered me, until you. You piqued my interest, challenged me even. I had only been interested in one woman before you."

"Luciana."

He nods. "Yes."

"I'm sorry you lost her."

He takes a deep breath and looks me over. Normally, I would give him more to look at but not now. Out of respect for her, I didn't take it to that place.

"I loved Luciana, without doubt. I won't question anything further. I feel it would be disrespectful to her."

"You mean...the car accident? Did he...did your father cause it?"

"Two cars," he shakes his head. "I remember two cars. When I woke in the hospital, I found out that she was dead, that I had some small injury to my hand and that it was ruled an accident. I never liked Thor, but I had him look into it, long ago. He had left school and gone to the police academy and as I said—he is an asshole, but he is a good man. He could find nothing, but he told me he was sure it was my father's doing. Thor was...very fond of Luciana. She chose me over him. He told her getting mixed up with me was stupid. At her funeral he wouldn't even look at me, but then, no one would."

"It wasn't your fault." I reassure him, as I run my hands through his hair.

"That is the cross I carried every day. I have finally accepted it. My fa...that man being dead allowed me to set it down and walk away. You, Melyssa, have given me hope. The cross is a memory that will never be forgotten. I will owe you for the rest of your life for trusting in me."

"You don't owe me anything."

"I owe you everything. It is my honor and privilege to be loved, to feel love, to accept it and give it back. I owe you everything, but I promise and threaten you, I will always take more from you than you are willing to give. I will demand it, Melyssa. Some things I cannot change."

"I would never dream of changing anything about you." I smile evilly. Now that the serious part of our conversation is over, I am ready and willing to take it to that place. So is Elsa. I reach for his belt. "Don't change. Especially not that part."

How to Tie The St. Andrews Knot

-The wide end of the tie should be on your right side and the other end on your left. The tie should be inside out.

-Cross the narrow end over the other end. (Now three regions)

-Bring the wide end over the narrow end. (Left and right region)

-Bring the wide end under the knot from the right to the left region.

-Bring the wide end over the center.

-Bring the wide end underneath the tie knot from right to left.

-Bring the wide end under the narrow part of the tie from left region to center.

-Bring the wide end down and pass the loop in front. Make sure the knot is tightened.

-Use one hand to pull the narrow end down and use the other hand to move the knot up until it reaches the center of the collar.

Playlist for SABATO

Do You Wanna Know ~ Arctic Monkeys
Our Truth ~ Lacuna Coil
The Army Inside ~ Lacuna Coil
Trip To Darkness ~ Lacuna Coil
Bread and Butter ~ Hugo
Stolen Dance ~ Milky Chance
Take Me To Church ~ Hozier
Believe ~ Mumford & Sons

About the Author

MJ FIELDS

MJ Fields' love of writing was in full swing by age eight. Together with her cousins, she wrote a newsletter and sold it to family members. She self-published her first New Adult romance in January 2013. Today, she has completed five self-published series, The Love series, The Wrapped series, The Burning Souls series, The Men of Steel series and The Ties of Steel series. The Norfolk series has two title self-published so far.

MJ is a USA Today bestselling author and former small business owner, who recently closed the business so she could write full time.

MJ lives in central New York, surrounded by family and friends. Her house is full of pets, friends, and noise ninety percent of the time, and she would have it no other way.

[More from MJ FIELDS](#)

MEN OF STEEL SERIES
FOREVER STEEL
JASE
JASE & CARLY
CYRUS
ZANDOR
XAVIER
Forever Family
And
Family

TIES OF STEEL SERIES
ABE
DOMINIC
SABTATO

The LRHA Legacy Series
A collection of series that follow the Links, Ross, Abraham, and Hines families through several generations.
Each series can be a standalone but is so much deeper read in order.

The Love Series
Blue Love
New Love
Sad Love
True Love

The Wrapped series
Wrapped in Silk
Wrapped in Armor
Wrapped Always and Forever

Burning Souls Series
Stained
Merged
Forged

And the latest releases
Love You Anyways
And Love Notes

Ava links story will be coming out in summer 2015

The Norfolk Series
Irons
Irons 2
Irons 3

CONNECT WITH MJ FIELDS

Email – mjfieldsbooks@gmail.com
Website – www.mjfieldsbooks.com
Facebook – http://tinyurl.com/mjfieldsfb
Tsu-https://www.tsu.co/mjfields
For more on the Ties of Steel series, sign up for the newsletter on MJ's Facebook page or at
www.mjfieldsbooks.com
Would you like to receive text messages from MJ Fields?
Text MJFields to 96362
Standard texting fees apply
Follow MJ on Spotify and listen to songs that inspired this and many of her other books!

To Ally,
We will someday discuss….
I love you more.

SABATO (THE CROSS) TIES OF STEEL BOOK FOUR

What's next for Steel? I am so glad you asked...(insert obnoxious laugh / snort)
Coming fall 2015

]

STEEL TOTAL DESTRUCTION
SERIES BOOK ONE

MEMPHIS BLACK

By:
MJ Fields

PROLOGUE

October 25th, 2007

I look in the mirror one last time, my hair is longer on top that it is on the sides. The gel I use to style it makes it look messy and black instead of dark brown. With my black boots I stand six foot three. I having spent an hour at the gym every night after school, I finally have great definition. I'm stage ready.

I walk out on stage with my guitar strung around my neck, pick in hand, waiting for the nerves to consume me. But they don't.

Why? Because I'm a damn *legend*, that's why. The stadium is sold out and the crowd is going wild.

"Hello New Jersey!" I hold the mic out for the crowd's roar. They give me exactly what I want.

"I am Memphis Black, lead singer and guitarist extraordinaire for"—fuck I hate this part. The band, what the hell is the band's name?

"Black Hawks," my sister Madison whispers.

"The Black Hawks!" I yell to the 'crowd.'

"That name is so lame." I hear my sister's friend Tally giggle.

"You two, out."

"No, you said if we video taped this, you would…"

"Out!"

"Come on, it's our first dance, we need to learn how!" Madison stomps her foot.

"Well, you didn't hold up your end of the deal, now did you?" I lift the guitar strap over my head.

"Come on, please," Madison says, eyes huge.

"Yeah please," Tally joins her.

I consider telling them to fuck off, but they'd tell Mom. I consider a simple 'no,' but they'd tell her that, too. So I choose the safest answer: "Fine. But you both have to shut the hell up."

Tally covers her mouth, looking horrified. Girl is a train wreck in epic, adolescent proportion. She has kinky brown curls and a ribbon always wrapped around her head. Freckles bridge her nose and dot her face, and she always wears cartoon character t-shirts, today it's Care Bears.

"What now, Talls?" I huff.

"You said—"

"*Hell*?" I laugh.

"Yeah, you did." She giggles again.

"You know what? I think the both of you should just stay home. All freshman girls do at a dance is stand in a corner, giggle, and look like dweebs." I look at my sister. "Mads, a boy asks you to dance? You'll start laughing and snorting." Next, I point at her friend. "Tall, you'll get some big ass grin." I roll my eyes when she covers her mouth again—little girl can't handle a curse word to save her life. "Just keep smiling and laughing, and they'll think there's something wrong up in those crazy heads of yours. Besides, you're both in that—I don't know, awkward stage: braces, boobs just budding...."

Tally covers her mouth again while Madison starts to get really pissed off.

"I mean, look at that hair. Mads, you're so use to wearing a ball cap you have permanent hat head. And you," I can't resist taking one more shot at Tally. "How the hell are you gonna get a comb through that kinky mess before Saturday?"

That's when Madison finally screams for Mom. Tally just looks at me like that cat from the cartoon, the one with the big green guy. *Shrek*? Yeah Shrek. Puss , Puss in Boots. That's what her face looks like.

Looking back at her, I almost feel kind of bad for giving them a hard time.

Mom comes in then and gives me the third degree, She tells me, 'Girls are sensitive when they're going through changes," and that I should 'be more thoughtful.'

Finally, I can't take it anymore. "Okay Mom, fine. I will buy into their little girl fantasies about that girl, with the blue dress, the one with the mice that turn into horses—"

"Cinderella." In spite of herself, my Mom laughs.

"Yeah. Her."

Her face goes from amused to suspicious. Mom face. "What exactly are they doing in your room, anyway?"

"They were supposed to be taping my performance." I try not to smile as she gives me that look. I know exactly what she's about to say—that my rock star fantasies are just as lame as some dumb fairy tale with talking mice. "It's not the same thing, Mom. This is my *dream*, something I can actually make into a *career* one day."

"I know, Memphis." She pats my back, smiling. "But maybe *their* dream is to dance."

Sexual Awakenings: Volume One
The Walz

By
Angelica

Text copyright © 2014 Angelica Chase

All rights reserved.

No part of this publication may be reproduced or transmitted in any form by any means, electronic or mechanical, including photocopying, recording, or otherwise without written permission of the above author. The only exception is by a reviewer, who may quote short experts in a review.

Published by Angelica Chase, Independent Author

Cover Design by Juliana Cabrera, Jersey Girl Graphics

Editing by Edee M. Fallon, Mad Spark Editing

Interior Design and Formatting by Juliana Cabrera, Jersey Girl Graphics

This book is a work of fiction. Names, characters, and incidents are the product of the author's imagination or used fictitiously. Any resemblance to any actual persons, living or dead, events, or locales are entirely co-incidental.

FALL

I lit candles all over the house in only the scents he would tolerate. I covered our topiaries with soft, clear lights, and arranged fall flowers and large cornstalks into vases around the living room and porch. I loved fall, and by the way the house now smelled and had been transformed, it showed. Grabbing my pumpkin spice latte, I sat in my reading chair on the porch, watching the leaves sway in the cool breeze. I was already cold, but refused to go inside, soaking up the last of the sun as it made its way behind the trees, basking in the feeling in the air. Everything seemed clearer, crisper, and cold days were rare in the south this early in the season. Receiving an incoming message on my tablet, I tapped it, finding nothing new. He wouldn't be home for dinner. It was a good thing I hadn't bothered to cook. I knew better. A year straight of eating alone will do that to a woman. I opted for another night of wine and my vibrator.

Once inside, I chose my favorite bottle of red and poured a healthy glass. Surveying my beautifully decorated home, I rolled my eyes. What was the point? Maybe he was right. The last time I had decorated for the holidays, my husband had asked that same question.

"We don't have any children. We hardly have company. Why even bother?"

Prick. We didn't have children because he had a vasectomy three weeks after our wedding without telling me, only for me to find out in the first of many viscous arguments that ensued. We didn't have company because he was too occupied keeping his own, busy with his constant need to stick his dick in their throats. It wasn't enough for my husband to have one affair; he was in the midst of two.

I was not a woman scorned. Fuck that. I was a woman who had been freed, and too lazy to leave him, having no desire to start another relationship or leave my beautiful home. Alex was never here, ever. What was the point of giving up my life for a ghost I barely lived with? I took my wedding ring off months ago. He never noticed because, in all honesty, I couldn't remember the last conversation we had.

And then I remembered.

"You never loved me did you?" I asked as he entered the house after another late meeting.

"Sure, I love you. Why are you acting so out of sorts?" He ran his hands through his hair, a signature move on his part that I used to find sexy. A stranger to me at that point when we had originally been so close, he stared at me as if I disgusted him, and I returned it. We had been best friends before we were lovers. We'd shared everything. I didn't even recognize the man who now took his place. There was not a damn thing wrong with me or the way I looked. All of his fucked up issues of infidelity were his own.

"I'm not an idiot. Don't play innocent, Alex," I snapped.

"Drink your wine, honey," he said dryly, pushing past me.

That was our last conversation. When he was home, he called his mistresses from his office. I heard every word, because I listened. I listened to strengthen my resolve. I had already decided to ask for a divorce after Christmas. New Year, new life, I guessed. He would let me keep the house and I would let him keep most of his money. He had plenty of it, due to old money passed down from his parents, and his newfound success at his advertising firm. I supposed he thought that since I wanted for nothing, I should just accept my circumstances as a good little wife, go shopping, get pampered. The truth was, I mourned my relationship with my husband, or at least the man I knew before things fell apart. The most frustrating aspect was he refused to admit anything was wrong; the man that had proposed to me knew something was wrong with me before I did at times. He was attentive and nurturing and...human. My tears saddened him, my smiles and laughter fueled him. He'd loved me.

I shook off the small amount of pain making its way into my chest. I had no more room for self-pity. I had done it all. I had worked out, tried new hair, new clothes. I had even gone so far as to get Botox. The only conclusion I came to after a few months of being refused in the skimpiest of lingerie was FUCK HIM. FUCK HIM. I had tried to make my marriage work. He was more interested in seeing it fail. Our relationship was too far gone from what it used to be. There was no trust, and definitely no lingering love. I had spent hours crying over him, now I just wanted my freedom. And freedom was becoming more important than comfort. I had to get out of this and soon.

I sipped my wine, thinking how completely unsatisfying it all was. I had waited until the age of twenty-nine to get married. It seemed the sensible thing to do after a few months of dating Alex. I couldn't even remember the last time we had made love or fucked. My last attempt to keep the home fires burning had failed miserably.

"We aren't a couple of fucking horny teenagers living out a fantasy, Vi. We aren't making a porno, and what the fuck are you wearing?"

I gave up that day, throwing every single negligee I owned away and burying any remaining hope. Sex with Alex was never exactly hot. It had been enough because I had honestly loved him.

Drinking the last of my glass, I poured myself another. Sex, now there was something I was tired of living without. I had my trusty toy. God, how I loved that thing. Battery maintenance promised endless minutes of pleasure. The thought alone had me wanting to reach for it.

I was thirty-two years old, sitting in a big, beautifully decorated house, imagining the next session with my vibrator. I heard the shatter of the wine glass before I realized I was the one who had thrown it in anger.

This is not my life! This is not who I am. This shit...this waiting, much like my marriage, was over!

Things were about to change and change today. First, I had to come up with a plan.

***

Sex, or lack thereof, was what set me off in the kitchen. I missed it. I wanted it. I needed it, but why? I'd never really had sex like most adults. Well, those adults who I envied, which included pretty much anyone who was having their needs met at this point. I abstained from having my own affair because, for a short time, I held out hope. Now that my mind was made up on divorce, I no longer had to justify my reasoning. Sex was a necessity for me. I had waited long enough. My body was starving for touch, my lips bankrupt from a lack of kisses. While a relationship didn't appeal to me, at least not immediately, the thought of a good hard fuck made me insane with want. Not that I'd ever been satisfied sexually.

My experience consisted mainly of missionary, with a few sporadic moments here and there in various positions. Alex was not well endowed and had by no means made up for it throughout our years together. I wondered what it was like to be with a man with a big cock. I moaned at the thought, never once having an orgasm from a man's dick. My girlfriend Molly told me that without a vibrator I may never have one. She insisted girls who came with men inside them were either porn stars with amazing acting skills or had been divinely gifted in that department. It was a myth to me, an orgasm from a man's cock. I'd had fantasies for years about the possibilities of sex. All of it interested me, especially the kink. Alex would look at me as though I was insane when I suggested anything out of our norm. I would get hot and bothered reading all of my dark erotic romances and begged him to try some scenarios with me. Looking back now, I can kind of see his point on why that might seem a little strange. It just wasn't realistic.

Do these people really exist, the people that explore the forbidden? Of course they do, but where were they? Certainly not on the outskirts of Savannah, GA. I laughed at the thought. I'd do good to find a decent looking, well hung, hardworking man in this area period, let alone one that would explore my sexuality with me. Then again, what if? I mean, surely the insatiable and erotic sexual cravings of people are not limited to only large cities.

Where in the hell would I look for something like that here?

Of course there was the web, but some, or most, of those sites had a virus attached. I'd delved into porn a little when my imagination couldn't do it for me and I needed a little extra something. That got old as well. I was tired of watching. I wanted the experience. Pouring myself another glass of wine, I ignored the shattered glass on the floor. Who the hell would care about the mess anyway? After all, it was only me here.

***

Hours later, after watching Jimmy Fallon, my curiosity brought me back to the web. Fuck it; I'd been the well-behaved, jilted wife long enough. I wanted to know what was out there, especially those like me who shared the same curiosities. I would love to know if any other women in Savannah had a fascination with kink. After a few hours of searching, I stumbled upon a site advertising a local adults only page. There was a large triple X on the screen and a flashing advertisement of what looked like a bar in or around Savannah, but my excitement was stifled when I realized there was no address. After a quick Google search for the bar, named The Rabbit Hole, I came up empty, and gave up. Yawning, I threw my tablet beside my pillow and laid my head down to watch Nightline when I heard a ping.

I looked at my tablet to see an incoming message asking for the password. After careful thought, I had nothing. I typed my plea.

Hint?

Rabbit Hole.

Not helpful at all. Shit. The possibilities were endless. I studied the XXX on the screen and saw an Alice in Wonderland cartoon encased in them. Inside the rabbit hole, in the middle X, was Alice kissing another Alice on the cheek as she held her pointer finger to her lips.

Making the best guess I could, I keyed it in.

Don't kiss and tell.

I was immediately brought to the homepage, asked to create a username—Blue_Alice—and started navigating my way around.

It was a chat room, and from the subject matter floating in boxes around the screen, it was definitely a no holds barred kink fest. Perfect! At least the curious vixen inside me wouldn't have to show her face for now. I sat for hours in the various chat rooms reading the conversations. Most of them consisted of people hooking up and then agreeing to email in private. Great, hours on the site and I had only gotten a little hot reading what appeared to be an open and unashamed twosome having really kinky message sex. I could read a book and get hotter than this. I was just about to grab my trusty silver bullet and a new erotica book when I got an incoming message.

MadHatter: What are you doing here?

I froze, feeling completely busted. I shook my embarrassment off quickly. I had knocked on the damn door, so far so good, why the hell not? I typed my reply.

Blue_Alice: Looking.

MadHatter: For what?

Blue_Alice: Anything but what I'm doing.

There, honesty. Honesty was good.

MadHatter: Why so blue, Alice? Bored housewife?

Blue_Alice: Fuck you.

MadHatter: So I'm assuming I'm correct?

Blue_Alice: Maybe, what the hell does it matter?

MadHatter: We don't do married here.

Blue_Alice: I am getting a divorce.

MadHatter: That's not a new one.

Blue_Alice: Keep your boring ass chat room.

MadHatter: Temper, temper.

Blue_Alice: I could do a better job turning people on than this bullshit.

MadHatter: Wow, you really need a thick cock in that sassy mouth.

Blue_Alice: And I suppose you're the one who will be giving it to me?

MadHatter: Why not me?

I felt my cheeks grow hot and took a deep breath. Okay, now we are talking here.

Blue_Alice: Fine…talk to me.

MadHatter: Why are you here?

Blue_Alice: You already asked me that.

MadHatter: And you didn't give me a good enough answer.

I thought about it. Going into this with honesty would be the only way I would truly get what I wanted. But is this what I wanted? What if he was some nasty, fat perv with bad skin and greasy hair? Then again, he may have thought I was some nasty troll with a huge gut and overgrown forest in my pants. I shook my head, indignant at my own stereotyping. *Not cool, Vi.* This whole scenario meant taking a chance. I had been teetering on the edge of this for years, if I was honest with myself. I wanted to be fucked ruthlessly, worshipped and tortured, brought to levels of sexual awareness I'd only dreamed about. I was sure, no positive, I had an undiscovered fetish or two. Honest, I'll be honest.

Blue_Alice: I want to explore a part of me I've kept hidden.

MadHatter: Why?

Blue_Alice: Because I don't have anything to lose.

MadHatter: That's dangerous.

Blue_Alice: That in itself is why I am interested. I want to be fucked in ways I've only imagined and I'm tired of only feeling half full. I have cravings and I'm ready.

A few minutes later, I was sure the conversation had ended, then a ping.

 MadHatter: I'll be in touch.

 Blue_Alice: Wait!

Okay that seemed a little desperate.

 MadHatter: What?

 Blue_Alice: Who are you?

 MadHatter: I'm the guy with the thick cock you'll be wondering about tonight while you play with your toys.

 Blue_Alice: Charming.

 MadHatter: I can be.

And he was gone, if it had even been a he. For all I knew, it could have been a she. This too fascinated me. I thought of women and my sexual boundaries when it came to them and decided one leap at a time. Although women appealed to me from the waist up, I had no desire to explore the waist down. Then again, I'd really never had the opportunity.

      ***

The next day, I brought my iPad on every single errand with the chat room queued up. He could see me, he knew I was waiting. I looked desperate, but I needed this! I felt it in every part of me. I needed to be sexually free. I'd slept with six men in my thirty-two years. Two one night stands, one when I was in college and the other right before I met my husband Alex. The rest were boyfriends and not one of them was a freak, well not in the sense that I wanted them to be. A few got me off with their mouth, but it wasn't earth shattering. It was more or less a struggle and an enormous amount of effort with constant murmurs of "Are you close?" during what seemed to be rigorous work. So I rarely got off.

I had, as the mysterious messenger predicted, taken my toy to bed last night, imagining the man behind our brief chat. I was hot in a way I hadn't been in months at the possibilities alone. This had to be explored. I felt like I was a sexual creature on the verge of finally introducing myself. Once I was home, I unpacked my groceries, praying for the fucking iPad to ping. Just ping! When I got nothing, I decided to forgo cooking and treated myself to dinner at Tubby's, a nearby seafood restaurant on River Street. I sat on the balcony watching the boats glide down the river while the sun set. Couples passed by below me on the busy street holding hands and smiling while I dined alone. Minutes later I got my usual message from Alex letting me know he wouldn't be home tonight and I rolled my eyes. Why did he even bother at this point? God, how I hated him.

Later at home, I thought about looking up some listings to show. I had a real estate license I rarely used and knew it was getting close to time to put it back to use. I was good at it, and I enjoyed it, but when my marriage fell apart I dropped it completely. I had stayed at home for a month solid after hearing Alex's first conversation with one of his mistresses. I didn't need to see anything. The prick had no issue talking openly with her behind his office door. If you are going to cheat, at least have the smarts and decency to hide it. The devastating thought that he didn't care enough to hide is what really drove the knife into my heart. A few months after I had questioned him about his distance, I realized he had no intention of revealing his indiscretions to me. He was simply that fucking stupid. I heard every word he uttered to those women. It was eerily close to the way he used to speak to me. It hurt me horribly at first, now it just made my stomach turn. Why the fuck was I still here? What more reason did I need?

He cheated, our marriage was over. I hated him. Why didn't I just ask for a divorce? PING!

A wave of adrenaline shot through me as I looked at the screen. It was an address. It was obvious why. It was an invitation and one that came way too soon for my comfort.

Well that would be a hell no. I wanted to at least have a conversation longer than a few short sentences before I agreed to a rendezvous.

    Blue_Alice: Hello?

No response came. I already knew the address would be my only message tonight. It was a challenge. He wanted to see what I was made of, if I was willing to step out of my comfort zone. All the reasonable reactions raced through me.

What kind of person barely introduces himself and then gives an address to a total stranger?

Then again, what kind of person tells a complete stranger they want to be fucked six ways from Sunday?

 I stared at the address for what seemed like an eternity. Okay, I could drive by. What's the harm? I would just look around, scope the place out. I could do this. Throwing my blanket off my legs and retiring my yoga pants, I took a scalding hot shower. I Googled the address with a towel wrapped around me, fear creeping into my thoughts. My search, of course, showed only results with possible directions. It had to be a home address. He gave me directions to his home? I shook off the towel, covered myself with scented lotion and took in my body. I had long legs and curvy hips, a little extra weight made them even more pronounced. My breasts were pushing a C-cup, and though they weren't perfectly proportionate to my hips and ass, I was fine with them. I pulled out a thin black sheath dress that collared at the top, hugging my neck snugly, slipped on my spiked red heels and put on my best face. Thick eyelashes and perfectly painted red lips later, I ran my hands through my dirty blonde hair that I'd ironed straight. I was ready.

Two small glasses of wine and a mini-breakdown later, I corked my bottle and made my way to my car. *You can do this, Vi. You can also back out at any time.*

My cell had no issues navigating the address. My screen map timed my trip to thirty minutes, and in thirty minutes I could be in the midst of possibly the best or worst situation of my life. Then again, I couldn't imagine anything worse than the one I was already in.

I had enough heart left to give, I just didn't give a damn enough to use it. This wasn't about my heart; this was about a thirst I'd fought long enough. This would be good. This could be my something to look forward to.

Come on Violet, divorce is not death and you've got a lot of living to do.

The Sexual Awakenings serial should be read in order:

Part 1: The Waltz

Part 2: The Tango

Part 3: The Last Dance

Part 4: Curtains

MJ FIELDS

MERCILESS RIDE

A Hellions Ride Novel
Hell Raisers Challenging Extreme Chaos

By
Chelsea Camaron

Merciless Ride

Copyright © Chelsea Camaron 2014

All rights reserved. No part of this publication may be reproduced, distributed, or transmitted in any form or by any means, or stored in a database or retrieval system, without the prior written permission of Chelsea Camaron, except as permitted under the U.S. Copyright Act of 1976.

This is a work of fiction. All characters, organizations, and events portrayed in this novel are either products of the author's imagination or are used fictitiously. Any resemblance to actual events, locales, or persons, living or dead, is entirely coincidental.

1st Edition Published: September 2014
Whiskey Girls Publishing
Cover Design by: Jessie Lane
Images by: | Magnolia Ridge Photography | Shutterstock
Cover Model: Jacob Sones – Photo taken by Scott Hoover
LoveNBooksBoys ~ Ellie
Editing by: Asli Fratarcangeli and C&D Editing

Intended for mature audiences only

This book contains strong language, strong sexual situations, violence, and rape. Please do not buy if any of this offends you.

This is not meant to be a true or exact depiction of a motorcycle club rather a work of fiction meant to entertain.

Although part of a series, Merciless Ride can be read as a stand-alone novel.

CHAPTER ONE

Unexpected

~*Tessie*~

No, no, no, don't die, dammit. Fuck my life.

It is two in the morning, I just got off work from the bar, and tonight has already been a long damn night. We have been busier since the Desert Ghosts Motorcycle Club arrived in town. They must be working with the Hellions on something to be here, returning as often as they do.

Staying in this small place, they only have two options for a spot to grab a beer. *Tiny's,* where a man that is far from tiny will be serving them, or find me and the girls at *Ruthless.* Since they are in business with the Hellions, they come to *Ruthless.* Although not Hellion owned, it is known as their place to grab a drink and unwind.

I am on my way to pick up Axel, my son, when my little Honda Civic begins dying a slow, painful death as my dashboard lights up like a Christmas tree. I have just enough time to pull it safely to the side of the road before it shuts off completely.

No! This can't be happening, I think to myself as I try to restart the car.

Turning the key over in the ignition, I am left with silence surrounding me. Click. Click. Click. Nothing.

Looking over at my cell phone, I think of my limited options for aid. Who can I call at two in the morning to come give me a ride?

I don't want my mom to have to get dressed and then get Axel dressed to come out here. Plus, I am still going to need to have the car towed. I knew I should have signed up for one of those automotive clubs, but damn that would be another bill. A bill I certainly can't afford.

Picking up my cell phone, I dial the one person I know that can help me get a ride and get my car towed all in a quick manner as well as keep it within a reasonable budget.

"Hey, Doll, sorry to call so late," I say when she answers.

"No problem; what's wrong, Tessie?" she asks, the sleepy tone in her voice reminding me normal people don't keep my kind of schedule.

Shit, I woke her up. I feel even more guilt now, but she is one of the few friends I have. Plus, she will come get me, no question, since Tripp and Rex are away on a transport. I would've been tempted to call Rex; however, I have promised myself no more. Luckily, he is away, so the urge is gone, leaving me with Doll. If they were home, Rex would've been at the bar tonight, either to troll for fresh pussy or give me an orgasm in the stock room before the night was over. Rex and I have a fucked up history - one centered around sex, sometimes a little more, but mostly it is just about getting off. Well, that was until recently when I made the decision to cut him out of my life as much as possible.

"My car broke down out on Miller's Hill Road. It won't start back up and I need to get home. I'm sorry for bothering you. I didn't know who else I could call," I say as I hear a noise in the background.

Doll is mumbling something, but I can't bring myself to focus on her as my blood runs cold when I hear Tripp's voice say *his* name.

Shit, Rex! He can't come get me. No. No. No. He cannot come with me to get Axel. Panic is setting in as I run through how this night is going. He will ask me where my son is. He always asks me about Axel. My plan was to get Doll on her way and call my mom to keep him overnight. If Rex is too close, I won't have time to make the call. Then he will wonder why we can't go get him.

"No worries, Tessie, Rex will be there shortly to get you," I hear her say his name, snapping me out of my thoughts.

"Rex? I th… thought they were on a transport," I stammer, questioning why he is back.

"Oh, they got back about an hour ago. Tripp heard you talking so he called him while we've been on the phone. He'll pick you up and get your car taken care of. Do you need a ride tomorrow?"

"No, Doll. Thanks, you've done so much already. I gotta go. I need to call my mom so she's not expecting me right away for Axel." With that, we hang up.

Making a quick call to my mom, I ask her to keep Axel overnight for me. Since he's already asleep, this works out better for him anyway. Regardless of who comes, none of the Hellions are going to lay eyes on Axel.

Knowing my son is settled, I have to prepare myself to see Rex. I seem to lose all self-control when he's around. I always have. Boundaries, I have given myself mental boundaries with him. He is never going to grow up, so I have stopped holding out for that. He is also never going to commit to me or anyone else, for that matter. I have given up on that pipe dream. With that said, I have to set the boundaries for my body more firmly. No more allowing lust to takeover.

Rex is sex walking, period, end of story. He has shoulder length, dirty blond hair. Eyes that are piercing blue, a body that's got defined muscles, and ink that makes you want to lick every inch of his skin. The thing about Rex, he knows he is the whole package. He knows he looks good. He's confident in his bedroom abilities, as he should be. There is also this edge to him. The same edge that all the Hellions carry. The thing that draws the barflies to them like a man lost in the desert to water.

Headlights coming my way draw my attention. Then a wrecker pulls up in front of my little car. I hold my breath as the driver side door opens, my mouth dropping open when it's not Rex who climbs out.

At six feet tall, with broad shoulders and all muscle, the man coming to me is another example of the edge all the Hellions carry. His long-sleeved, black T-shirt pulls tightly against his well-defined chest, abs, and arms. His normally spiked blonde hair is hidden under an old, worn out, baseball hat. The jeans he is wearing are well washed and fit him like a pair of broken in shoes, comfortable perfection. Black motorcycle boots stop in front of me, drawing my attention back to my situation.

"Hey, Tessie, let's get you loaded up and home to your boy."

"Shooter," is all I manage.

"Yeah, baby, you get me. Rex called. He couldn't make it, but didn't want you on the side of the road."

This is the moment my heart should sink a little that Rex isn't coming to help me. What surprises me, though, is I don't feel short changed in the least bit. I don't feel let down. For once, I feel absolutely nothing for Drexel 'Rex' Crews.

~Shooter~

Damn him! Brother or not, right now, I want to kick his ass. I swear I heard him speaking to someone else as I answered the phone, *"Suck it harder, bitch."* Instead of dropping the barfly, he calls me to pick up his woman off the side of the road. Only Tessie isn't his ol' lady; she's just his back up pussy; the pussy he doesn't want to hold onto yet won't let go of, either.

Tessie is beautiful. She deserves so much better than Rex or any man the likes of us. She's petite, maybe five-feet-four, with dark brown hair and brown eyes that dance when she smiles. Her perky breasts are what most may consider small, but they fit her body perfectly. She has a round ass, but not overly large, just enough to really grip as she rides you. With Tessie, though, it's more than that. She is genuine, caring, and sweet. Loyal to a fault sometimes, she puts up with a lot of shit, not only from our club, but all the guys going into the bar.

I won't lie to myself; I have watched her for years with Rex, envious as hell. Tessie accepts him as he is, whatever he gives her. I have never met a woman who can easily understand and take a man truly at face value the way Tessie does, not only with Rex, but all of us.

I have been a patched member of the Catawba Hellions MC for five years now. My boss, Ryder, introduced me to the club after he patched in with the Haywood's charter. His wife Dina's father was an original before he passed away tragically in a car accident years ago.

I make the almost hour commute daily to work at Ryder's Restorations in Charlotte. Most days, I paint cars for him. Occasionally, I step in on some fabrication, but it's rare. The pay is good, business is good, and the guys at the shop are good. I could relocate to a place closer to work, but I don't want to be in the city. I like being close to my club and not having neighbors close by. This life is simple and calm compared to what I have seen in my past.

I am going through the routine of hooking up Tessie's car to the wrecker. My buddy here in Catawba has a towing and recovery business. He said he would come get her, but I couldn't do that to Tessie. She's a single mom, by herself on an old road in the middle of nowhere, and it is beyond late. A familiar face might make things a little better, especially since I don't know how disappointed she is over Rex not coming personally.

Glancing over my shoulder, I see she's watching me.

"Need help?" she asks, sticking her hands in her jean pockets.

"Nah, baby, I got it. Go ahead and get in. I'll be a few minutes, and then we'll get you home."

She nods at me before proceeding to get in the truck. The 1993 silver Honda Civic she has been driving certainly has seen better days. Once we get this to the shop, I'm going to give it a complete over-haul. She has a kid to get home to.

Jobs here are few and far between. The bar is really the only place she could go right now without leaving her mom behind to work in the city. It's a small town, people talk, and Tessie hasn't had an easy life.

With the car secure, I climb in behind the wheel to tow it back to my place. Looking over to the passenger seat, I see she has fallen asleep against the door already. Reaching over, I buckle her in, and she startles and wakes.

"Shooter, thank you."

"Anytime, baby. You need me to take you to your mom's or your place?" I ask, wondering if she needs to pick up her son.

"My house, please. Mom didn't want me to wake Axel."

The exhaustion is written on her face, but more than that there is loneliness in her eyes. I don't know why, yet I feel the need to apologize that it's me that came to get her.

"I'm sorry Rex couldn't make it."

"I'm not," she says, gazing out the window into the dark night.

How do I respond to that? Rather than involve myself in another man's business, I stay quiet. Her phone rings from her purse saving me from continuing our conversation.

"What, Rex?" she answers with a dull tone. There is a pause for him to speak. "Yes, Shooter came. I'm on my way home." Her brows draw together in frustration, but her voice remains impassive. "No, you can't come over tonight." She sighs deeply. "Rex, I told you, no more." Another pause. "You couldn't come get me because you were doing who knows what to some barfly. I'm not stupid. Rex, I told you, I'm done. The fact that you want to come over tonight shows the complete lack of respect you have for me. We're over and have been for years. Hell, we weren't actually ever officially together, so there is nothing to be over."

Her voice never raises, never sharpens. She is calm, cool, and detached as she continues after allowing Rex to reply. "We're nothing more than friends. Move on, Rex. I'm going to. Goodnight." And with that, she swipes her thumb across the screen to end the call.

She lightly bangs her head against the window as we pull up to her house where she starts to unbuckle. Quickly, I reach in my back pocket and get my business card out of my wallet.

"Look, Tessie, if you need anything, I don't care the time, call."

When she looks at the card then up to me, a slight smile crosses her face. "Andy 'Shooter' Jenkins. You look like an Andy."

"What?"

"In all the years you've been coming to the bar, I've only know you as 'Shooter' and 'Jenkins,' never Andy. You look like an Andy."

Made in the USA
Middletown, DE
08 August 2015